Aaron,
I hope you enjoy
the adventure!
—Brian W Peterson

CHILDREN OF THE SUN

By

Brian W Peterson

Children of the Sun
Brian W. Peterson
ISBN: 978-0-9904198-9-1
Library of Congress Control Number: 2015943548
Copyright © 2015 Brian W. Peterson
All rights reserved worldwide,
Icebox Publishing, Westport, CT

Cover Design by Melinda Patrick

Dedication:

This book is dedicated to the memory of my cousin, John K. Buttress. He was the best writer and smartest member of my family, and an outstanding man. Our conversations about God, life, and writing were often inspirational and always deep.

Acknowledgements:

Getting a novel published has more moving parts than an extraterrestrial spacecraft, or so it seems. Todd Wood and his people at Icebox understand those parts far better than I do, and without Todd not only giving me this opportunity, but his understanding of the process, this book would not have found its way to readers. My cover artist, website designer, and "oh yeah, I need one more thing" go-to lady when I was at wit's end, Melinda Patrick, was the calm one through it all. Besides possessing superior talent and producing superior product, she came up with ideas just as I ran out of them. My editor, Meticulous Mindy Peterson, made me second-guess myself once every three pages, which is something I hate to do, but exactly what she is supposed to do. She's my wife, so she's good at that.

The Lord has blessed me with a vivid, off-beat imagination. When I was a kid, imagining spaceships coming to get me was one of my more normal fantasies. Children of the Sun makes me look downright well-adjusted. My parents have always encouraged me to use my talents to the utmost, although my mother was always a little concerned about my fascination with Edgar Allan Poe. What's a little literary torture, murder, and dismemberment now and then?
From my sister, Sheryl, to friends and family who have read my writings and encouraged me over the years, as well as those who encouraged me during the process of publishing this book, I am fortunate to have been showered with praise and encouragement for what comes out of my mind. There are too many people to name and thank, but your support will always be remembered.

Without my wife's love, patience, and understanding, I would be mowing five acres of grass right now and would have never published any of my fiction work. She has had to put up with living with a dreamer for a long time.

Family and friends, from the bottom of my heart, thank you all.

Brian W. Peterson

Chapter 1 - Together

Hours before, the sun had disappeared beyond the field of corn. The now-darkened field sloped upward toward a large wooded area that separated a small town from many miles of corn fields, soybean fields, and the occasional dairy farm. The glow of the town to the south was a soft yellow smudge of light above the trees. At the edge of the woods was a football field-sized area of bare dirt that was a popular hangout for area youth. The growing corn stalks and nearby trees served as a useful visual barrier between their summer parties and reality.

The monotony of small-town life for the fledgling adults was broken up symbolically by the woods and practically by the marijuana and whiskey that was making the rounds. A Metallica song boomed out of a portable compact disc player, providing a soundtrack for the beauty of the southern Indiana night, even though no one seemed to notice what they were missing in the heavens.

On this cool, moonless night, Orion the Hunter had already chased Taurus the Bull out of the sky. The Gemini twins were preparing to drop below the horizon and Leo was not far behind. But with the amount of cannabis and alcohol in their bloodstreams, the partiers would have been lucky to see only one lion or one set of twins.

Some of the teens had wandered off in couples, headed to seclusion deeper into the cornfield or into the woods. But Stevie and his cousin, Ralph Barton, along with their buddy,

Billy Sharp, were more interested in just kicking back, chatting away about the future.

"Not me," Stevie blurted out his thoughts, unaware that he was beginning to lose control of the ability to distinguish reality from imagination.

"Not me what?" asked cousin Ralph. In stark contrast to Stevie's short, thin frame, Ralph was tall, broad-shouldered and built for football. As he lay on his back in the soft dirt at the edge of the cornfield, Ralph's Chicago Bears t-shirt barely contained his bulky chest and rippled stomach muscles. His curly hair scarcely budged in the gentle breeze.

"Not me what?" said Stevie, looking confused.

"I dunno. You said it, not me," Ralph responded.

"I'm not lettin' go of my dreams, that's not me what," Stevie said with a fair amount of sobriety and certainty.

"Yeah, you and the rest of us. Mom says if I don't get my grades up I ain't goin' nowhere on a football scholarship, and I think she's prob'ly right."

"That's ridiculous," Billy chimed in. "Why do you think those guys take underwater basket weaving classes in college? Nobody on the football team makes good grades 'cept the quarterback, and that's why he's the quarterback."

"Nah. I gotta have good grades or the scouts'll just go away," Ralph insisted. "I've gotta lay off this junk here and concentrate on gettin' the grades up. I only got one more year to go." With that, he flipped his joint in the direction of the field of young corn stalks.

Stevie looked impressed. "What about the Jack?" he asked.

"Old Number Seven hasta go, too," he said with a sense of melodrama. Ralph realized that, in the middle of the night, in the middle of nowhere, he was making a choice to go somewhere, to chase a dream rather than stay to farm the land. In his mind, there was not much of a difference between staying in his hometown and going nowhere. "I gotta get outta here."

"I like it here," Billy protested. Tall, lanky, and a longtime friend of the cousins, he was more of a tag-along than anything else. The cousins enjoyed his humor so they never seemed to mind his presence. Plus, he was on the football team, as a receiver, with Ralph, so that was good enough for the larger of the two cousins. "Whaddya got against this place?"

"I love it here," Ralph explained in earnest. "It's a great place if you like farmin' and the good life. But the NFL doesn't come through here. The lights, the action, the women- they don't visit Nowhere-ville."

"I'm with Ralph," Stevie stated with more certainty than ever. The effects of the night's indulgences seemed to fade quickly with the subject of conversation revolving around his favorite topic. "The future is bright for those willing to strive toward their goals."

"Who said that?" Billy asked.

"I did," Stevie snapped. "Didn't ya just hear me?"

"Nothin' happens here, Billy," Ralph opined as he pointed into the dark distance. "The future is out there, beyond the farms and the small towns and the friendly people. The future is away from here. Nothin' ever happens here- not nothin' I'm interested in, anyway."

Stevie stood up hastily, as though positioning himself closer to the sky would aid his vision. "Check that out," he said as he craned his neck and chin upward.

Ralph leaped to his feet without speaking. Billy struggled to his feet and stood motionless, which in his state was an accomplishment.

"Tell me again, Ralph, how nothin' ever happens 'roun' here," Stevie mockingly challenged.

The group of teenagers who were scattered around the edge of the cornfield and on into the woods had yet to notice a light slowly descending upon them. Too slow to be a meteor, too large to be an airplane, the half-stoned threesome looked upward with a mixture of excitement, bewilderment and apprehension.

"Guys, it's a spaceship," Stevie declared.

"Uh huh, sure," Ralph laughed. "It's a helicopter. Look how it's movin'. It's floatin' down at us like a helicopter."

"Helicopters are loud," Stevie pointed out to his cousin. "That ain't no helicopter."

"Maybe it's a UFO," blurted Billy.

"That's what he just said, Einstein," Ralph scolded. "It's comin' right here, whatever it is."

By now, others had noticed the growing brightness of the descending light in the sky. With cries that the police were coming to bust them, several teens ran off into the woods. Others stood and stared, just as Stevie, Ralph and Billy stared. One brunette grabbed her blouse and ran into the woods, screaming all the way, her boyfriend running behind her, trying to catch up.

"Hear that?" Stevie asked. A slight rumble was growing slowly, from a barely audible sound to an ever-increasing roar of mysterious engines.

"It's gotta be military," Ralph reasoned. "Ain't no such thing as UFOs."

For the first time, Stevie looked away from the craft and at the young man who was both his cousin and best friend. He grabbed Ralph by the short sleeve of his Bears' t-shirt and tugged. "Together?" he asked knowingly.

"Together," Ralph responded without hesitation.

"What are you guys doin'?" Billy asked.

"If I knew I'd tell ya," Stevie answered. "But whatever we do, we're doin' together," he explained. "Ralph and I live together and we'll die together if that's what it comes to."

Billy looked down at the ground in thought as the brightly lit craft slowly settled down from the sky, ever closer to the Earth. "I'm with ya," he said with an air of firmness. He looked back and forth between the cousins who eyed him curiously. "Well if ya don't mind, anyway," Billy added.

"Hey, whatever. No problem," Ralph said reassuringly. "I don't even know if we know what we're doin'."

"But we do know it's a UFO," Stevie added.

"That we do," Ralph replied. "That we do."

Indeed, the teenagers were correct. Whatever it was, it was certainly unidentified, it was flying toward them, and the boys did not object that something extraordinary was happening in the fields of Indiana- in the middle of nowhere, as they always complained. The future was taking an unexpected and bizarre turn.

The roar of the craft deepened. The wind picked up. The gentle swaying of the young corn stalks gave way to violent jerks to and fro. The bright lights shielded the onlookers from establishing the identity of the craft until it nearly touched the ground. As the craft grew ever closer, the roar grew louder still. All brave souls who remained in the vicinity covered their ears with their hands.

It was not a helicopter and it was not an airplane. If it was military, it was something which no one in the Midwest had ever before seen. Maybe this strange, monstrous machine had been spotted in the deserts of California and Nevada, but never in the farmlands of Middle America. The behemoth had rounded edges and a smooth, almost shiny, skin. Despite the rounded appearance, it was not an aerodynamic-looking craft. It looked sleek, but not a sleekness for cutting through air.

It was less cylinder than oval, yet less oval than just a mountain of smooth blob, having little apparent symmetry. But at this point, no one considered the matters of symmetry or odd shapes. Had the craft landed in town near buildings, the boys would have realized that the machine was four stories tall.

Rather than wheels, the craft sported eight legs with oversized cupped feet. The brilliant landing lights and the growl of the engines concealed the rest of the craft in a mysterious glow of light and sound. Had the light cast a favorable glow, onlookers would have seen what amounted to windows- small port holes that presumably allowed people-creatures- on the inside to see out.

As the craft touched down over the top of the corn stalks, settling into the soft dirt, the white landing lights were hidden from view. Apparent to the ten or so teenagers still brave enough to stand their ground, the truth was obvious: this was a craft that was not built on Earth.

Despite the fact that his heart pounded from the adrenalin rocketing through his arteries, Stevie thought clearly enough to turn to his cousin again. "Hang with me, Ralph."

"I'm here," big Ralph's quivering voice responded.

Billy moved his mouth slightly but no sound came out. He was sure that he would stick with his friends, but only because he was now too afraid to be away from them.

The roar rapidly subsided. Gasps of fear and disbelief spread through the small crowd. A couple slowly emerged from the woods to witness the extraterrestrial event, the boy fixing his pants to ensure that they were now fitted to his body properly.

When a bright beam of white light bolted from the spaceship onto the gathering crowd, all but the three young men gave their best cockroach impersonations, scattering into the woods at top flight. The three friends who remained quivered from head to toe, unaware that they were alone with this huge alien ship.

What transpired next was witnessed by at least a half dozen youthful onlookers who stopped their flight through the woods to watch events unfold. The number of "eyewitnesses" varied in the following days, as some who turned high tail would later claim to have seen it all. Some told the truth, some repeated what the actual witnesses observed, and some exaggerated with tall tales akin to what can be heard in bait shops, near prime fishing holes, or in bars and offices as bored city men distort their golf games. Stories varied from honest accounts to whoppers fit for supermarket tabloids. And the supermarket tabloids paid.

Another point of ridicule was the claim that, when a giant door opened like that of an armored personnel carrier, the youth were stunned to see humans- an adult male, an adult female, and a small child- exit and disappear into the corn field. Nearly everyone agreed that Stevie, Ralph and Billy all entered the large spaceship, never to be seen or heard from again. The tabloids paid well, so stories later abounded about lasers disintegrating the three into thin air or monstrous aliens dragging them away.

One problem of credibility would forever haunt the real witnesses: to one degree or another, they were all high on various drugs. Seeing a spaceship drop from the sky only yards away can sober one rather quickly, but between the goings on of the teenagers and their vices, and the silly stories coming from those who had fled, skeptics were plentiful.

There was one bit of evidence that was beyond explanation for the voices of a reasonable explanation: high or not, the kids could not have crushed the corn stalks and left behind the prints of a large, heavy vehicle. Underneath the landing gear, the corn stalks were not merely bent or swirled into shapes- they were pulverized into powder, as if some other force was at work other than mere weight. From the air, the outline of the ship was not visible on the ground, though many expected otherwise; the youth explained that the landing gear extended downward enough to ensure that the body of the craft did not touch the soft Earth.

One other oddity left locals and scientists alike intrigued: the craft all but melted some of the corn stalks. The stalks that touched the craft did not burn, they just melted into little balls of green putty. Heat should not have had this effect, so theories abounded and scientists visited the site in efforts to understand exactly what had occurred.

While the carousing youth were widely dismissed, the story of three humans exiting the craft was ridiculed. Surely their senses and recollections would have been keener had they not been high, the skeptics reasoned. Others argued that with their senses dulled, their imaginations could not have been activated, thus they were telling the truth. The effects of the drugs, still others reasoned, would have produced wild stories. Some saw reason to believe while others found reason to disbelieve. It was all in the mind of the beholder.

The alleged arrival of aliens did not shake the community the way that the disappearance of the three youth managed to rattle their nerves. The three were neither heard from nor seen again. Mothers wailed and fathers searched, but without accepting the story of the spaceship, no one could ever explain the disappearance of Stevie Barton, Ralph Barton, and Billy Sharp.

No one dared to explain.

*   *   *   *   *   *

The next night, a crowd of hundreds, some said a couple of thousand- from southern Indiana, northern Kentucky, and western Ohio- lined the edge of the woods and the vast corn field. All waited in expectation or with great skepticism. Yet they waited. It was a Saturday night. Church services started early the next morning. Some grew impatient as midnight fell upon the countryside.

To the astonishment of the many who remained, in the distance a craft appeared to land near the horizon. "That's Tucker's farm!" shouted one local man. "That's Tucker's farm!" he repeated, excitement gushing out of his throat. Many in the crowd made mad dashes for their cars, but the efforts were in vain. Before most could get their vehicles started, the craft had launched itself away from Earth. They watched as the spaceship streaked across the sky, toward the western horizon, as it appeared to fly into the head of Leo, the celestial lion that on this night seemed to protect the alien spaceship from the hoards of earthlings.

Sixteen years would pass before the spaceships returned.

Chapter 2 - The Appointment

The humid Indiana summer night was similar to that of sixteen years prior when the spaceships came. The infamous spring night had long since faded from daily conversations, but the feelings of fear and apprehension never quite lifted from the small, isolated town. Had three of their own not disappeared on that first night, perhaps the people would have allowed the consecutive nights to fade peacefully from their memories.

On this summer night, in the same field, near the same wooded area, the spaceships descended. Now, however, a few houses dotted the eastern edge of the expansive corn field about a half-mile north of the woods. The town had grown by only a few hundred people in the succeeding sixteen years, but they happened to grow, by chance, near the site of that exciting night. The heart of the town still lay on the far side of the woods, but the owner of the corn field had successfully eased his burden of limited cash flow by selling off part of the land.

The spaceships seemed to come straight down out of Cygnus, the celestial swan that flies above the river of stars that we know as our Milky Way galaxy, as the constellation approached zenith.

*   *   *   *   *   *

As if from a frightening nightmare, David Steele shot up into a sitting position in his bed. Without alarm and without the aid of light, he calmly but swiftly slipped into a pair of jeans and pulled on a t-shirt in the total darkness. After stepping into a pair of tennis shoes, he was on his way. Without further delay, he exited the house through a side door that led to the nearby corn field.

He walked along a path worn down from years of farming equipment having made the trek to the fields and back. David's house was one of those near the fabled alien landing that occurred when he was just a toddler. Now, he was about to witness firsthand a similar event.

Walking like the zombie that chases the hero's girlfriend in a 1950s B-movie, David ignored the lights streaking across the night sky and stared straight ahead. With his arms at his side he slowly marched forward. He appeared to be a candidate for examination as a sleepwalker.

The streaking lights transformed from pinpoints to discernible craft. A dozen small craft zoomed around the countryside, as though on the lookout for potential enemies-or witnesses. The closer the mothership came to the ground, the closer the small, agile craft came to the landing site.

Blues, greens, yellows, oranges, and reds flashed through the sky in erratic paths. White spotlights searched the corn field and the woods. The small craft defied known aeronautic limits with their sudden jerks and changes of direction. Following the fast moving flying ships were high-pitched sounds of machines unlike David had ever heard.

Intense beams of white light from the ships rapidly covered every square inch of the landscape as David drew ever near the patch of ground that was about to become a landing site.

If he cared- which he obviously did not- David would have had a difficult time making out the shapes of the scout craft. The flying ships moved much too quickly to be properly defined in the moonless sky.

By the moment, the roar of the mothership grew closer, louder, forcing the air to vibrate around the young man. The fluttering of his thick but straight brown hair gave the only indication on his six-foot, two-inch frame that there were forces pressing against his body. The darkness hid his brown eyes, which, if they could be seen, would reveal that they were glazed over in his zombie-like state.

David, oblivious to his surroundings, followed the invisible pull from some invisible tractor beam. He was not a curious onlooker, rather he was about to become a participant- whether by choice or by direction an observer could not have been sure. The broad-shouldered, muscular 18-year old quietly marched forward.

When he reached a certain spot in the hard dirt path, David turned and walked a few strides into the field. The young corn stalks did not fill the edge of the field, leaving soft, dry dirt to fill the void up to the wide equipment path.

Without warning, a small craft zipped past his head. David did not so much as flinch. Another craft, which looked to be about twenty feet long, came to a sudden stop only a few yards to his side. A beam of light unexpectedly cast a brilliant cone of white into the edge of the woods. A young teenage couple sprinted away into the woods in fear for their lives.

The lights, the roar, the dust in the air- all were oblivious to the young man as he stood patiently waiting for his appointment to arrive.

All the while, the mothership descended until it rested on almost exactly the same patch of ground as its predecessor had sixteen years earlier, crushing corn planted in the same Indiana soil. Without disturbing the locals, an extraterrestrial vehicle over five-hundred feet in length and three-hundred feet in width landed on Earth's soft soil. Rather than a shiny, rounded behemoth as was its predecessor, the mothership was a large but dark craft with many jagged angles and odd elevations. Like its predecessor, it too lacked aerodynamic grace; however, the large vessel, with its angles and protruding pieces of black alien substance which gave an appearance of Legos stacked willy-nilly, had a look of a fearsome machine.

Windows were not evident on this craft. In fact, nothing was evident. It was a large, odd-looking chunk of technology that would defy any earthly scientist who studied it. That it was a flying vessel was obvious only because it had just landed on the soil.

David never wondered how fearsome the inhabitants of the spaceship must be. He never wondered why he was in the field or why he had ventured out in the middle of the night. He merely followed the irresistible pull- a pull from what he did not know and did not contemplate.

The roar subsided but did not cease. The lights dimmed but did not darken completely. If he had desired, young David could have seen the stars above or heard dogs barking in the distance, but he had neither such awareness nor desire. His appointment had arrived. That was his only conscious thought, and that thought may not have been a conscious one.

A large door slowly dropped from underneath the mothership, allowing interior light to pierce the darkened field. Two men- humans, they appeared to be- walked from within the ship to the bottom of the ramp. David advanced to the ramp's end and looked into the eyes of the creatures. Whatever they were, human-like creatures no different than David in physical composition, wore military uniforms. Reverently, the alien men bowed.

*　　*　　*　　*　　*　　*

David's blue jeans and Cincinnati Reds t-shirt were obscured by the sheet that covered him. As his unconscious body lay prone on the table, he was unaware that the alien men were in the process of opening his skull in order to perform brain surgery. The makeshift operating room had all the makings of any sterile, well-lit, visually unattractive operating room found in civilized hospitals on Earth.

The doctor in charge, like the other five people in the room, was completely covered, with skin exposed only around his eyes. He stood above the top of David's head, absorbed in his work. To the doctor's right, his primary assistant stood, waiting. The others were lesser assistants, not as well-trained in the science of medicine.

As the doctor completed the task of opening a small area of David's skull an inch above his right ear, the primary assistant deftly reached into a pocket of his smock and pulled out a microchip. The others had no reason to notice the assistant's movements. On the table in front of him, lying next to David's right shoulder, was a microchip that was identical in appearance to the chip that the assistant furtively produced.

Unseen to the others in the room, sweat poured down the assistant's lean body underneath the medical clothing. If nerves were audible, even the unconscious David would have heard the deafening sound.

Yet the assistant moved easily, nimbly sliding the official microchip on the table nearer to his own body. He then grabbed with tweezers the microchip which he had pulled from his pocket and picked up a small hose that had a graphite nozzle on the end.

With the push of a button, a blue laser leaped out four inches from the nozzle. The harmless beam then received the microchip from the tweezers in the assistant's other hand. Quickly the assistant covered the microchip on the table with the glove that covered his left hand. Immediately, the doctor took the laser device from the assistant and slowly inverted the tool, which now firmly gripped the microchip, and pressed the microchip and laser beam deep into David's brain matter, into the inner temporal lobe.

"Doctor, our time is limited. We are vulnerable to attack," boomed a voice over an unseen intercom speaker.

"We have just finished inserting the chip," the doctor replied. "We can fuse him and allow him to wake up slowly on his own while we travel."

"Plans have changed. A Rebel ship is uncomfortably near. Fuse him now," the booming voice ordered. "We cannot risk our destruction with him aboard."

In a matter of minutes the procedure was over. The chip was inserted, the small piece of skull was replaced, a different laser was used to seal the opening, and unless someone knew what to look for, the imprints of surgery were invisible underneath David's brown hair.

The assistant casually tried to pick up the microchip that had rested on the table and was now supposed to be under his glove. It was gone. The sweat poured faster from his pores. If the chip was not on the table, that could only mean that it had fallen to the floor. Discovery of his traitorous act was now possible.

The doctor reluctantly gave orders to prepare to bring David from his induced slumber. Other assistants grabbed tools and moved to different places around the operating table to make the order a reality. The primary assistant seized the moment of activity to step away from the table and quickly scan the floor. When he spotted the microchip, he stepped on it and attempted to grind it into dust by slowly rotating his shoe. He could not risk being spotted bending over, picking up the chip. In his mind, he did the next best thing.

*　　　*　　　*　　　*　　　*　　　*

The darkened field and its surroundings had not changed. The clear summer night revealed the stars as brilliantly as ever. A slight breeze was not enough to hide barking dogs in the distance, but with the darkened, small spaceships sitting idly in the field, the only oddity was a dull roar that emanated from the mothership, which was known as the Prince Tinian.

The twelve small craft simultaneously came to life. The whir of the Prince Tinian rapidly increased from a deep, low sound to an increasingly louder rumble that vibrated the ground. The spaceships all lifted in unison.

David Steele, the clean cut "good kid" that the town admired had a secret that even he did not know until he stepped off of the spaceship. He stood motionless as the small craft slowly floated upward and toward the rising Prince Tinian. As four separate docking bay doors opened, the ships disappeared one by one in quick succession. In just a few seconds all twelve were gone, hidden by the doors that sealed the ships inside the mothership.

Once the parade of ship dockings was over, the Prince Tinian ascended rapidly. At around 2,000 feet, the mothership leaped upward and to the west, ripping off a sonic boom that awakened people for hundreds of miles. As David watched, what appeared at first to be a satellite or a high-flying airplane opened fire on the Prince Tinian. Thin red lasers shot toward the fleeing spaceship. Within seconds, blue lights flickered toward the enemy vessel, signifying return fire. The light pattern was repeated multiple times. All was quiet on the ground, despite the ferocious light show above.

Uninterested, David walked home in his stupor.

*   *   *   *   *   *

The bridge of the Prince Tinian was awash in noise-noise that would have seemed like utter confusion to a visitor. The crew was in the midst of battle. Every noise, every shout, every movement had purpose. The shouted commands and proper military confirmations of orders received and carried out filled the air in between muted explosions and the whine of engines. The ship rocked back and forth like a roller coaster about to go off its tracks. Long, thunderous explosions rumbled through the craft every time the Prince Tinian fired at the pursuing enemy destroyer.

In the middle of all the noise and commands, a young man dressed in the same dark jumpsuit that served as a military uniform for the entire crew entered the bridge.

"Admiral. We have an urgent matter in the surgery room."

Admiral Artimus Praeder, the most senior officer in the service of the King onboard the ship, slowly turned his head and stared at the soldier in disbelief. His tall, wiry frame masterfully hid his physical potency. Before he had entered the Academy, Praeder was a mere grunt fighting the Rebels in ground combat. He was known to have once snapped a Rebel's backbone in half with his bare hands over his knee after his laser pistol was out of ammunition. His reputation grew from that moment on. His full head of gray hair only added to the aura all these years later. His hands never lost their iron grip. His voice remained stern and strong. His eyes were like blue flames. The man was a legend, and few had the courage to voice disagreement, let alone challenge him. That the Kingdom would send an Admiral on a mission to a distant solar system underscored to all the importance of their task. But to send a legend inspired awe throughout the military, not to mention the inevitability of the mission's ultimate success.

"Urgent matter? Shall I ask you to oversee the small matters being executed here on the bridge while I am away?"

"Well, uh, sir. I am sorry, sir. But sir, Doctor Bogome is-" His sentence was halted by a shout from a flight crew member.

"Admiral! The Banu has broken off pursuit."

Admiral Praeder turned his attention back to the young ensign. "Doctor Bogome?"

"He is near hysterics he is so angry, sir."

The Admiral's cocksure manner instantly transformed into alarm. Praeder followed the ensign down a narrow white hall, down a speedy elevator that only lowered them two floors, and down another narrow white, staid hallway. In the meantime, two armed soldiers joined the pair, leading the way.

The doctor had spent his volcanic energy by the time the four military men entered the operating room. He held in his palm a partially crushed microchip. He spoke without greeting.

"It is damaged beyond control, I am certain of that."

"What happened?!"

"I am not sure, but I am positive that I inserted a microchip into my lord's brain," the old, gray-haired doctor replied without hope.

The Admiral was about to erupt. "Then what is that?!" he shouted.

Humbly and with great embarrassment, the doctor avoided eye contact. "It is failure, sir. I do not understand-" He broke off in sudden realization. "But maybe-" he interrupted himself again with his own thoughts.

*   *   *   *   *   *

The foursome had become a five-some as the two armed soldiers, the ensign, Admiral Praeder and Doctor Bogome marched down the narrow hallway. Their purpose was of extraordinary importance in the minds of all. If their mission was in vain, more than just the mission failed. Of all missions, Praeder thought ruefully, why did this one have to be plagued with Rebel spies?

Admiral Praeder was certain of one unalterable fact as he walked the walk that seemed to take forever: there would be no trial, no judge, no jury for traitors on his ship.

Punishment would be swift and it would be announced to all onboard. Those who collaborated with the Rebels would pay the ultimate price, period. Praeder would see to it that everyone had the opportunity to see a dead Rebel spy.

*   *   *   *   *   *

 In a small, evenly-lit white room that looked like nearly every other room in the austere spacecraft, the frail-looking medical assistant stood with his back against the wall opposite the entrance to his private quarters. A tiny pill rested in his left palm and a small glass of water was firmly gripped by his other hand. The approaching footsteps were not mysterious to the young traitor. Death was approaching his door.

 The doorway of the entrance opened up and immediately the two armed soldiers burst in, laser rifles aimed at the doctor's young assistant. In an instant the pill was into his throat and water chased it down. In the mere seconds from the time the soldiers entered until the Admiral made eye contact with the double agent, the latter's eyelids began to slowly close.

 Information would not be supplied by this turncoat.

 What none of them- not even the spy- knew was that the tiny microchip was neither blank nor loaded with faulty information. The Rebel thinking had been to leave the prince clueless- to do anything more ambitious was to invite failure. They could have attempted to have the prince self-destruct or to destroy the ship, but their knowledge of the

Prince Tinian was too limited for that to be a viable option. Instead, the replacement chip contained correct but limited information that would prevent the Crown's doctors from quickly identifying the real problem. Reopening the prince's skull would have been a last resort, so there was no need to rush that option.

Had the prince fallen into depression or begun acting in a bizarre manner, the Rebel leadership reasoned, a second surgery quickly would be ordered. Better to cause confusion upon which they could capitalize during the prince's journey home rather than try to do too much and accomplish nothing.

*   *   *   *   *   *

From an unlit bedroom, a man sat on a small chair as he gazed into the night, elbows on the window sill and hands on his cheeks. A feeling of hopelessness crept into his stomach as he watched David walk down the pathway toward the house. David disappeared from his view, then the creak of a door could be faintly heard opening and closing again. From the darkness came a middle-aged woman's soft but distressed voice. "Why didn't they take him?"

"I do not know," he muttered, unable to hide the disarray that had become of his thoughts. "I do not know."

Chapter 3 - Reading Minds

Midwestern summers are made for baseball. Forgotten are the cold winters and the blustery spring days. Winter is either wet and cold or dry and cold, but always cold. Southern Indiana usually escapes the bitter cold, but temperature can be a relative matter. Spring is warm one day, chilly the next, and usually windy. Great thunderstorms rumble across the Great Plains, through the heartland, and across the great expanse of farms, small towns and cities, on their way to the eastern seaboard, all the while producing heavenly light shows that strike fear in some and awe in others.

But there is no time as pleasant in the Midwest as that short lull between the fading of spring and the onset of full-blown summer. The calendar marks the end of school, summer's brutal heat usually stays away until Independence Day, and the countryside is in bloom.

Spring also brought to David and his friends the sound of wood on leather. At least when his team was up to bat, that was the sound that made the world go 'round for him.

David enjoyed high school baseball, but summer baseball was the real thing. No indoor practices or fielding grounders on the basketball hardwood because of the weather. No practices in forty degree temperatures. Lots of travel. Besides, school was out and high school was gone forever. He and his buddy, Johnny Young, were headed to the desert Southwest for a four-year last-stop before heading to the Majors via the minor league farm system. Nothing but time stood in the way of the Big Leagues.

Philosophical views on baseball and the weather were far from David's mind as he crouched behind home plate. The six-foot tall toothpick of a pitcher glared in at David for a sign. The pitcher's sandy blonde hair, which hung nearly to his shoulders, stuck out at odd angles from beneath the sides of his cap. David discreetly displayed to Johnny the sign: his middle finger.

The right-handed pitcher went through the windup and let go with a fastball. The sound of baseball colliding with ribs could be heard by the outfielders.

The batter doubled over in pain. Slowly, he lifted his head and attempted to straighten his body. He looked out at the skinny pitcher and deduced that he could rip him apart, but he knew that Johnny's best friend was only two feet away. The batter would not dare assault Johnny with David in the same county.

Wincing in pain and holding his ribs, the batter-runner half-stumbled, half-strode toward the skinny 18-year old pitcher for all of two steps before quickly readjusting his path down the chalky white line and on to first base. He was not about to pick a fight in a league game, much less with that horse David Steele behind him.

The umpire walked purposely to the mound.

The batter's coach was not intimidated by the young athletes. "That's crap! That's crap! Throw him out blue! That's payback! Are you gonna allow that, blue?!"

The umpire was not the least bit concerned about the rant. His pocked face and nearly permanent scowl made him look just as mean as his deserved reputation. The former Marine carried himself as though he were still in the Corps, and whether the scowl was real or shtick, nobody ever dared to find out.

When the umpire arrived at the mound, his no-nonsense attitude registered with the skinny young man. "I'm warning both teams, starting with you. That's the last batter you pluck today or you're going home early. Got it?!" Johnny did not see color in those eyes, only iron. The young pitcher was flippant and irreverent, but he was not stupid enough to mess with the broad-chested block of a man who was the umpire.

"Yes sir."

The batter-turned-runner, now safely on first base, felt emboldened to restore his pride. "Come on, ump! Throw him out! If it wasn't intentional then he's dangerous! The guy can't pitch!"

Johnny turned and glared at his suddenly brave victim while the taunting continued.

As the umpire made his way to both benches to warn the coaches, David jogged out to the mound. The two had been best friends since they met in their Kindergarten class. They hunted quail and deer together, fished together, got into trouble together, and most important to both of them, they played baseball together. There was nothing like the chemistry of Johnny pitching and David catching. When Johnny was playing first base or left field between starts, baseball just was not quite the same for the two comrades.

"Thunk!" David tried not to laugh at his own description.

"That good, huh?" They both burst out laughing.

"That good," David affirmed.

While the opposing coach continued to make his case for Johnny's ejection, the buddies on the mound soaked in just another joy of baseball.

"I see you remember the sign for a bean ball."

"Hey, even if you didn't call for it, I was drilling him anyway, man. You've hit two dingers and driven in all our runs and then he tries to behead you?! Uh uh. Ain't happenin' when I'm on the mound. I'm just glad they don't have the DH. I wanted my crack at him."

David laughed again. "You got your crack at him, all right. You 'bout cracked his ribs. That was your hardest fastball all day."

"Hey, I'm adding muscle," Johnny said with a sly grin. "Been workin' out. But until I get that fastball in the red zone of the ol' Jugs gun I gotta be crafty."

"Crafty means moving the ball around, throwing to different locations, not throwing everything high and out over the plate."

"I'm changing locations. First time I hit somebody in the ribs all day, wasn't it?" Again the pair broke into laughter. They were cracking themselves up and no one noticed. All eyes were focused on the argument that was winding down in front of the opposing team's bench.

*   *   *   *   *   *

The small manual scoreboard behind the left field fence, which was manned by a grade school boy who was making a few bucks, showed that the game was now in the top of the ninth. The home Cardinals led the visiting Bulldogs 6 to 3.

The batter boldly dug his spikes into the dirt of the batter's box to the left of David. David pointed his index finger down and toward his left spike- fastball inside. Johnny was never a big threat to bean batters- despite the earlier shenanigans- so batters felt comfortable digging in. David would have none of it, even with the game about to end.

Johnny fired a fastball high and tight that seemed to take the air out of the batter's lungs as he leaped back, out of the box.

"Two and two," the umpire casually announced.

The batter nervously reestablished his footing in the box. The game had been more eventful than most due to the earlier incident, and the batter was not sure whether Johnny would risk ejection from this game and an automatic suspension for additional games.

Johnny stood on the rubber, his right hand on the baseball nestled in his glove. He peered over the glove to get his pitching instruction from his buddy.

David displayed two fingers. Johnny shook him off. Again David flashed two fingers, but he was met with the same response from Johnny. David slowly and subtly nodded his head as he flashed two fingers again. The silent argument ended as Johnny went through his windup and launched a curveball that broke rapidly down and away from the right-handed batter. The batter desperately flailed at the elusive spinning white sphere.

"Steeerriiiie!" bellowed the burly ump.

David caught the last pitch of the game and flipped it toward his team's bench. He greeted his friend with a handshake and high praise. "Great pitch!"

"Great pitch-calling. You knew, though, didn't you?! You knew what I wanted to throw, but you wouldn't call it!"

Johnny was surrounded by teammates who either shook his hand, slapped him on the back and shoulder, yelled their praise, or did all of the above.

"That's why we're teammates," David explained with complete sincerity concealed by a smile. "I read your mind and then set you on the straight and narrow."

"Well I know how you think, too, pal." They both laughed. Laughing was what they did best- besides baseball.

*   *   *   *   *   *

On the side of a grass-covered hill overlooking the ball field, with a 180-degree view of Indiana farms and scattered clumps of trees and roads, David looked up into the sky, pondering how he would ever find the words to share his secret with his buddy. The slow-moving cumulus clouds drifted from horizon to horizon. The soft breeze seemed to blow the right words away from David's mind.

David recognized that, during the game, he never noticed how deep the blue of the sky was. He never noticed the clouds until they obscured the sun. But after home games and practices, he and Johnny often came to this spot on the hill, where they could simultaneously chat and notice that indeed there was a world spinning around them.

Most of the teenagers they knew did not take the time to see anything outside of their own realm. But the pair had talked about what made Indiana life so good, and they knew that in the desert, where they would soon find themselves for the sake of baseball, the skies and landscape would be much different.

It was on this hill where they often prepared for the future- or preordained the order in which the future should move. They had foreseen their own rise on the baseball diamond and were on the verge of correctly foreseeing their use of recently signed college baseball scholarships. Many offers had poured in, but the decision was never in much doubt. The future was as neat and tidy as their plans, they believed.

Both lay on their backs, knees propped up for comfort. Only David's pickup remained near the ball field below. Everyone else had left almost an hour earlier.

The small talk of the baseball game had ceased. The hill always seemed to inspire the philosophical and the faraway. Their dreams, so well thought out, so genuine and heart-felt, were about to unravel with a few uneasy sentences, despite the years of meticulous construction.

"Something's goin' on, Johnny," David announced in his drawl, which was a blend of the Midwest and the South.

"Whaddya mean?" Johnny asked in the same drawl.

"I don't know how to tell ya," David replied slowly.

"Must be something in the water."

"Why's that?"

" 'Cause things are changing with me, too."

David's interest rose as the conversation prepared to switch from the casual to the serious. "Such as?"

"Such as, I'm not goin' to ASU," Johnny answered, again with little feeling.

David seemed to deflate. Reality was setting in. The dreams that the pair had so carefully created, ideas that they had cultivated and nurtured, had already begun to fall apart. Now the reality of the collapse was being confirmed. "What happened?" he asked, as though he already was aware of news that should have stunned him.

Johnny paused in order to word his response carefully. "Priorities are changing. What was once important is being overshadowed." He paused again, reading David's reaction, trying to read his mind. "I thought you'd be mad at me."

"Arizona State. Year 'round baseball. Far, far away from these basketball nuts. It was the perfect dream. Another step in the perfect plan." David's words floated above the pair, conjuring up visions in both of their minds. Together- yet quietly and separately- they relived their times together on the diamond, the countless hours inventing dreams of baseball exploits yet to be experienced in the Major Leagues.

"I know. I agree." To David's surprise, Johnny suddenly changed subjects, as though the new subject was somehow related to the collapse of their dreams. "Face it, we both have interesting families. My dad always acts like somebody's gonna jump around a corner and kill him and your aunt and uncle are raising you to become the next General Patton."

"I know more about military strategies and theory than I know what to do with: Napoleon, Caesar, Khan, you name it," David confirmed.

"And I know more about paranoia and seclusion by watching my dad. But what changed with you?"

Again there was a pause as the right words were sought by David. "You go first 'cause you'll think I'm bonkers. Go ahead."

"Bonkers, huh? This I gotta hear."

"Let's just say," David said with hesitation. "I can't tell anyone 'cept you."

"Now I'm really curious. Tell me."

"I'll give the signs, you throw the pitch."

Johnny laughed. "Always forgetting the pitcher's the most important guy on the field."

David laughed, putting himself at ease.

"I don't know yet," Johnny searched for an honest explanation without revealing too much. He was not accustomed to keeping a secret from his lifelong friend. "My dad…" His thoughts trailed off as a small cloud briefly obscured the sun. "I don't know how to explain it. He said some things to me. Not his normal rantings."

"What things?"

"When I understand it, when I translate it, you'll be the first to know."

"But you know you can't go to ASU?" David asked with a soft mixture of incredulity and annoyance.

David wondered to himself why the question even mattered. He knew that he himself was not going to Arizona State, so whether or not Johnny went, the grand dream was dead. But somehow, illogically, he was annoyed that Johnny also was breaking the pact.

"Yeah," was all that Johnny could manage.

Johnny's curt, one-word response warned David to leave it alone. Besides, how could he ask Johnny to be more specific about his hand in ending The Dream when he was not even sure that he could offer his own explanation?

A long silence, which usually was allowed to pass for a full five minutes without posing a threat to either young man, now seemed to only build tension between the two. It had been years since they had argued about anything significant, but the tension that brewed was less like anger and more like a foreboding presence.

After a long two minutes, David broke the thick silence. "Things are changing, Johnny."

Neither saw the old, battered mid-'90's pickup truck approach the hillside after pausing at David's newer model royal blue truck.

"So what's changing with you?" Johnny asked as he laid back down.

"It's hard to explain. Something really weird happened. Something I can't fully explain. Something that has-"

The old pickup honked when it reached the base of the hillside. The friends sat up in unison.

"I'm riding home with David," Johnny yelled.

Albert Young, a man in his mid-fifties and of slight build like his son, yelled back without exiting his truck. "Something important has come up," he shouted at his son. The elder Young's streaks of gray in his hair and hard-bitten face matched perfectly with his bitter, solitary approach to life. None of the locals knew him and none cared to know him once they spent more than two minutes with him.

Young- he was "Mr. Young" to David- carried on his shoulders the attitude of a man who had been through a war and come away with many emotional scars, yet no one knew whether he had or not. No one dared- no one cared- to ask. He was an unpleasant man who had a perfect relationship with the town: he did not wish to mingle with them and they did not wish to be around him.

Johnny looked apologetically at David. "Something's goin' on, and it ain't good." With that, the would-be Arizona

41

State pitcher climbed to his feet and made his way down the hill.

"See ya at practice tomorrow," David called after him.

"Yeah," Johnny said without conviction.

After the truck finally disappeared from sight, David resumed his position where he could watch the clouds traverse the brilliant blue sky. Over and over in his mind the words repeated: He's gonna think I'm nuts.

*   *   *   *   *   *

The small town hardware store was just like hundreds of others in hundreds of other small Midwestern towns. Hand tools, power tools, household chemicals, lawn tools, ammunition, and a variety of guns were for sale. Faded asbestos-laden twelve-inch vinyl tiles covered the concrete floor, with old merchandise display cases creating narrow aisles. Designed by men for men: not a man cared whether the hardware store setting met anyone's aesthetic expectations. It was one place a man did not mind shopping- or just ogling tools.

Phillip Steele, tall and stocky and looking every bit of his fifty-five years, seemed as if he were at home in a hardware store. His rugged-looking face complemented his short gray hair. Wherever he had been and whatever he had experienced, Life seemed to have left an impression on his face and in his expressions. His calm demeanor belied his almost constant wariness. The careful observer would have spotted his frequent glances over the shoulder or his mild trepidation when leaving his house or walking down the street. It were as if Steele thought that an unwanted surprise could strike at any moment.

His pleasant manner hid from the townspeople his lethal physical skills. But these days, he had no need for such skills; he just seemed to worry that the need would never go away.

Always concerned with what the town gossipers had to say- though he seldom repeated such gossip- his awareness of what others thought was heightened by the events of the previous night. Spaceships, aliens- the talk of the town and the outlying areas could be of nothing else. More than ever, Steele had to know what everyone was saying.

Steele quietly fondled a box-ended wrench as he listened to the men near the cash register. A man who looked to be about 60 years old had the floor.

"… And my house shook and the pictures was a rattlin' and I swear I thought we was havin' one of them California earthquakes," August Symington sketched with words for the others to see. The old man was actually 71 years old, but his physical condition and soft face effectively hid his age.

A young man of 20 years, a store employee and another area native by the name of Rick, listened intently to the tale being spun as he leaned against the cash register.

The third man, himself not any younger than the tale-weaving Symington, was dying to ask questions. Old Quincy Adams, his lips starting to move every time he thought the elderly man was finished with a sentence, was bound and determined to get to the bottom of the ruckus of the previous night. He took the opportunity of a pause in the story. "Did ya see all the lights?"

"Hell no," the story teller bellowed. "I was takin' cover under my bed!" The seriousness drained away as he paused. "Ma couldn't figure out where I was 'til I hollered at her to get under the bed, too."

The young clerk laughed, but old man Adams was taken aback. "Jan wouldn't fit under the bed!" he shot out, without considering whether Symington would take offense.

Instead, Symington was tickled by the thought. "Ain't my fault. She woulda fit when I married her." With that, they all laughed and Adams gave out a quick clap with his hands.

When the laughter subsided, it was obvious that they were not going to get distracted from the subject at hand the way men usually do when story tellers and comedians are present. Rick kept them on track. "They say some kids were hiding in the woods and saw the whole thing."

"Oh, I doubt that," responded old man Symington. "Ya got some folks sayin' they saw little green men and all that."

Adams saw another opportunity to provide input into the conversation. "All the idiots come out of the woods when they get a chance, don't they?"

"Out of the woods!" Rick howled. "That's a good one." They all laughed some more at the accidental pun.

"Just like fifteen years ago, ever'body was sayin' the same things then," Symington recalled.

The laughter was suddenly squeezed out of the room. The young clerk asked with a sense of awe and dread, "You guys really believe there were spaceships?"

"Damn right I do," Symington said without hesitation. "What else woulda made those marks? 'Course I believe there were space ships!"

Adams changed his tune slightly. "It was probably an earthquake. They have them sometimes, you know."

"Earthquakes don't leave swirly marks in the fields."

"But they weren't those deep swirly marks like in a movie, they were just faint indentations," Adams replied defensively.

"Or make lights in the sky," Rick ventured.

Now old man Adams was in a bind. Being the voice of reason wasn't panning out. He wistfully looked around the store until he spotted Steele, who was still pretending to be interested in box-ended wrenches. "So whaddya say, Phillip?" he asked, looking more for backup than Steele's true opinion.

"Just like fifteen years ago, wasn't it?" Symington half asked, half told.

"Sixteen," Adams corrected.

Steele thought about it for a moment as he eyed the three men. "I was not here sixteen years ago. I moved in a couple of years after that happened."

Symington felt as though he had won the geriatric battle. "I'm tellin' you boys as sure as I'm standin' here. My

45

house is just behind those woods off to the southeast and nobody coulda felt it the way I felt it. It wa'n't thunder, it wa'n't no earthquake, and it was a spaceship."

"So the spaceships return, fifteen years later," Adams said with amazement.

"Sixteen."

"But for what?" Rick needed to know.

"Not for me," Steele said matter-of-factly. "All I know is, not for me."

"Sixteen years ago another one came the next night," Symington reminded them all.

"Just an earthquake," Steele said plainly.

"Probably," Adams nodded with satisfaction. It was settled.

Chapter 4 - Information Gap

Phillip Steele's two-story house was located at the end of the street before the street elbowed around a corner and out of the neighborhood. Located in a subdivision at the edge of the now-famous "spaceship field" and over a mile from the main section of town, the fourteen-year old dwelling looked like a country farmhouse, despite its age and the fact that it was on less than an acre of land. The nearest neighbor's house on either side was one hundred and fifty feet away- in Steele's mind far enough for privacy yet close enough for a certain degree of fitting in. The two-story white house with the wrap-around porch only lacked a picket fence for it to appear on the cover of Country Living magazine.

At this moment in his living room, Steele realized that there were no news helicopters flying around, although had he bothered to look he would have seen two news vans and over a dozen cars camped out at the edge of the nearby field.

In the living room, a few feet in front of a very old cloth-covered couch, sat a 32-inch television. The house was decorated in a country style of light blues and beiges. Paintings of horses, barns, fields, and cowboys filled the walls. The only modern furniture was David's swivel rocker and a loveseat. In a day and age of high definition television, the standard TV looked antique, as well. In the adjoining dining room, the solid oak table was antique, as were the end tables and other wood furniture.

Conspicuous by their absence, there were no old family photos on the walls, only the paintings.

Steele sat on the couch while his nephew David sat on the old, deteriorating swivel rocker. David stared at the television, even though the volume was turned down.

Grace Steele entered the room from the kitchen, carrying a glass of water for her husband. She was the anchor of the household, never one to raise a fuss about herself while endowed with super-human doses of patience and kindness. When David needed consoling or just to get something off his chest, Aunt Grace was there. Her small frame gave her a dainty look and her gray hair perfectly matched her image.

Grace's facial expression betrayed the seriousness of the conversation that was about to commence. David sensed her grave countenance but failed to understand just how serious this matter was to a great number of people.

"Tell me," David's uncle began. "What do you now know about yourself?"

"I am Prince Andrew Chateau, son of King Andrew Chateau the Second, benevolent ruler of our home planet, Craylar." David paused, as if expecting that the whole matter was a bit too crazy to be believed by his down-to-earth relatives. "I have been hidden here for protection," he continued. "Soon I will return to aid my father in ruling his kingdom and to apply my abilities in putting down the Rebellion. My brother Tinian was poisoned by a rebel before I was born, so father elected to send me to Earth until I reached adulthood."

David spoke for another five minutes, while his aunt and uncle grew more apprehensive with each tick of the second hand of the antique oak clock which sat on the mantle. "You and Aunt Grace have subtly trained me for my role in my father's Kingdom," David said as he reached the conclusion of his new knowledge. "Someday I will be the king of Craylar, and hopefully the Rebellion will only be a memory by that time."

David loudly exhaled as if he had just finished a great physical task. His aunt and uncle did not share in his relief.

"Is that it?!" Steele asked, as if shock were about to overcome him. His intense brown eyes shouted out his unhappiness. His usual wariness was heightened more than ever. His concern reached a level higher than his usual daily passive paranoia. He suppressed the fear that threatened to encompass his entire body. He allowed his thoughts to quickly peruse a checklist of dreadful reasons why his nephew sat in front of him rather than on the spaceship, headed across the galaxy, but he quickly choked off emotions before they could develop.

"That's it."

"Five minutes?! Five lousy minutes?! You should have had three hours worth of information!"

"Three hours?" David laughed. "I wasn't on the ship for very long. How would I know three hours worth of stuff?"

Steele was obviously disgusted. Grace, in her typical style, was a mixture of calm and concern. "What do you think?" she asked her husband.

Steele sighed loudly before answering with a weak, "This is not good." Something was wrong- something was disastrously wrong- but the elder Steele was fearful of expressing such a dark concern. He could only stew in his juices. His head angrily jerked to and fro as he desperately tried to find an answer to David's deficient knowledge. Mentally limber and logical, this time a solution eluded him.

"What?" David laughingly asked, like a kid being left out of a secret.

Steele did not care about David's questions at the moment. "What about the stalkers?" he asked.

"The Rebels sent here," Aunt Grace explained, finishing her husband's thought.

David was clueless. "I don't understand."

"Someone was sent here to kill you," Steele explained. "Someone came the next night- it is part of the town's folklore- and we received communications telling us that others had come. Think, David. Think. Are you sure you do not have information about stalkers?"

"Stalkers? Here to kill me?! Wait a minute, now. All I did was follow whatever urging it was to go to the spaceship, which I don't even understand. Why would someone kill me?" David tried to stay calm, to demonstrate to his aunt that he had absorbed her lessons, but his first true test was not going

50

well. His stomach was beginning to churn and sweat had just begun to appear on his skin over his entire body.

David's mind flashed that there were reasons after all that his uncle taught him military strategies and his aunt taught him to deal with adversity with a level head. The thought was quickly pushed aside by the sentence that still floated in his head: Someone was sent here to kill you.

"They arrived here the day after we did," Grace gave as an explanation, although to David the statement explained nothing.

"Who? Who are they?"

"We were hoping you would know," Steele said dejectedly. "Rebels, of course. But who specifically? We do not know."

Always the optimist, Grace hazarded a guess. "Maybe they gave up and went home."

Steele shook his head to note his disagreement.

"David," Grace asked slowly and patiently. "Why didn't they take you last night?" Her cadence was a sure sign to David that she felt troubled underneath her cool exterior.

"Were they supposed to?"

"Yes," Steele nodded. "They were supposed to."

"What about you?" the thought suddenly occurred to David.

Grace answered because she perceived that her husband was not in the mood to speak more than necessary. "We're to leave at a later date. We didn't want to suddenly disappear and accidentally send a signal to the Rebels that you were on your way home. We figured that since we've made it the entire sixteen Earth years without an encounter, they can't possibly know where you are or who you are."

"Who I am?" David asked as he became more confused.

"David," Grace said gently. "You're Prince Andrew Chateau, not David Steele. We were fortunate enough that you took after your mother more than your father- in looks, anyway. I'm sure the Rebels brought with them photos of your father when he was young."

"So what went wrong last night?" David asked. He felt that growing sense of his uncle's fear that something had gone terribly wrong- something that could jeopardize his life.

His earlier shyness of speaking with Johnny about this weird turn of events was fading. He needed to talk to his friend, to unload and seek advice. David may have been the more intelligent of the two, but they always relied upon and advised each other. David needed to talk, and his aunt and uncle did not fill that order. "I'm so confused," he half exhaled, half spoke. "And how did I know to go into the field, anyway?"

Grace glanced at her husband and saw that she should be the one to answer such a minute and insignificant detail. "When you were a baby a rudimentary chip was placed in your head. They-"

David interrupted. "Rudimentary? But what-"

Grace was beginning to share in Steele's mental exhaustion. Rarely one to interrupt, she did so now without thinking twice. "David, I need to finish this thought," she said, firmly but with at least the pretense of patience in her voice. "The microchips are far more advanced these days, apparently. Besides, you cannot plant too much knowledge into a child's head without causing confusion. You were just a toddler when we arrived here."

Uncle Phillip came back to life, with no patience for the direction of the meaningless questions posed by the boy prince. "Listen David, right now I cannot seem to be able to communicate with the ship. The situation is unstable right now, so it is time for you to get acquainted with some items that I have for you. You are to carry the laser I give you wherever you go. You are to trust no one. No one! Not friends, acquaintances, not anyone."

"What's gonna happen?" David asked, though not really sure whether he wanted to hear an answer.

"We wish we knew."

David looked at the television. "Look!" he shouted.

On the television, the Steeles saw a fleeting image of the nearby cornfield. As Steele turned up the volume with the remote control, a US Air Force General was on the screen being interviewed. "At this time," the General stated firmly. "I cannot confirm or deny the presence of Air Force aircraft in the areas in question."

A reporter, whose presence was only known because his hand and the microphone he held were visible, was not satisfied with the answer. "Sir," he began. "What about the reports of lights flashing across the sky and the sonic booms in many mountain and western states?"

"As I said," the General replied. "There are areas- plural- in question. Son, if we had the ability to put on a light show like the one described by all these people, we'd put that show on every Fourth of July."

The reporter paused, grasping the denial of Air Force involvement. He had expected more evasiveness, with more "cannot confirm or deny" statements rather than "we would if we could" admissions. "General, do you know why Indiana, particularly southern Indiana, seems to have so many UFO sightings?"

"I don't know anything about UFO's or what that has to do with the Air Force."

David was amazed. "It's a national story!"

The reporter was heard in a voice-over. "The General was either unable or unwilling to provide further information."

The news anchor appeared on the screen. "Thank you, John," he said. "To other news now," he said. "Due to the recent terrorist attacks on US Naval ships in the Strait of Hormuz, the price of oil today-" Steele muted the television with the remote control.

Unbeknownst to David, Grace had watched him throughout the news story. She had watched with a motherly, caring eye. She knew that if David failed to learn the many lessons that she and Steele tried to teach him over the years, their stint on Earth was an incredible waste of time and the Kingdom could be in jeopardy. She continued to eye him carefully as she verbalized her observation. "You seem to be in an alternate world right now, David."

David did not attempt to hide his excitement. He gushed his words like a small child would. "I am. It's neat, but it's weird. I mean, to find out one day that you're not who you are, that's weird. I don't know what to think, but I know I don't like the fact that somebody wants to kill me." His last words were slower and reflected the sobering thoughts that danced between his ears.

"You will get used to that," Steele responded, as though he were reassuring the young man. "You will find other things to worry about."

But worry was only part of David's problem.

Chapter 5 - Empty

In his bedroom, David sat at his desk, in front of his computer. Behind him, the walls were covered with posters of baseball players. The bookshelves that ran along one wall were full of books about baseball, military leaders, and war strategies. The gold, metal coat tree had baseball jerseys and jackets dangling from the hooks and was topped with baseball caps. An old glove rested on the edge of his dresser, waiting to fall to the floor. Except for the military books, everything was baseball. Even his mouse pad was of old Riverfront Stadium.

The light blue carpet was littered with baseballs, his catcher's mitt, dirty socks and t-shirts, and a small plastic bag that contained a bulb for the rear turn signal on his truck—which he knew he would eventually remember to change.

Nothing in the room hinted at David having an interest in any other sport. No footballs, no basketballs- nothing but baseball. Whether it was books by the late Major League umpire Ron Luciano or biographies of players from Babe Ruth to Ken Griffey, Jr., every book, fiction or not, was about the Great American Pastime. Yes, football was now king in America, but baseball was the soul of America. World and national events were mere backdrop for the great stick-and-ball chess game.

His desk was cluttered with sundry papers, stationery items, and forms printed out after he completed his registration for college. Copies of papers left behind by the last scout to visit lay under the computer monitor, mixed in with brochures from several players' agents who had tried to convince him to forego college in favor of a head start in a Major League organization.

If he would have dug through the messy stack, he would have also found documents from the San Diego Padres, who had drafted him just weeks prior to this day. The Padres decided that a late-round pick was worth the gamble, but David stuck to his guns, just as he said he would. The Padres were enamored not only with his hitting, but his smarts- baseball smarts and life smarts. They correctly judged that he still had room to mature, but they liked the thought of this six-foot-two, two-hundred and thirty-five pound slab of a kid crouching behind home plate in their beautiful downtown stadium. He had the "make-up," as scouts had called it, to be a Major League catcher. He knew how to call a game, to keep a hitter guessing, to change location and speed on batters. He thought several pitches ahead during each at-bat, and scouts could see from the stands his ability to run a game.

But Johnny was not drafted by the Padres. In fact, Johnny was not drafted at all. He, too, had earned a scholarship to the baseball paradise in the desert, but right-handed pitchers cannot get away with a lack of velocity on the fastball- at least according to conventional wisdom, they cannot. So no Johnny, no David. That simple. Each year in the future David would make it clear to all teams that he would not come out of college early, and by that time Johnny would have matured enough physically to become more attractive to scouts.

Then, and only then, could they allow themselves to be split up. The odds were great, if indeed Johnny were to be drafted as they hoped and dreamed, that they would be drafted by different teams. They could accept that for the Big Leagues, but not sooner.

For now, the Major League teams, the scouts, the papers on his desk- they would all have to wait. Despite what he typed in his text, baseball was not on his mind at the moment. Before he hit the "Send" button he read the text out loud. "Johnny, what's going on?! Let me know how you are. We need to talk. We both have stuff to say." He hoped it would be soon.

*   *   *   *   *   *

For the first time in his life, David felt like a basket case. Unable to concentrate on anything and unsure of what would become of recent events, one series of thoughts reverberated in his head: Who am I? Who is Prince Andrew Chateau? Who is David Steele? Why hadn't anyone told me all this before now?

He was not who he thought he was. His best friend was avoiding him. Bizarre happenings surrounded him- and those happenings were done in his name.

Baseball, Arizona State- all of it. It all seemed so distant now.

Johnny had not been at practice for a second time. It had now been three full days since the two had last spoken. Sending e-mail and texts seemed to help David, but not the situation. Sending the messages was the only way he knew, other than going to Johnny's house, to do anything constructive, to make progress- except that no progress was being made.

Johnny's father had rather remarkably declined to ever have a telephone installed in their house. As far as anyone knew, there was no one in the county- likely the entire state- who did not have a phone except the Youngs. Johnny was not allowed to have a cell phone, either; every text that David sent went to the Young computer, to their e-mail account.

Yet, a phone line had to be installed when Johnny was granted permission to have Internet and e-mail access. When the day came, David did not bother to ask about the obvious contradiction. He just accepted it as another weird facet of Albert Young's existence.

Twice a day over the prior two days, David had visited their house. Twice a day he left the house disappointed. He was sure that they- or at least Mr. Young- were home on every occasion, though he could not prove it.

David's despair and depression stretched into that third day of not speaking with Johnny. He was having difficulty absorbing the materials given to him by Phillip. Hunger and sleep became optional. His mind raced when he was supposed to be sleeping- reliving his recent past, worrying about his friendship with Johnny, simultaneously petrified and jaded about his future.

Besides the confusion in his own life, David was disturbed that he could not be there for Johnny. Apparently, Johnny was enduring his own troubled times. He had hinted so on the hill after their last game. Now out of contact, David was certain that something was wrong. Johnny would not just disappear. He was having problems and David could not be there to help.

Since the entire misadventure had begun, David had regressed emotionally until he was now recalling every possible memory shared between the two young men. Their first few years of friendship were not particularly strong, but they were little boys at the time. Baseball slowly pushed them together until they had become tight like a knot in string- only by cutting the string could the knot be untangled.

When Johnny took up pitching at age 10, David had the bright idea that they would make a good battery on the diamond, so he learned to be a catcher. Given David's growth spurts, catcher was the natural position for him. Eight years later, the pair was attracting scouts from universities and professional teams; then David actually had been drafted. Eighteen years old and plotting a career in the Big Leagues-what could be better than that? They asked themselves that question with regularity.

Acquiring drivers' licenses had briefly threatened the baseball careers of the boys. David's penchant for fast driving and Johnny's reckless streak were a bad combination.

In time, and without incident, they realized that maturity was a necessary commodity. The fast driving slowed somewhat. The recklessness faded. Oh, they were still young and male and seemingly invincible creatures, but life was lived in the context of baseball, and they knew that broken arms or legs could interfere with their dreams.

They had their share of girlfriends, but they agreed that girls were too big of a distraction to worry about for more than one or two dates. It caused them angst with the local girls, and several of the young ladies beheld the two with eyes of contempt. College would be a completely different kind of life, they reasoned, at a university with a far higher population than their little town- and the entire population was their age. Girls could wait; there were goals to attain. Getting into college had to come first.

He recalled specific events, specific times and places. He chuckled quietly with each good memory. There were few reasons to frown about their past.

*   *   *   *   *   *

David was about to burst. He had not confided in anyone other than Johnny for years. Emptiness permeated his thoughts, his emotions, his being. The schematic of the Prince Tinian that lay in front of him was incomprehensible at the moment- David did not even know how his uncle had gotten his hands on the plans to the ship that David had so recently boarded.

From time to time, Steele would enter David's bedroom to check on the younger's progress. These were plans delivered several years ago, the uncle explained to the nephew. There had been two such contacts over the past sixteen years. But there was much with which to be concerned that was more significant than the delivery method of information. There were plans, strategies, and the history of the Kingdom and of the Rebellion. There was terminology to be memorized for commanding a destroyer in space. There were names and places to learn. There were leadership methods popular on their home planet. There was extensive work to be done.

David was the most suspect about the histories of the Kingdom and the Rebellion. The Kingdom, his literature attested, had been around for centuries. In that time, the monarchies had become increasingly benevolent. Rebellions would come and go, but the method of rule remained monarchial.

When the Chateau family seized the throne five generations ago, David learned, it was to expel a corrupt king and queen. Only the lower class and a fortunate few among the upper class had survived the rule of the Banus without fleeing. Under David's ancestors, dissent from the Banu clan was dealt with swiftly and harshly. The early Chateau monarchy was marred by violent uprisings and brutal repression of lawbreakers. Blood flowed freely.

Craylar was again united as one people, one government. Uprisings were nearly constant events. Long ago under the Banus, before David's family had gained control, revolts were crushed to the point of overkill in order to send a message to the people. Under the last two generations of Chateaus, revolts were met with patience, negotiation, and then reconciliation. Regional self-rule was not allowed, but harmony was preferred over disorder.

Perhaps that is what bothered David most. More than the lack of the democracy and republicanism that he had been taught in schools on Earth, more than the disconnect between his own life and his people, David found it difficult to accept the convenient message that everything before the reign of the Chateaus was so bad and now everything was so good.

It was too perfect.

When David's grandfather ascended as King Andrew, the pace of unity and harmony accelerated. David's father, King Andrew II, continued policies that promoted economic stability for all classes, and the middle class finally reemerged completely.

It all sounded so nice. But, David wondered, if he was so benevolent, why did the Rebellion rise up? If the terror of the Banus had been so thoroughly discredited, why did the leader of the Rebellion keep that family's name?

Over the course of the three days of despairing about Johnny and trying to digest his uncle's materials, David's cynicism grew.

He understood military strategies and leadership. But strategies and ideas from "home" were supposed to have been included in the now-famously absent chip. Steele struggled to improvise. He could not adequately educate the young man in a brief amount of time- particularly because Steele did not know everything that would have been included on the chip. He had no way of knowing all of its content.

His home planet of Craylar was closer to the center of the galaxy than Earth and in a different spiral arm, yet David's thoughts were with neither world; his mind might as well have been in another galaxy. The Kingdom and Rebellion were not important. All that mattered to him was the mysterious disappearance of his buddy and the need to share thoughts and feelings with him. The blueprints of the Prince Tinian and their command lingo could wait.

No experience was ever complete without sharing it with Johnny. The same was true for Johnny. No high or low was ever capped until the other knew about the event. Now, in the midst of his agonizing and despair, David needed Johnny's friendship more than ever.

$$* \quad * \quad * \quad * \quad * \quad *$$

The fit of depression and anxiety did not lessen on their fourth day apart. After being burdened for so long- burdened with the weight of a royalty that did not seem real- David was bursting at the seams to talk to his best friend. He was used to confiding his darkest thoughts, his boldest dreams, and if ever there was a time to confide, this was it. E-mails had gone unanswered. The lack of news, of mere conversation, was gnawing at him. He must speak with Johnny. He must unburden himself.

He thought these thoughts a thousand times. If ever he needed his friend, it was now. The weight of the world intensified with Johnny's unexplained absence. This had never happened before, this silence between the two- it was the same thoughts over and over. This had never happened. Where was Johnny? On and on. Over and over. The repetition was beginning to cripple his thought processes.

He knew that Johnny's words were measured when they lay on the hillside after their most recent ballgame. He knew that for Johnny to detach himself from David in that manner could only mean that Johnny's father was the culprit. The "old man" to which Johnny frequently referred truly was not old, yet his behavior did seem to be that of an 80-year old coot.

The two friends were always candid with each other, so their last conversation weighed heavily on David's mind as he knocked on the door for what was now the second time of the day and eighth in four days.

The town had returned to something close to normal. The talk was gradually dying down, though not gone. Although David had not noticed, the news helicopters hovering overhead, shooting footage of the now-empty field, were gone. The news vans were not parked nearby. Curious on-lookers had wandered back under their own rocks. A few reporters lingered, but most had gone home.

He stood on Johnny's porch, not knowing what to expect. Johnny would not be a problem, David surmised. It was Mr. Young who was strange, not Johnny. Young had a sense of paranoia like no one David had ever before seen. He had heard the explanation for not owning a telephone, but he had forgotten it because it did not make sense. He could not fathom opposition to owning a telephone while owning a personal computer. Nor could David ever figure out Young's refusal to attend Johnny's baseball games.

The thoughts of Mr. Young's bizarre behavior continued. The odd hours he kept. His intense reclusion. His avoidance of meat in supermarkets, though he was not a vegetarian. There seemed to be no rhyme or reason to the old man's conduct.

Standing on the Youngs' porch momentarily kept his mind off Johnny, ironically. The problem with Johnny was Mr. Young. It had to be.

Townspeople and farmers alike professed to not know the man. Many would not have recognized him when they saw him, except for his occasional appearances at the grocery store, the bank, or the hardware store. No one knew where he got his money, or when he had ever worked. They did know, however, that he had not worked since moving to the area.

On the single occasion that David's aunt and uncle met Johnny's dad, Young seemed to have been in the midst of a drug trip. His movements were jerky, his eyes dark and brooding, his brain never rested and his body never let go of the perpetual tension that seemed to rule his frame. If anything illustrated the weird nature of Albert Young, it was that after all of the years of the two boys' friendship, Phillip and Grace had only met him once.

David often thought that Johnny may be built like his dad, but the similarities ended there. Johnny possessed none of Young's paranoia and bizarre mood swings. Instead, Johnny was open with his thoughts and confident in his manner- two characteristics which Young did not have. The best way that David had ever summed up the contradictions between father and son was that the son was normal. That said it all.

David had many hundreds of encounters over the years with Young, but rarely were many words spoken between the two. Often David felt like he was being sized up by the man, as if David's character and demeanor were always being judged. David rarely complained to Johnny about this unease around his father, but Johnny was quick to volunteer that his father was a kook. Johnny had a certain degree of fear of his dad that David read as half fear and half respect.

This time, thankfully and to his amazement, Johnny answered the door. As could be anticipated, instead of the usual Johnny, the now-aloof friend seemed startled at David's presence.

"We gotta talk," was all that David could say. His mind was too cluttered to state his case any other way.

Chapter 6 - Revelations

The two friends walked casually through a clearing near Johnny's house. Unlike David, Johnny lived out in the country, isolated from other houses, two miles from the nearest neighbor. Two nearby farms were carved up by twenty acres of woods and a crop-less field owned by an out-of-towner. Somehow- David was not quite sure just how- Johnny's dad came into ownership of the wooded acreage. By bordering the field and the two large farms, Young had the seclusion he craved.

With all of their talk about dreams and goals and success, the inseparable young men believed that a rural life was the best way to finish out their lives. But there were times- many times- when David and Johnny the teenagers lamented the lack of entertainment spots and the city nightlife, yet David and Johnny the budding young men realized that life was more than action and living for the moment.

The two chattered over small talk until they were in the middle of the field. Subconsciously, David wished to be apart from the world when he revealed his secret. He did not want to have interruptions or eavesdroppers. He desired that implied separation from reality. He just wanted to unload, in private, onto his best friend this secret burden that had pressed upon him for days.

They laughed as they recalled insignificant memories. Now comfortably in the middle of nowhere, David patiently waited for the moment.

CHILDREN OF THE SUN

"Old lady Johnson wasn't too happy with us," Johnny laughed as he finished a story of reminiscence.

"That's an understatement." More laughter. David's brain pursued a segue. "Remember how we used to call ourselves 'children of the sun?'" he reminded his friend.

"We were from the inside of the Sun," Johnny recalled cheerfully.

"And that's why we played ball so well in the heat," David finished the sentence.

The laughter and happy thoughts were so warm inside David's heart that he considered backing out of souring the moment. But they were adults now, he thought. Adults are supposed to know, instinctively, when the time is proper for laughter and when the time is proper for tears. Nothing could ruin a happy moment like a bucket of seriousness, but the bucket must be emptied now, David thought. Now. His mind and heart seemed to be in conflict, but he could not figure out if his head said 'stop' and his heart said 'go,' or if it was the other way around.

Johnny was unaware of David's battle, yet he had his own reasons for reminiscing- his own secret reasons to bathe himself in sentimentality. "We were gonna build a spaceship to take us to the Sun," Johnny recalled. "And we got caught stealing lumber from Kenny's dad."

More laughter. More discomfort. More memories rushed into their minds which they needed to suppress. Then silence.

The silence finally became so thick that Johnny sensed that whatever David's problem was, it could not be fixed with laughter. David's need for dialogue was not a matter that he should take lightly, Johnny thought to himself.

"We really gotta talk," was all David could bring himself to say. Only when he saw the warmth and compassion in Johnny's eyes did he muster up the necessary courage. But even that courage seemed to falter.

Thinking that he knew the reason for David's struggles, Johnny filled the void with what had previously brought unease between the two young men. "David, I ain't goin' to ASU. I'm gonna be leaving soon."

"Leaving? Where?"

"Far away. I'll explain later. That's why you'll have to go to ASU without me."

"I'm not goin' either," David said, his confidence in his mission growing once again.

Johnny was sincerely saddened. "Don't lose the dream on account of me."

David changed the course of his path through the field, then stopped when he was ten feet from the friend he now could barely face. "Last week," he started, then interrupted himself with a deep, loud breath. "Last week changed my life." The ten second pause that followed seemed like ten minutes to David. "Johnny, that spaceship… this is nuts!"

Again David turned and walked away, only to stop after a few steps. This time, he told himself, his mind racing, his palms sweating, I have to say this and get out from under this. He turned to face his friend.

"You're gonna think I'm bonkers, but that spaceship the other night came for me," David blurted. There. He felt better. The load on his shoulders and chest indeed had been lifted, but he was not aware that it had transferred to his best friend.

David put his head down and stared at the ground. He awaited the inevitable ridicule to follow.

Johnny's eyes filled with horror. He had to conceal it. He must. It was now time for his world to spin out of control. The thought of leaving the only true friend that he ever had was bad enough, but this? He must have heard him wrong. Surely he meant something else. There must be a logical explanation. The thoughts all convened in his brain instantaneously. Dozens more flew in and out of his mind without hindrance.

David still could not look his friend in the eyes. It all sounded so absurd. Spaceships. Aliens. He himself an alien! How crazy was that?

Johnny spoke in a voice deeper than normal and with more fear than ever before. His words came out slowly, measured. "What do you mean, David?"

That's it, David thought. He thinks I'm nuts, too. He'll want me to get psychiatric help or something. He lifted his head to look his friend in the eyes. "I mean they came here for me. I was supposed to go with them but something went wrong."

"Who?"

"The spaceship people."

"Take you where?" Johnny was devoid of patience. He wanted answers now.

"I can't explain it," David heard himself say as he desperately tried to explain it to himself. "Listen, I know I sound crazy, but I think I'm gonna be leaving soon, too."

"David! Tell me you're kidding!" His voice rose, reflecting the growing anxiety within him.

David laughed. "I know it sounds crazy. I don't blame ya for what you're thinking. You think I'm crazy, too."

"No," Johnny blurted. "Just tell me you're not getting on that spaceship!"

The combination of Johnny's words and tone placed David's thoughts on another track, even though he continued the conversation. Something in Johnny's response was illogical to David, though the teenaged prince was too emotionally drained to connect all of the dots. "I have to go."

"Why?"

"It's a long story."

"Tell me," Johnny implored, desperation rising in his voice.

"I said it's a long story."

"I don't care. Tell me why you have to go!" Johnny demanded.

David could no longer stand still. If he were to retell the story, he had to walk. The pair walked a giant circle around the field as David gave the long version of recent events, including conversations with his aunt and uncle. Johnny forced himself to remain silent, absorbing every detail.

Soon the sun would set. Given the events of the past few days, the last thing David wanted to do was worry his aunt and uncle. It was time to wrap up the story so he could go home.

"You don't seem too amazed by all this. I figured you'd laugh me right out of the county."

Johnny shrugged.

"That's it?" David asked in disbelief. "That's all you've got to say- a shrug? Nothing else?"

"Did they give you a weapon?" Johnny asked, innocently enough.

"No."

"How are you supposed to communicate with them? How will they know when to come back?" Johnny was probing but David failed to notice.

"I don't know. My uncle communicated with them somehow. But he hasn't told me how yet."

"When are they comin' back?"

David began to wonder if he should be annoyed by all of the detailed questions. David had just told him the most incredible, unbelievable story that either had ever heard- so David thought- and yet Johnny merely asked about the details. A little shock was followed by lots of instant acceptance and a barrage of questions.

"I don't know when they're comin' back," David answered. "I think my uncle has to signal them." David was astounded by his friend's overall reaction. He could not help himself but to ask, "You really believe me?"

"Yeah, I do," Johnny replied nonchalantly. "I believe you."

"You're kidding?!"

"No," Johnny replied matter-of-factly. "And you'll never believe why."

Baffled, David took the bait. "Okay. Why?"

"Because sixteen years ago my dad and I came to this town the day after you and your aunt and uncle did."

"Yeah, and…?"

"David," Johnny explained slowly and patiently, as if trying to explain two plus two to a four-year old. "My dad has been looking for you for sixteen years." Johnny's tone lacked the appropriate emotion for the statement, so David missed the import of the meaning of the words. There was no dread, no misgiving in his voice. It was just a matter of fact.

Unlike David, he had been fully prepared for this moment for months. The preparations had begun three years ago by his father, who slowly broke in the young man incrementally. After three years, Johnny's education was completed, with the biggest revelations coming only recently. Slowly but surely, Albert Young had made sure that his son was prepared when the time came. Johnny knew that the day would arrive when he had to have a long talk with David- he just did not know that David would be part of the story, part of his father's preparations.

"I don't get it," David said, his eyes searching Johnny's eyes. "Looking for me how? Why?"

Johnny stared back into David's eyes. With their eyes momentarily locked, David knew. He did not know instantly- the understanding grew in short leaps. But he knew. The longer he knew, the deeper a sick feeling grew in his gut. His mind raced in search of answers, for ways out of this burgeoning nightmare. Darkness spread across his soul, obscuring optimism in him that wanted to believe that everything would be all right. This understanding growing within him was like a nasty, wicked beast rising up out of the depths.

After many seconds that felt like long enough to destroy a lifetime, David could only whisper a single word. "No." He sunk to the bottom of his nightmare.

The thought of the nightmare fading was crushed by Johnny's deliberate, cold response. "Yes."

"No, Johnny. No way. No way!" David physically came to life as he fidgeted with his fingers and hands, running them through his hair, then shoving them into his jeans pockets and immediately pulling them back out, repeating the steps multiple times. His feet slowly kicked at the ground. His hands changed direction to tug at the bottom of his t-shirt. His skin tingled. His heart rate increased and his breaths quickened. This just could not be happening. His temples began to hurt as the blood vessels pounded. A cold chill swept his sweaty body.

"Why else-"

David interrupted. "Be serious, dammit!" His throaty response sounded like the growl of an angry Rottweiler.

"Why else would I be so understanding?" Johnny asked impassively. "I should be shocked, right? Your best friend tells you he's a space alien. How would you react? Unless you understood. Unless you were one yourself."

David turned and walked away, just far enough to have separation between the two young men who had been best friends only minutes before this awful moment. Maybe we still can be, David thought. His physical reaction was matched by revulsion inside his mind. Thinking clearly seemed difficult. He repeatedly and firmly pressed one hand up against his face and wiped sweat away from his nose, eyes and mouth.

Johnny continued. "We figured out that your aunt and uncle came to this area. I was a baby and didn't know the difference, but my people figured it out."

"He was the stalker sent to find me?"

"He isn't allowed to return until you're dead. After a few years he gave up, so he stayed in touch with the Rebellion and they figured he could watch for a ship when they came to pick you up. They would watch for a Crown's ship leaving the frontier."

"And you guys would track me once I got on the spaceship?"

"Not track," Johnny explained with nerves of steel. "Kill." Johnny's disconnect from his emotions frightened even himself. Albert Young had long ago convinced himself that the prince- whoever he might be- had not stayed in the area, thus his search had ended. He convinced himself that when the Crown's spaceship returned to Earth, it would land in another part of the United States, another part of the world, perhaps, and that he and his father would be picked up in time to join the pursuit.

And Johnny was taught to share those same beliefs.

Johnny never imagined that his family's mortal enemy was his best friend. He was mentally prepared for almost anything- but not this. By sheer force of will, he would not let David see in his face his own trepidation and horror at this turn of events. Johnny had a destiny to fulfill.

"Lovely," David said, though he could have verbalized a different thought out of the hundreds that seemed to clutter the interior of his skull.

"My dad has waited patiently for all these years," Johnny said, almost glowingly it seemed to David.

Ever the optimist, and one to hide behind denial whenever possible, David pulled out another of his many thoughts. "Well, me and you can put an end to this war."

For the first time, a genuine emotion overcame Johnny. With sincere sadness he uttered the unbelievable news. "David, I have to kill you."

David stood in the field, motionless. Johnny's words stung him but produced no emotional outburst. The revolting words should have both incensed and frightened him. He was already physically ill- more pain heaped onto his head had little effect; yet David still stared at Johnny in disbelief. Just like that- "I have to kill you." Nothing to it.

Despite the sadness in Johnny's voice, there was something terribly astonishing about a lifelong friend calmly making such a pronouncement. How could he do that, David wondered? How could he say such a thing and mean it? How could friendship be thrown away so easily?

David could not instantly recover from the loss of a long friendship, of possibly being dragged into a war he did not understand, of the emptiness he felt inside. His facial expressions were a mass of bewilderment and pain. The pain had grown, spread throughout his body. But now the pain could do no more damage, no matter what other ridiculous assertions Johnny made.

Johnny tried to explain the unexplainable. "My dad has trained me for this moment. It's why I'm on Earth. I just don't know why it has to be you."

"What do you mean, "trained" for this?" David was incredulous. He felt his jaws tighten. His lungs felt as though they were slowly but steadily being crushed.

"My dad was afraid that he'd be punished for not finding you," Johnny explained. "So he felt the need to train me, to mentally prepare me for my role in the Rebellion."

Ever the one with noble intentions, David refused to grasp the commitment he heard in his new adversary's voice. "What about our friendship?" he asked.

"What about it?" Johnny asked, unblinkingly.

"You really think you could kill me?" David asked, thinking that he had just framed the argument that would trump Johnny's entire cold, disgusting attitude. Together,

David thought, we will end this silly war and continue our friendship as it always has been.

"Some things are more important than friendship," Johnny coolly replied.

"There's no way!" David exploded, his voice racing through the quiet countryside.

"David, I have to. I don't want to, I have to." Johnny's steady, icy response surprised them both. The die is cast, he thought. He was not burdened with all of David's philosophical dances around the central issue of what reality had in store for the pair. He saw in his mind what lay ahead and he accepted it. "It's my destiny."

"You're sick!" With that, David turned and angrily marched away, across the field and hopefully, he thought, out of this nightmare. Those three words would haunt his memory for the rest of his life. They were closer friends than any other friends he had ever observed. But Johnny only spoke of his destiny.

As he headed across the field, toward the long gravel driveway of the Young residence to reach his pickup, he began to wonder if he would be able to walk the entire distance. He was emotionally spent and physically ill, and now expending physical energy was intensifying the sensation of illness. His breathing was labored and his body was covered with sweat. A quick doctor's observation would have resulted in the prognosis that he had the flu. If only that were so.

Johnny did not bother to give chase. Hand to hand, scrawny Johnny did not stand a chance against the bearish

David. But there were other ways, he thought, as he watched David go. After all, it was his destiny.

*   *   *   *   *   *

David drove home with his mind in complete turmoil. Johnny's cool declaration of impending murder unnerved the young man. Had one of his former classmates made such statements, David would have knocked the classmate into the nearest emergency room thirty miles away. But this was Johnny. They met in Kindergarten. They thought alike. They read each other's minds. They played baseball together. They were best friends. They were inseparable. They were soul mates.

They were enemies.

Chapter 7 - His Own Rebellion

Phillip and Grace Steele had no doubt that something was wrong. Their nephew was always amiable and extroverted. He just never seemed to have bad days. But in the days that had passed since contact with the Royal Fleet, David had been far from agreeable. He had become moody and distant, prone to spend his time either alone or with his baseball team.

But when David entered the house and walked through the living room without a greeting and with an almost angry step, they knew. What was supposed to have been so easy was now a mysterious, potentially dangerous situation. When David entered, their ongoing conversation of the previous twenty minutes had been about that mystery.

Why did the military ship fail to take the prince with them? Logically, it appeared to them that the captain of the vessel must have believed that the situation was too dangerous. But if that were so, why come at all? Why not wait until another time- a safe time- to land on Earth?

Why did David know so little? They obviously implanted a memory chip into his brain, given that he now knew at least some information.

This and more was eating at the Steeles when David hurriedly passed through the living room and rushed up the stairs to his bedroom. He had never before acted in such a way, and now their worrying took on an added dimension.

*　　*　　*　　*　　*　　*

David had no idea what he was going to do next. During his drive home, he had failed to complete a single, coherent thought. One thought begun in earnest gave way to fifty succeeding, confusing thoughts.

Night had fallen during his drive, and the darkness which usually brought him peace of mind and perspective failed to do so. The clear southern Indiana night did little to clear his crowded mind or ease his extreme tension.

Now, alone in his bedroom, coherence was no closer to his mind. He looked at the baseball posters and wondered what had become of his life. For days he had agonized over the concept of living a lie, but decided that the description was inaccurate. He had agonized over the fact that he was not who he thought he was, but that was too distastefully whiney.

David failed to accurately identify exactly what concept haunted him. He was royalty of a warring alien people while living on the outskirts of a small town in the farmlands of the United States on Earth. He could not even explain that one to himself.

Of one thing he was sure: he was deeply confused before he shared his experience with Johnny. Before then he thought that his life could not get any worse.

He was determined that his friendship would survive. Of course this is a dark moment, he thought. Of course things seem to be falling apart. This was merely the beginning. As time wore on- time! That was what he needed. He needed to spend time with Johnny, reminding him of what a nutcase Mr. Young was. Reminding him that they long ago swore an allegiance to each other. Only the Big Leagues would separate them, they had vowed- and vowed repeatedly.

David opened the top drawer of his dresser as his thoughts bounced between hope and despair. Underneath his socks he uncovered a palm-sized gray laser gun that his uncle had given to him days before. While the thoughts of Johnny and the last several days raged within his head, David slowly caressed the odd weapon.

Not shaped like a gun, the laser was actually shaped like an extra-wide sheetrock knife with the blade hidden. Rather than a trigger like that of a gun, the firing mechanism was a button that had to be pushed. The safety, which protected from accidental discharge, was a switch that slid to one side.

Aiming seemed awkward. He stepped in front of the mirror affixed to the back of his dresser and confirmed his suspicion. Unlike his .308 or shotguns, he could not comfortably draw a bead on any specific point. Out of curiosity, the little boy in him wanted to fire the weapon. He was too acquainted with weapons to perform such a foolish stunt, but the urge was there. This weapon is so small, he thought. Surely it could not do too much harm. To the mirror, he had no doubt it would do harm. But to a person? They must have given him the "junior" laser, he figured.

He moved around in front of the mirror as if he were a Hollywood action star, but he could not get comfortable with his attempts to aim at his own face in the mirror. Lining up a shot proved difficult. He had no doubt that aiming while under pressure would be challenging.

He had lied to Johnny about not having a weapon, but at the moment of utterance he was unsure why he had lied. Having seen Johnny's reaction, he now argued with himself whether the lie was prudent. On the one hand, he thought, if Johnny were buying into this destiny thing, then having a weapon to protect himself was indeed prudent. On the other hand, what was the big deal? He already owned two shotguns, a rifle, and a semi-automatic pistol- as did his now-former buddy. Johnny not only knew of the guns, he had fired each one himself. Was a little toy laser gun even necessary? He would rather carry his .40 caliber Sig Sauer, he thought. He preferred the feel of the P226 any day over this over-sized sheetrock knife.

With an emphatic thrust of his hands, he buried the laser gun under the socks in the drawer. Then he thought better of it and placed the alien weapon on the wood lip formed above the drawer, underneath the dresser's wood top. The overhang inside the unit meant that something resting on the small surface was not visible when the drawer was opened. Someone searching his drawers would automatically look under clothing articles. But the lip above the top drawer, which jutted inward four inches, was wide enough to hide an item as small as the laser.

As he closed the drawer, he instantly forgot about the prospect of firing the strange laser gun. Immediately his mind returned to the thought of arguing his case to his friend. He could not bring himself to accept the term "former friend."

*   *   *   *   *   *

Grace thought that it was a good sign when David descended the stairs. Whatever it was that bothered him this evening, she thought, will or has already passed. Quickly she realized that she was wrong. She noticed his walk as he entered the room and then as he fixed his eyes on her husband. He had that swagger that he rarely demonstrated, but it was an attitude of fieriness that she recognized as a signal of his readiness for battle- but not their collective battle; not the battle on behalf of the Crown.

She grabbed the remote control that lay on the couch next to her and muted the television. Steele looked up from the couch at David just as the young man was about to speak. Little did David know that the television was simply background noise as the couple plotted out the next few days- or however long it took for the Prince Tinian to return- as well as what they would do without David until the ship returned to recover them.

David did not bother with feigning courtesy and trivial greetings. Rather than sit in the swivel rocker, he chose to stand. "Uncle Phillip," he immediately launched into his purpose for entering the room. "Tell me, how does my father justify a monarchy?" It was half question, total accusation.

Steele quickly debated with himself whether he would take the bait, but the mild-mannered man was much stronger and more courageous than David ever realized. He thought for a moment as he eyed the young man with great caution.

When David's temper flared, he mused, he was like a caged lion being let loose. A stupid lion at that. Steele's aversion to using contractions sounded odd when he became angry, but it was in fits of anger that his focus narrowed, ideas and thinking came easily, and his pronunciation became exceptionally crisp.

Steele's maturity quickly overcame splinter thoughts that threatened to develop in the recesses of his brain. "He is a benevolent ruler, David." His slow pronunciation of the boy's name was a subtle sign that the young man should watch his step. David was not interested in subtleties.

"Tell me more," he ordered firmly, folding his arms emphatically, as if to demonstrate his skepticism.

"His father focused the kingdom on matters important to establishing peace, and he was able to establish order. Your father was the next king. There had been generations of difficult times, because of our ancestors and the rebels, so your father's primary concern was bringing economic prosperity to our people. He did that through policy and through entering into peace treaties with other civilizations-other planets. Thanks to your father and grandfather, more people are free now than ever before.

"The Banu name is both a family name and, if he is still alive, the name of the current leader. He is a charismatic, brutal man who is determined to not only take back the throne for the Banu family but to kill every Chateau he can find. He is dangerous, and he must be stopped."

"That sounds like a lot of propaganda crap to me," David snarled, darts shooting from his eyes.

"David!" Grace cried out.

He ignored her. "So you molded me into this student of military strategy for this?!" David continued angrily, his words dripping with a tone that was a call to battle.

"Yes, and that is why I was so upset that your memory chip did not have military information on it. You were to have your knowledge merged with our people's knowledge."

"And what about the Rebels?" David demanded.

"What about them?" Steele was quietly losing patience, but his exterior did not betray his thoughts.

"How do I know that they're not freedom fighters? How do I know they're not the ones in the right?"

"David!" Grace gasped. Her hand shot to her mouth at the sound of such foul words.

Steele's exterior was now unable to provide cover for his thoughts. "I will say this as calmly as possible." He was trying to convince himself of the need to maintain his composure, even while his taut face and slightly trembling hands betrayed his anger. He did not care whether he exploded at the boy, but Grace did. "I have given you time to deal with all this. I have stood back and let you go through the emotions and shock that the chip would have prevented. But now it is time for you to get past some things and go forward. There is a battleship out there waiting to take you home. You have a purpose, a mission. You are not prepared for that mission and we need to get you there fast."

David felt that his uncle was changing the subject. He was not concerned about missions right now. But Steele was going to make sure that David listened.

"I have assembled some items in the den," Steele continued. "You already have the laser in your room and you and I will go out somewhere where you can practice firing it-we will go tomorrow. But the other items are of the utmost importance." With each sentence, Steele's voice and nerves steadied, his tension eased. "You have already learned many things you need to know. The items in the den are here in case times become dangerous, and for communication."

David was forgetting his arguments against the Kingdom and the war. Steele could see in David's face the transformation from the bullheaded kid into a curious child.

"These supplemental items are all we have until our destroyer returns. I wish it could be another way, David. I really do. But life is this, and you have to deal with it, and you have to move forward with rapid advancement of the materials you have been reading these past few days. You have to be ready mentally when the ship arrives to take you back home."

The room fell quiet. The tension in the air dissipated. Even Grace, the worry wart, had quietly released her tension through her lungs.

Slowly, thoughtfully, the mature David began to speak, though his critical nature still controlled him. "Why didn't you tell me any of this before?"

Steele was not in the mood for a performance review, no matter how polite. "You would not have been able to keep all this to yourself. You are just becoming a man. A boy cannot keep all this to himself. You would have been a danger to yourself, to the cause. Responsibility can only be sensibly doled out with maturity."

Again the silence returned. The angry child who entered the room minutes before was quickly struggling to reach for the manhood blooming inside him. I have to deal with this, he thought to himself. He was not quite sure how he would deal with it, but he was going to try. The one thought that he must hide from his family, he told himself, was that he had met the enemy.

"David," Grace interrupted the young man's thoughts. "We didn't expect this either. In fact, we don't completely understand what's going on. They were supposed to insert the chip as you flew away, back to the Kingdom, back to our part of the galaxy. I'm sorry we weren't better prepared for this."

David looked at his aunt, then his uncle, and weakly nodded. Too many thoughts collided with one another for him to respond with any degree of coherence. Finally, when he realized that he had to say something, he blurted, "I have to digest all this." With that, he left the house through the front door.

Phillip and Grace were not impressed. Things were not going well, they both agreed.

"If he is our best hope," Steele muttered angrily to his wife. "Then the Kingdom is in a lot of trouble."

"What are we gonna do? This is awful!" Grace asked, fighting back tears.

"I am rethinking whether we should allow him to go out in public, keeping up the facade that all is normal." But Steele was not through, and he was not about to hide anything. They had traveled too far, waited too long, to deal lightly with adversity. After years of time passing uneventfully, every minute now mattered. He knew that he must act decisively. "First, I am going to hide the communicator. I do not want him in communication with the ship until he is ready and I sure do not want them picking him up when he is acting like this. No telling what he would say to them."

"But what are we going to do about him? To prepare him?"

"I should kill him!" His voice contained no irony, no humor.

"Phillip!"

"Oh, I am not going to kill him. But only because he is my brother's son and the best hope for the Kingdom. Without him, our male blood line ends. Besides, no one back home would understand and I do not want us to go down in history as traitors. So..." His thoughts trailed off momentarily. "Killing him is not an option."

Grace could no longer hold back the tears. Her frustrations and fears had been suppressed for too many days.

Chapter 8 – Destiny

"Tell me," Johnny began slowly. "What would happen if we converted the prince to our side?"

Albert Young instantly knew that something was afoot. His menacing dark brown eyes glared into Johnny's, probing. His eyebrows moved slightly closer together. The mild bags underneath his eyes moved closer to his eyelids, forcing Young to squint to see. His lower jaw moved upward, slowly, about to force his teeth to clench. And this was not his angry look.

Johnny had become accustomed to such probing, but his ability to conceal thoughts and feelings from his father had never improved. The man could read his son through a brick wall.

"And how would you go about such a task?"

"Well, I- uh, I guess through persuasion."

"There are many forms of persuasion."

"Verbal persuasion."

Young's steely gaze bore through Johnny's eyes and into his mind. Johnny looked away for relief.

"Why would you want to persuade the son of the King to oppose his own father? Why do you think that would succeed? That would take time." Young's words were spoken with his typical dry, harsh tone, no matter the subject. "It would be quicker, easier to simply kill him." Easier was emphasized with the elongation of the word and more air escaping from the harsh man's harsh throat as he slowly enunciated.

Johnny thought about his response, desperately trying to not show weakness to his father. "Don't you think that the prince would be an incredible ally? A crushing psychological victory for us and against the Kingdom?"

Young almost smiled. He was a vile man, and a man of vicious tendencies, but so far as anyone knew- anyone except Johnny- he was simply cold. He was, to the outside world, a quiet, aloof man who could have been just as easily an intensely private individual or a serial killer. He was not one of those people about whom others would comment if a heinous crime had been committed, "We would've never dreamed he was capable of this." He abhorred contact with others. He trusted no one and desired to interact with no one. Relationships were "not his thing," as David once observed.

Ironically, it was this attitude that may have kept him from finding the prince. He never considered how he could find the prince if he never interacted with potential suspects.

"Psychological victory," the elder man continued. "I like that way of thinking. But we are not talking about a lieutenant defecting or sabotaging a Royal fireworks display. We are talking about the successor to the throne. Psychological victories often preface substantive victories, but this- this is too important to worry about psycho- in fact," Young interrupted himself. "In fact, the prince's death would be the ultimate psychological victory in the pursuit of defeating the Kingdom!" The thought brought excitement to Young's voice and brain.

Johnny slowly exhaled. He had vacillated between resolve and compromise. But he knew that, with his father, there would be no compromise.

Young's deep brown eyes again pierced Johnny's soul. He knew- simple deduction. "It's David." He paused for effect. "Isn't it?" He knew that Johnny cared about no one else except for his father and the one friend. The other boys and girls were good acquaintances, at best. Yes, there were others to whom he referred as "friends," but deep down, the boy did not really mean it.

Long ago, Johnny had begun training himself to control his outward reactions. Subtle changes in his face and demeanor were only perceptible to the careful observer. His father was such a careful observer. Johnny's muscles tightened throughout his entire body. His teeth clenched even though his lips remained relaxed. His facial muscles tightened and his eyes narrowed slightly.

"How long have you known?" Young asked softly. The man seemed to not have a heart, except in rare moments with his son. But he understood that this was painful for Johnny. He understood how important this friendship was to him. At that moment, he also understood that he would have to double down on ridding Johnny of this foolish impediment. Friendship was not going to get in the way of the mission.

It was Johnny's turn to glare with a hard stare. Internally, his mind raced with a dozen lies as possible responses. But it was no use. "Just two hours ago."

The two studied each other's eyes.

"How did you know?" Johnny asked.

"There's only two things you care about- baseball and David. In fact, when you got into a little trouble with that girl Donna, I was a bit relieved."

"Oh good gosh! Besides, Donna and I, we-"

"I don't want to hear anything about Donna," Albert scolded. "Let's stick to the larger picture. I was not about to allow a misguided sexual liaison interfere with our purposes. That's why I did what I did to Donna's father. Now, what about David? When are you going to fulfill your destiny?"

"My destiny? I thought it's yours," Johnny lied.

"I failed, Johnny." A sullen expression crossed Young's face. "I should have found and killed the prince within days or weeks of our arrival. A battle cruiser orbited the sun in anticipation."

"I know, I know. You've told me. You never found him and the mission was much more difficult than anyone had imagined. But isn't there a better way now?"

"No!" Young shouted. The Albert Young of old was back. The soft talk with his son was not working. "My day has passed. I could have returned to Craylar a hero had I succeeded. But now," he lowered his voice. "Now, you can be the hero. You can set the stage for your ascension to the throne. It can be you!"

"But I can-"

"No!" Young was not interested in any words that followed 'but.' "You are destined to be King. Of that, there is no doubt. You can enter the gates of the Royal Court with honor and dignity. You can take your seat at the head of the government with authority!"

Young's pause was not an opening for further argument, and Johnny knew it. As desired, the young man absorbed the meaning of his father's words.

"It was because of destiny that I failed. You are destined to be compared with my cousin, our great leader, Banu. It is with me- and by extension you- that he held great hope. It is you who he intends to succeed him someday. Never was it me. I'll be too old then. You- not me, not anyone else- are to be the second King of the restored House of Banu, after our cousin someday abdicates. He knew that I would train you from here if our stay became extended. Someday you will be Banu the Second, John the First, whatever you want to be. But you will be the King of Craylar!"

Johnny stared past his father, in awe at the thought and at a year's worth of emotion coming from his father in such a brief amount of time. He had heard it all before, but the thought was still spectacular. The intensity, the almost crazed fervor with which Young spoke the words was befitting of a salesman trying to peddle explosives to a would-be terrorist. His appeal was flawless to the teenager. A little murder between friends wasn't such a big deal, after all- at least not coming from Mr. Young. The elder man meant every word with a passion that was only exhibited in moments such as these. Johnny liked that passion; he loved that message: King!

And unlike David, he understood the depth of the statement. He was prepared for the future.

"Do you understand the importance of destroying the prince?" Young asked, intensity flooding his words, syllables hissing past his lips.

"I do."

"Good," Young continued. "I failed. You will not."

"There is no other way?" Johnny half asked, half stated.

"There is no other way. You must kill him. If we destroyed their ship and stranded him on this planet, they would send another ship. If we found a way to convert him, they would capture him and reprogram his mind. There is no other way."

A sense of dread welled up inside of Johnny. The thought of killing his best friend was easier given his upbringing, but still a reprehensible thought- even to the offspring of Albert Young- Albert Banu. "And you cannot take this from me?" As soon as the words had been launched he realized how wimpy, how weak they sounded- he sounded. Before he could interrupt the trajectory of the weak words with strong ones, his father fiercely swatted them out of the air.

"You must learn, son. You must learn to kill, to control, to take power when it stands before you. Killing is power. This is not a unique idea. Causes fail, empires fall when those in control are afraid to wield power, to kill. You must learn the ways of reality, not pious fantasy. Friends can be replaced, but there is only one destiny."

Johnny swallowed hard. He had been wonderfully focused in his training, his father had told him. But now, with the fate of a people potentially resting on his shoulders, he would require extra resolve.

"Consider this," Young said absent emotion and melodrama. "Your final two lessons."

"Two?" Johnny asked. "What besides destiny?"

"Temptation."

Johnny's mind drifted, the words "destiny" and "temptation" echoing in his head. Destiny he understood. How temptation would play a role he did not know. But he did know that he rather liked his destiny.

"I will kill the prince. Don't worry." The words and tone convinced his father, and they nearly convinced Johnny himself.

*   *   *   *

*   *

Johnny thought over the words for nearly an hour in the peace and quiet of the Young home. Solitude was easy to come by given his father's inability to carry trivial chatter and mundane conversations. He could sit in the middle of the living room, as he was now, and be surrounded by silence. Nearly anywhere in the house was a quiet place.

He had never resented David. David was bigger, stronger, and more highly regarded as a baseball player. David seemed- to others, anyway- to be smarter, and he had a much sunnier disposition. But Johnny was faster- quicker- and his pitching abilities were on the rise. He was more cunning, more manipulative than David, and they both believed that such traits counted toward intelligence.

Unlike David, Johnny did not fret about matters- if he made a mistake he was over it in minutes. Unlike his brawny friend, though, he did not forget when the mistake was made by someone else. He was unforgiving toward everyone except his father and David. No one else was worth the time to forgive. If someone made him mad enough, that person did not exist, in his imagination, at least. That person became a non-entity, the same way everyone, on two planets, became non-entities to his father.

If Johnny liked someone, he exhibited a selflessness that ran deep. He was committed to a local charity that helped families at Christmas, largely because he liked the trigonometry teacher who headed up the efforts every year. Through the program, he learned to enjoy helping people and, to both boys' surprise, his father did not make him quit.

When Johnny was away from David, he could be gloomy and sullen, almost depressed, so dark was his personality. When with David, he was much more affable. Johnny dismissed the changes in attitude to genetics, laughingly claiming that David's influence could override that of his father's.

After an hour alone in his thoughts about his current situation, he continued to struggle with what he should do about David. He knew, but he did not want to know. The attraction of being a ruler along with David was exciting, but he knew that it was impossible. Each week, it seemed, he learned more and more about his home planet, the bloody, internecine civil war, and his destiny.

Despite his deep affection for David, his buddy was a prince- the prince. The last male in the line of Chateaus in a society that did not permit queens. But he was more than that: he was the enemy- not just the enemy like a Royal soldier was the enemy. No, he was the very face of the enemy. The only offspring of the hated King- and the young prince barely even knew that.

Johnny loved David as his very own brother, but he was not his brother. Regardless of what he had been, he was now the enemy. There was nothing complicated about it. Because he was the enemy, Johnny had to forget about friendship. Destiny would bring him power and glory- something that a mere friendship would not bring. And unlike his bewildered best friend, he understood every aspect of the past, the present, and his glorious future.

On this Friday night, the young man who normally worried about neither plans nor organization decided that he had an idea worth pursuing: He made his way to the computer and looked up a website. He had made up his mind, he told himself, that he was ready to kill.

It was not often, but it was the case now: he had a plan.

Chapter 9 - The Town's Gone Mad

"Vern and Tommy's Game Rooms of Fun" was the awkward official name of the arcade and pool hall. The local kids just called it "Vern's." It was housed in a relatively new building located just off of downtown- relatively new when compared to the town's center. Downtown consisted of one city block of old brick buildings parted by a one-way street. Main Street, which flowed southward through downtown, returned to a normal two-way traffic flow on both sides of the downtown section.

A pharmacy, a barbershop, a liquor store, a bank, a small grocery store, a tattoo parlor, and the hardware store where Phillip Steele had participated in the debate about the alien spaceship, were the stores located in this short strip of land. The other three storefronts were empty.

Just to the north of downtown, in what used to be the service area of a car dealership, Vern's attracted dozens of youth each night. The front of the reinforced cinder block building, where at one time a showroom of new Buicks, Oldsmobiles and Pontiacs caught the eyes of passing motorists, was now occupied by a regional clothing store chain.

Vern's was only accessible from the back alley, and that was just fine to the youngsters who made the frequent trek downtown to pass time amongst friends. To many of the kids, there was something exciting and mildly deviant about a dark alley entrance- even though the goings on inside were quite innocuous. While some of the kids remained at home to play their computer games, many still enjoyed the old-fashioned habit of socializing with peers at the arcade.

Inside, the large rectangular room, with the walls and floors fully finished, expertly hiding the history of the former auto service area, was a room divided in half between video arcade games on the one side and a half dozen pool tables and sundry table games on the other. Teenagers played air hockey, foosball and similar games in an area near the pool tables.

Back in one corner, near the soda machines and the entrance to the restrooms, at the farthest pool table from the door, two couples shot a game of pool. The pair of vivacious young ladies and two burly young men were not burdened by the serious complications of life the way their good friends David and Johnny were so burdened. Had a stranger observed the behavior of the baseball-playing best friends and then watched the four youngsters at the pool table, the stranger would have failed to see any similarities between the two groups.

The teenagers were not as concerned about the future, either. The boys were already in the process of mastering the family farms, and there was no need for college. The girls likely would marry local farmers or area or regional small businessmen. Why fret about the future when the present was so comfortable and the future promised more of the same?

Both Bobby and Junior were large in every part of their bodies- heads, hands, chests, legs and feet. Bobby looked like he could pick up a three-hundred pound sow and carry it on his shoulder. Junior looked as though he might be able to carry Bobby and the sow. Bobby had too much fat hanging from his gut; Junior did not. Bobby was six-feet tall and checked in at 305 pounds while Junior was four inches taller but only twenty pounds heavier. Bobby had the brains but Junior had the muscles. Along with David, the three had been the biggest boys in the high school. All were born within months of each other and all were now recent graduates. The football coach, who never convinced David to play, was understandably sad to lose Bobby and Junior.

Karen and Lisa were cousins who looked like sisters. The short, striking brunettes had heads of hair that seemed to match their bubbly personalities. They exuded a contentment rooted in an understanding of a concept which many of the local kids their age did not grasp: what you now wish you could escape would someday be the best memories of your life. Just like their mothers, the girls were likely never going to live anywhere else in the world- in the state, for that matter, once college was over with- and the knowledge kept lit within them a glow of happiness that they could not thoroughly explain.

But at the moment, Karen was not as happy as she normally was. "Why do I always get stuck with Junior?" she demanded to know.

"Because," Lisa coolly reasoned, her blue eyes enhancing the coy smile directed at her cousin. "You have the patience to deal with him."

Junior walked over to Karen and bent down enough to rest his large head on her small shoulder. Karen could not take it any longer. Her laugh filled half of the large room until the sound died away near the video games.

"Ya hear that?" she asked mockingly. "You're my ball and chain in pool."

"Ball in chain, huh?" His gruff voice was in sharp contrast to her sweet country melody. "I thought wives are the ball in chains."

"Humph!" She walked off, trying not to smile.

David cautiously entered Vern's with the timidity of a mouse standing in the middle of a field at a bird sanctuary. He was accustomed to dominating on the sports field and holding his own, at worst, everywhere else. Even big Bobby and bigger Junior, who outweighed David by seventy and ninety pounds, respectively, recognized that, despite their size advantage over him, David moved with both strength and speed. He might not be considered cat-like, but David's powerful arms and legs perfectly concealed any discrepancy in speed. Young men size up even their buddies, and all three shared a triangle of respect.

Never one to successfully put on an act, David's approach to the pool table was marred by a poor performance. His mind had not slowed in nearly a week. In that time, he had not seen friends outside of his baseball team. It was no secret that something was wrong with him, but he tried his act, anyway.

"Hey guys," he said cheerfully. The "hey" was weak and the "guys" was forced, resulting in an unnatural cadence.

"Hey David," they all said, nearly in unison.

"So what's up?"

"Just whoopin' up on Karen and Junior," Bobby laughed.

"Poor Karen," David smiled knowingly.

"Have you seen Johnny?" Lisa asked. It was a genuine question of curiosity, but David was instantly suspicious-more like paranoid.

"Uh, no, uh, why?" The response was defensive and he knew it. Delivered with the smoothness of a three-legged dog walking on ice, he thought.

Even thick-brained Junior noticed the awkward response. As Lisa answered, Bobby looked David over closely. "No reason. He just said he'd be here tonight. Ain't seen you two around for awhile." With David in her sight, she bent down and took her shot. The clanking of the billiard balls turned all eyes to the table.

David hated the lack of conversation. An entire three seconds had passed and no one had spoken. It was killing him. They must know that something was wrong. They must have talked to Johnny, who told them everything. Whose side would they take? He began to sweat along his hairline and under his arms.

Bobby's words did not help put David at ease. "Said somethin' 'bout he hopes you're comin' but I told 'im I didn't know why you wouldn't. It's pool night and you'd show."

"Was that it?" David's paranoia was seeping out of every word.

The clank of billiard balls was followed by a loud, "Aw man!" The youngsters turned to the table in time to see the Eight ball drop into the corner pocket. They all busted out laughing, except David.

"You did it again!" Karen laughed with a touch of frustration.

"We win again," Bobby laughed.

Junior shook his head. "One day," he swore as he laughed, "I'm gonna learn how to hit what I'm aimin' at."

"You wanna play?" Bobby asked David.

"That'll be the day, Junior," Karen replied to her pool partner. "I've never seen you hit what you're aiming at yet."

David shook his head in the negative at Bobby. David was not in the mood for fun and games. Odd place to come then, he thought to himself.

"It's not fair sticking Karen with Junior all the time," Lisa said, feeling sorry for her cousin.

"That's fine," reasoned Bobby. "You can be his partner."

"Oh no," she laughed. "Karen, same teams again."

"Junior, aim for their balls and maybe you'll knock in ours!" Karen scolded.

David could not get into the spirit of the moment, so he grabbed a chair next to the wall. He sat down and tried to tune out his friends. How much longer would they be his friends? When was he going to leave his home in favor of a place that was supposed to be his real home, he wondered?

The new pool game began. All eyes split time between the table and David and his obvious discomfort. For his part, David split his attention between the table and his many conflicting thoughts. He was too nervous to look his friends in the eyes. He had forgotten why he had even come to Vern's- oh yes, he wanted to get away from his aunt and uncle and his entire situation.

Fear was rising up inside David.

As he sat near his friends, but in a world all his own, one sentence played repeatedly in his brain: "David, I have to kill you." The words had been mentally edited by David with the sadness in Johnny's voice now gone. No matter about what he thought, those same words leaped from his memory banks and played again and again like an unattended car alarm in the middle of a quiet country night.

The fear seemed to become a physical phenomenon. It rose up, out of his stomach, up his esophagus, and into his throat just below the back of his mouth. He could almost taste it. Simultaneously the fear dropped through his intestines and down his legs. His lower back and buttocks tightened. He curled his toes and squeezed them tightly into the bottom of his feet inside his tennis shoes.

His mind went back to why he was even at Vern's. Again- for maybe the hundredth time in the last hour- he argued with himself. Johnny could be persuaded. No, he could not. Nothing could make such a close friend turn on him so quickly. But Johnny's words said otherwise. There was this whole war thing. He was a prince. Johnny was- no, Johnny's dad- he was the enemy. This could all be worked out, reasoned away- but only if Johnny was willing to reason. Was he? Would he be willing in the near future?

At given moments, David was prepared to die for the sake of reason, for the sake of sanity, for the sake of friendship. He imagined that Johnny, too, would make such an effort. But at other moments, he was not so sure. He was not so sure about anything.

When Johnny walked through the door of the arcade, David spotted him from across the large room. Fear struck him like a baseball bat hitting him in the gut. The paranoia sent shivers throughout his body. It was justified, he told himself. Johnny was here to kill him. Why else would he have inquired of Bobby unless David's presence was important to him? David's heart raced. He could feel it pounding against his ribs. His hands trembled and the sweat poured. If he did not act correctly, death could only be minutes- maybe seconds- away.

The foursome at the table would not have given much thought when David headed toward the restroom had he not nearly leaped to his feet. They also could not help but notice that only seconds after David was gone, Johnny approached their table.

Karen saw him first. "Hey, Johnny."

"Hey."

The others chimed in with the response of "Hey."

Karen looked toward the door of the men's restroom as it eased shut. "What's with David?" she asked with confusion and a touch of tension in her voice.

"Whaddya mean?" Johnny asked, fixed on her words.

"I don't know. He's distracted or something."

"Well," Johnny feigned concern. "Maybe I better check on him." Johnny casually headed to the restroom.

Once inside, he dropped the act. He quickly crouched and looked under the partitions of the stalls. No David. As he raised up, he saw the metal garbage can, upside down, in front of a small open window. The window was six feet off the ground and small enough that a person of David's size would have to struggle in order to squeeze through the opening.

Johnny stood on the bottom of the upside-down can and angrily peered out the window, toward downtown. He stepped down and examined the window. Could David really have crawled through?

A clever grin washed across his face as he slowly turned to the three bathroom stalls. Without warning he pushed open the door to the first stall, fully expecting to see his former best friend. No David.

He repeated the maneuver with the two remaining bathroom stalls to no avail. No David and time was wasting. He lit out of the restroom, past his friends, through the arcade, and out the front door.

The friends stopped and stared for a moment. The world had been wobbling strangely for days now. Junior, bent over to take another errant pool shot, was the first to register an observation. "Short conversation."

"I tell ya," Bobby said as if in an argument. "It's that spaceship. Whole town's gone mad since that spaceship came."

"Who else has?" Karen wanted to know.

"Whole town. Old man Barnes. The sheriff. Marty and Ellen," Bobby answered.

"But Marty and Ellen were already kooked out druggies," Lisa reasoned.

"I heard the National Enquirer was here," Junior added. "Marty and Ellen have already been interviewed."

"So has the mayor," Bobby said, still convinced that everyone's actions were suspect.

"Big bucks for talkin' to those guys," Junior said as a grin slowly grew across his large face.

Bobby was still lost in his thoughts of a world gone mad. "Along with the four of us, David and Johnny are the only sane ones left."

"After tonight, I'm not so sure about those two," Karen added.

Junior's grin continued to grow. "I say we get in the tabloids," he said with a devilish tone to match his grin.

"How would we do that?" Lisa asked. "We didn't see anything."

"Tell 'em what they wanna hear," Bobby answered.

"Yup." Junior was convinced now of his own idea.

"Cool," was the only way Bobby could sum up the idea. "Cool."

Chapter 10 - Always a Plan

No matter the night, cars were always parked in front of The Trough. Foreign and domestic, bottle, can and tap, The Trough had the largest variety of beers to offer outside of Louisville and Indianapolis. Owner Andy McGown could get his hands on any beer his customers desired. Not wanting just the bar scene, he had a liquor store in front and a bar in the back of the joint.

McGown claimed that some people came from miles away and others changed their routes while passing through the region in order to stop by and stock up on their favorite alcoholic drinks. Given the very fact that he stayed in business and that there were so frequently new faces in The Trough, he was probably telling the truth.

Amidst all of the cars parked diagonally on both sides of the one-way street, Johnny quietly but feverishly hunted for David. He had to be here, Johnny reasoned. His truck- still parked outside of Vern's- had not been moved. Slowly, he worked his way up the opposite side of Main Street from Vern's and checked underneath the cars in front of The Trough.

Johnny knew David. David was watching him at this very moment, he believed. David would not just flee into the night and leave his truck behind.

The sharp scream of a startled woman pierced the darkened downtown area. Johnny ran toward the brief sound, which came from a neighborhood behind Vern's. He ran down the alley, past the yard of an elderly woman. The old woman stood beneath her porch light. She yelled over her chain link fence as Johnny ran by her. "It's okay. He just scared me. He-"

Johnny had already disappeared into the night, pursuing a distant shadow. A person far ahead passed near a streetlight, running. Johnny knew to whom the shadow belonged.

*　　*　　*　　*　　*　　*

David, though in good physical condition, was spent. Perhaps, he thought, it was the emotional drain that had taken a toll. The past several days had been almost unbearable for him. His life had been drastically changed and he was still not up to the task of properly accepting such change. Regardless of the reason for his exhaustion, he was panting like a Saint Bernard on a summer day when he decided to hide in the darkness, next to a large oak tree.

The long residential street was poorly lit, with only one streetlight for every two blocks. Down the street from which David had come, a car turned a corner and briefly illuminated a person who was trotting in David's direction. He recognized the lanky figure without difficulty. David sighed loudly at the thought of additional exertion. Certainly it must be about time to begin his campaign of reasoning with Johnny, he thought.

David stepped from a dark yard and onto the sidewalk, which was broken up over the years by tree roots pushing up the concrete. Most of the streets did not have sidewalks, but Central Street was one of the few that did. Johnny spotted the movement from two hundred yards away- just enough of a glow from a streetlight near David did the trick. With a burst of adrenalin, Johnny raced down the uneven sidewalk, hoping that the many trees would shield him from light- unaware that he had been spotted already.

David looked back in time to see his friend closing on him rapidly. Time to run again, he thought. He started off in a jog, but his mind moved much faster. What about just stopping? They were both tired, and he could squish the smaller Johnny if necessary.

He came up with a new plan- a plan that would surprise his friend and allow him to tackle and pin the smaller youth while he talked sense into him. David quickly changed direction and darted into the front yard of one of the houses.

The moment that David suddenly changed his path was the same moment that Johnny completed his move. In one motion, Johnny dropped to one knee, drew a hand-sized device from his pocket, and fired a brilliant reddish-orange beam of light toward David.

David heard the sizzle of the laser as it cut the air behind his head, narrowly missing him. The sound was a foreign one- so much so that David did not realize that he should be afraid. As he looked back in Johnny's direction, he felt a blow to the back of his head, shoulders, and mid-back that sent him flailing through the air and into a row of bushes that lined one of the houses. The body blow, the earsplitting explosion, and the orange ball of fire that shot into the air all arrived at the same time.

Momentarily stunned, David rolled out of the bushes and sat up. He saw pieces of flaming metal fall back to Earth.

David was intelligent and quick-witted. He had an uncanny ability to read a situation and to react calmly and positively. One glaring weakness was his unfortunate ability to push himself into a state of denial when the character or actions of friends were in doubt. But as he sat for those brief seconds, watching the pieces of an automobile come crashing onto the street, neighboring yards, and onto the flaming car itself, he could deny the obvious no longer.

Perhaps he could reason with Johnny before, but not now. He still managed to suppress the thoughts about Johnny's true intentions. He still managed to hold onto the elusive hope that this was all Albert Young's doing. His ideal view of Johnny was not dead, but it would have to be pushed to the back of his mind.

As neighbors poured out of their houses and into their yards, David ran through the same yards, which were now lit up by burning debris. The confused neighborhood saw flashes of two young men run by them, but they knew not who or what or why.

*   *   *   *   *   *

Sirens blared. The southern portion of the town was alive with fear and curiosity. A crowd of three dozen people gathered: some stayed in the doorways of their houses, some stood in yards and on the sidewalk, others stood in the middle of the street. They were accustomed to seeing explosions in their living rooms- on television- but not outside their homes, in their quiet little town.

It did not take a genius to know who they suspected. While the car burned itself out, just as many people watched the skies as watched the burning heap of metal.

*　　*　　*　　*　　*　　*

Sirens continued to blare in the distance. David had already crossed the four-lane U.S. highway that ran east and west, splitting the town in half, and he continued to head north through the next residential neighborhood. From the old downtown area, located in the southern section of town, and north toward the highway, the town was littered with pockets of noise, confusion, and fear. Across the U.S. Highway, all was quiet. That was about to change.

David could not see him, but he knew that Johnny was right behind him, in pursuit. What he failed to understand was that Johnny could match his desperation. While David was desperately trying to stay alive, Johnny was desperately trying to live up to his father's expectations. David did not want to get close enough to find out what caused the car to blow up, and Johnny did not want to return to his father with bad news.

David again stopped to rest. He was too far from his pickup. When the elderly lady screamed, he panicked. He knew Johnny was near, and he failed to plan a course of action. Anger rose up from his gut as he realized that his failure to use logic was putting him in danger. His previous plan ended the moment that it started- ended by Johnny's laser blast. But now, before he hatched another plan, he needed to rest.

David leaned up against a house as he caught his breath. His mind carried him back to lessons that he had learned: Alexander the Great, Patton, Lord Nelson and his navy. He had studied it all, modern and ancient. Yet here I sit, he thought, running like a chicken that escaped the pen.

Competing for equal time were thoughts about Johnny, about their former friendship. No! I can't think that way, his mind shouted. The friendship is not over! I can convince him. I can change him back to normal, one half of his brain screamed at the other. I will reason with him.

David's biggest source of confusion was himself. One thought would be optimistic and idealistic, the next pessimistic and cynical. One moment he convinced himself that reason was king, the next he feared death at the hands of Johnny. He simultaneously plotted plans of action for retreat and for diplomatic progress. He was in emotional disarray, and he was working on becoming a mental mess, as well. He was so badly overanalyzing every thought, every action, every reaction, that he was rendering his analysis meaningless. He was paralyzing himself. Training is supposed to prevent this, he thought. But here he was.

David was far from his truck and far from ready to accept the fate of his friendship with Johnny. His glaring weakness seized him with an idea.

Before he could complete his plans, his body had propelled him off of the ground and onto a chain link fence that separated two properties. Lacking time or care to be cautious, he balanced himself by putting one hand on the support post for a carport attached to a house and stood on the top rail of the four-foot fence. He nimbly pulled himself onto the top of the metal carport and across to the composition shingle roof of the house. Within moments, he was perched at the peak of the one-story house.

Lack of planning had carried him far away from his truck, he reasoned. But this plan would surely end the entire mess. He did not know how the plan would work, he just had confidence in the existence of a plan. If plans were his security blanket, he was going to smother himself before this night was over.

In the distance, the sounds of the disturbance to the south subsided. The twelve o'clock hour had passed and, except for Vern's and The Trough, on a normal Friday night the town would have long ago shut down. But this was not a normal Friday night.

Crickets chirped, toads croaked, a few dogs barked here and there, and cars occasionally passed on the highway several blocks away. The peaceful small town evening was shattered by David's recovering robust lungs.

"Johnny!" He listened for a moment, but a response was not to come. "Johnny!" he shouted again. "Listen to me!" His casual speech pattern was gone. He enunciated his words, hoping that his wayward friend would not miss a syllable.

David paused as he realized how forcefully his voice carried through the night. Surely, he thought, Johnny was within ear-shot.

"You can't do this! You hear me? Think about what you're doing!" He paused to listen. All he heard was more dogs barking than ever. "Johnny! Our friendship is more important than this! You can't do this to us!"

Dogs barked, causing other dogs to bark in other nearby neighborhoods. The toads and crickets fell silent. A few porch lights came on at a smattering of houses. David began to sense the foolishness of his move, yet he was not deterred. A young man so logical and yet so emotional- denial somehow managed to thrive in that collision of forces. "Do you hear me, Johnny?!" he shouted again.

As David correctly guessed, Johnny was out there. He did not know from where David was yelling, but he knew by sound that he was closing in on the location. He was awash in confidence. He had his former friend on the run. Surely he's unarmed, Johnny reasoned, or he would've faced me down.

He darted from dark yard to dark yard, each time getting closer to the voice.

"We don't even know what this whole thing is about!" he heard David bellow. Interesting, he thought. David was paid the visit by his own people's ship and yet he doesn't know what the war is about. David knew less than Johnny had previously realized. No wonder he responded with confusion rather than resolve.

"You can't change reality just because someone says we're enemies!" That confirmed it. Johnny had no doubt that David was wandering around like an injured puppy. He had no understanding of the war, the meaning of the visit from his people's ship, or why he was about to die. Johnny stopped and chuckled at the thought. Here was his best friend for years, and now he was about to die at the hand of the friend who turned out to be the son of an assassin, not a mere friend.

Johnny pegged him as standing on the roof of Alfie Capps. Everyone considered Capps to be the most gullible guy in town- an auto mechanic who got ripped off by his customers rather than the other way around. Capps won't like what happens to his roof if I miss, Johnny thought with a laugh.

He moved in, quietly, closer.

David crouched behind the chimney and waited a full two minutes before he spoke again. Despite the persistent fear that he was only helping Johnny find him, he pushed forward with his "plan."

"How can you kill your best friend because of something you know nothing about?! Why would you?!" He paused, waiting to hear a friendly response.

"What do I gotta say? How do you convince someone not to kill his best friend?"

The darkness was momentarily parted by a blinding surge of reddish-orange that seemed to light up the entire roof. The pulse of light was nothing like David had ever seen. He had his back turned to Johnny's first shot, on the other side of town. This brilliant yet brief glow was a surprise. Though it disappeared within a second from the time it began, the illumination temporarily blinded him.

An explosion shook the house. The laser blast struck the ridge of the roof two feet to David's left. The force of the blast knocked David from his feet and sent him tumbling backward into the darkness.

Johnny excitedly rushed into the street and into plain view. A streetlight only a few feet away gave him a short shadow. He saw the rising puff of smoke and a chunk missing from the ridge cap. He reasoned that his shot must have missed the mark. He was certain that David was unarmed, so he did not feel the need to take cover.

Before Johnny could accurately determine David's condition and whereabouts, Capps himself emerged from his house. The middle-aged man's excitement was mixed with a dozen emotions. "What was that?! What's going on?!" he shouted as he ran into his front yard, with bare feet and dressed in a robe.

Johnny casually walked toward Capps. The idea of killing the man was appealing to him. He had yet to experience that thrill- a thrill that he would definitely taste when he successfully rectified his father's failure. But, he decided, killing someone now would complicate matters and could interfere with his primary goal- a goal that he must attain.

As did many people in the area, Capps recognized the local baseball star. "What's happening, Johnny?"

"I'm chasin' a space alien," Johnny said matter-of-factly. His response was as natural as if he were telling the truth- which, of course, he was.

"Space alien?! Don't you be smart with me, boy!"

Johnny casually sauntered up to the balding, heavy-set man who was now panting from the scare and the brief jaunt across the lawn. "No, really." He pointed to the roof where there was just enough light to discern that a five-foot long section of the ridge of the roof was missing and a charred area was left in its place. "Look what it did to your roof. Only a space alien coulda done that."

Capps' eyes bulged. It was true! The talk of spaceships and space aliens- all true. He stared at Johnny for a moment, gauging the young man and his statement's veracity. "Was it like a lizard? Did it look like a lizard?" His voice was quick with excitement and anxiety. His sense of curiosity was warped by the shock.

"More like a catcher." Johnny deadpanned. With that, he jogged through the yard and disappeared as he rounded the corner of the house, headed toward Capps' back yard.

"A catcher? An alien catcher?" Capps yelled after Johnny, even though the lad had disappeared. "What, did he have a mask on?! Shin guards? What the hell does that mean, like a catcher?!"

Johnny searched for David to no avail. Given that he was carrying a laser gun, he did not wish to be questioned by the police. Anything, including getting thrown in jail, that would inhibit his ability to kill David was to be avoided. With such thoughts in mind, he truncated his search and headed back to the street. He waved at the still-shocked Mr. Capps and several of his neighbors as he jogged by them. He responded with a "not yet" when asked if he had found the alien.

Then, just as David had done minutes before, Johnny disappeared into the darkness.

*   *   *   *   *   *

Exhausted and limping, David struggled the last few steps to his pickup. The five-year old Ford short-bed pickup might in fact become his bed, he ruefully considered. He needed to get as far away from Johnny as possible and sleep. His truck would be his home tonight.

*   *   *   *   *   *

At two in the morning, the country roads all should have been deserted- at least only a couple of cars should have been out at this hour. Instead, he saw headlights or tail lights on every road he traveled, and they were all going in the same direction. Certainly there was a big party going on somewhere, he thought. No other explanation crossed his mind.

But David was too tired to think at the moment. Even before he had become exhausted, the results of his decisions were not spectacular on this night. Better to just find somewhere to go to sleep, he figured. Aunt Grace and Uncle Phillip could worry all they wanted. He was in pain from his fall from Capps' roof and he was beat- completely drained of strength, sore from his fall, and emotionally empty. Only his landing on top of a metal shed had kept his fall from being disastrous.

David drove for a few more miles before turning off into a corn field. He locked his doors and then stretched out across the bench seat, eager to put this long day behind him forever.

*　*　*　*　*　*

Unbeknownst to David, at the edge of the woods near his house, a crowd of about two hundred people was gathered. People swapped stories about Tom Bagget's exploding Buick and what they saw or thought they saw. Other people told of what happened to Alfie Capps' roof and how Johnny Young was a brave hero, tirelessly chasing down aliens.

There was no consensus on what they were going to do if the aliens did return. Some passionately wished to catch a ride on an out-of-this-world flight, some wished to see for themselves what aliens looked like, and still others simply were not sure what they would do if a spacecraft landed or why they were even there.

Headlights from a few of the cars lit up the area. Three of the cars' headlights were pointed out toward the corn field, at the expected landing site, and two cars were pointed at the group so that they could see each other.

Capps himself was present and loudly complained to the crowd, "If they come back, I don't think we're all gonna fit." He hesitated for a moment, then lifted his shotgun for all to see. "But if they're as ornery as the one that blew up my roof, we may not wanna go."

Chapter 11 - Temptation

He did it- he had made the attempt, anyway. He had tried to kill his best friend. He could not admit to his father that while the attempt was genuine, once he left Capps' house he did not pursue the matter as diligently as his father expected. If he found out, Mr. Young would characterize such giving up as half-hearted. And his father would know-somehow- that he could have pursued the matter better and yet chose not to do so.

The thought of pleasing his father's cousin was nice, but at the moment he struggled with the realities of life, death, and friendship. The Great Banu- for it was rarely merely "Banu"- would be proud. The Great Banu would reward him. The Great Banu has a long memory. The Great Banu, blah blah blah.

Indeed, Johnny coveted greatness. He believed in destiny. He would kill David. He even managed to push away the question of "Why?" Why David? Why not someone else in the town? Why could there not be a better way? No, those thoughts had to be annihilated, just as the prince himself had to be annihilated.

Just play to David's idealism, Johnny told himself. David was easy for the pickings. Just appeal to his righteous belief in everything good and David could be manipulated like a dog being told to sit for a biscuit.

Like David, Johnny felt that their friendship was the most important aspect of his life. Baseball was their true love, but they made each other not only better athletes, but better individuals, better men. They pushed each other.

Unlike David, Johnny did not see grand schemes for success beyond every fence or envision the future constantly. With the exception of baseball and his friendship with David, Johnny had always lived for the now. The sun would come out tomorrow, but why did that matter today? He did not need hope, he needed destiny. Hope was wishful thinking. Destiny was a path- the path to greatness which now awaited him.

Yet he did not need to think of his destiny daily. He had known, to gradually increasing degrees, for three years that his destiny was beyond the stars. For three years, his father had filled his mind with stories of spaceships, Banu, the Rebellion, and life on Craylar- as it was and as it should be. For three years he hid the secret from his best friend. He did not know when that life beyond the stars would begin, so he allowed himself the pleasure of planning for the Major Leagues.

He did not know, that is, until the spaceship returned for David.

Johnny was being trained to be a leader- not a mere strategist, but a strong public character who could motivate and persuade, lead, and manipulate. Some things, he had heard over and over from his father, were worth achieving no matter the cost. Regardless of naysayers and do-gooders who said otherwise, sometimes the end did indeed justify the means. What some would judge as harsh or cruel was in fact a necessary vessel to arrive at a greater result.

Sometimes, people, innocent or not, had to die in order for others to live or for the greater good to be realized. It was that simple.

From David, Johnny learned the power of friendship and loyalty without ever fully subscribing to the preeminence of such concepts. One by-product of their friendship was the lesson that personal interaction was far more important than Johnny's father let on. Someone unknown was someone not trusted, Johnny discovered. But friendship brought trust. Trust opened the opportunity for control and, if necessary, domination.

David never knew that the anti-philosophical Johnny had turned upside down the philosophies which he had advocated. Johnny had spent a lot of time in thought over the past three years- just not as deeply in thought as David would have. Such thoughts were nearly the totality of that which Johnny hid from his buddy. Everything else was open for David to see.

Johnny did not fully grasp his theories of trust and domination in time to try them out on his friend. The evolution of his thoughts about such concepts were new to him. Then again, had he realized that David was effectively the Anti-Christ as far as his people believed, he would have made the time to engage David in subtle psychological battles.

The one thing that now scared Johnny about his friend was the latter's mental toughness. Johnny's father was continuously belittling and berating the mentally weak, but such a description was not applicable to his burly friend. In day-to-day friendships, one often manipulates another for inconsequential reasons. Manipulating David was a monumental task. Better to simply appeal to David's good nature rather than fight him. His good nature and idealism were his weaknesses and the only real paths open to manipulation. Any other method would run one into David's stubbornness.

Mentally tough, emotionally weak- that was Johnny's assessment of David.

Killing, Johnny reasoned, was final. To kill David was to kill his best friend, his only confidante, his own personal "Dear Abby." To rule a world was a bizarre thought. To do so without David's partnership was incomprehensible.

Johnny slowly walked toward the block-long downtown strip. The day had been long, and now night, though more than half over, would be long and sleepless. In four hours the sun would rise. Better to face his father with his failure- his partial failure, for he had made the attempt- now than to endure even more hours of dread for an unavoidable moment.

Just as the questions beginning with "Why" seeped to the forefront of his consciousness, he again pushed them back. While he did not enjoy the thought of actually committing the act, he knew that there could be no path to victory without killing his best friend.

He vowed to interrupt his thoughts any time "Why" came back to try to persuade him otherwise. He knew that he could not allow himself to think like David. David did not understand destiny; David did not even understand why events were unfolding as they did. Johnny could see the path laid out before him; David could not.

His mind jumped again. Maybe it was too many video games that originally convinced him that his laser shots at David would do no real harm. But with each shot from his laser on this night, reality became a little clearer. Now he reflected on those laser shots at David; at his need to control; his need to attain his destiny.

It was time to kill. Now.

*   *   *   *   *   *

As Johnny pointed his blue Camaro down the street, away from the remote neighborhood, and headed back out to the country roads, a strange inner glow overcame the young man.

David was not, for once, on the tip of his brain.

He drove through the countryside with a sense of fulfillment. He had acquired the desire to kill. He had wanted to know that feeling of power. He had wanted to know how killing felt. He had wanted to now master his emotions so that he felt neither remorse nor the victims' pain. To please the Great Banu, to achieve greatness within and beyond the Rebellion, there were certain natural reactions and emotions and hurdles which must be overcome.

The first hurdle had now been cleared. His father would be pleased- and the killings served a purpose.

His mind went back to his father. What the old man had meant by "temptation" was now apparent. He had spent over an hour attempting to kill his best friend and yet he still questioned himself and his purpose. He had struggled with the temptation to let David live.

But now his failure to kill the prince could be glossed over to some degree. To what degree he would only know by judging his father's reaction. His father would have no other choice but to recognize the importance of his deeds in the wee hours of the morning, just three-and-a-half hours before the sun would rise again.

The contradictions that previously reverberated through Johnny's mind had caused him pain, but at long last these contradictions were easing. The pain was now more lack of sleep than confusion. As he headed toward his house, he realized that he just wanted to get home, face his father, report the good and the bad, and get it over with. He needed sleep. He could worry about weighty matters in the morning. The day had been too long. The temptation had been too strong. Destiny would have to wait until morning.

Yet that inner glow, that feeling of budding power, welled up within him and sustained him on his drive home. The world would not know of his accomplishment until the sun rose above the horizon.

Chapter 12 - Denial Hits Home

The sun had been above the horizon for thirty minutes by the time David woke up enough to drive himself home. The wooded, slow-rolling hills and green fields of corn and soybeans that stretched far beyond the horizon were alive with red-winged blackbirds, cardinals, and sundry other songbirds. The sky was filled with puffy masses of white clouds. The air was already warm and the humidity pressed heavily against every living creature.

David's chest tightened when he rounded the corner onto his street and saw the police cars. Had a "black-and-white" and an unmarked county Sheriff car sat in front of his house just a week prior, he would have assumed that they were on business at another house. On this day, given all of the events of the past week, he knew. He knew they were at his house, and he knew that whatever had happened was likely horrible.

As he exited his truck, he took a deep breath. Life was disintegrating quickly, and the succeeding events were certainly going to fit that mold, he told himself. He did not even try to hope for the best.

Visibly trembling with great dread, he stepped up onto the porch as he approached his front door. The perspiration rapidly spread across his entire frame.

A county Sheriff's deputy exited through the front door before David could reach for the door knob. Tall and lanky, grayed but only 35 years-old, the beige-uniformed Daryl

Osborne was known throughout the area as the nicest deputy among a group of nice deputies. Seldom did they handle anything tougher than vandalism committed by mischievous youth or illegal discharges of firearms, so a corps of Joe Fridays they were not.

Even away from the big cities famous for their violent crimes, an occasional event would occur that no one would admit could ever happen in their own town. The locals would express genuine shock at a heinous crime that would appear once every twenty or so years. Today marked that twentieth year.

"David, stay here, will ya?" It was half request, half command.

Again the word 'horrible' came to David's mind. The only question was how bad. "What's goin' on, Daryl?"

"A lotta people are doin' weird things and are on the streets and that kinda thing, with the spaceships and all, ya know."

To David, Osborne's half-attempted and half-finished thoughts made no sense. "Don't put me off like that. What's going on?"

"The Thompsons down the street, their kids were walking by a few hours ago- well after midnight. They saw someone leaving here."

"Did we get robbed? Where are Phillip and Grace?" His mind happened upon an acceptable explanation for the commotion.

"Yeah, it was a robbery," Osborne said as he put his arm around the younger man and led him down the porch steps and into the yard. "But it was also worse than that."

As David let the words sink in, a voice from within the house yelled out, "Osborne, come here, please."

"Stay here," Osborne ordered. It was an order that David could not abide.

Osborne entered the living room, unaware that David was only steps behind him. A man that David knew only as Detective Palasky, a plain-clothed detective that David had seen only a few times before, stood in the room. In his mid-fifties, his salt-and-pepper hair made him look distinguished. Put a blue suit on him and he was convincing as a businessman or a Secret Service agent guarding the president of the United States. His voice was deep and manner serious.

Palasky stood over the motionless body of a man spread out on the carpet. "Osborne, I need your help. I can't figure out why there's no blood on the carpet."

At the sight of Phillip Steele's dead body, David stepped from the porch and through the doorway. Palasky cringed upon seeing the youth. David grasped the door casing in an attempt to support himself.

"Son?" Palasky knew David should not be in the room.

"Oh, no. David! I told ya to stay outside!" Osborne turned back to Palasky. "This is David Steele, the victims' nephew. He lived here with them."

"I'm really sorry, David."

David gathered his strength and walked the short distance to the limp carcass that used to be his uncle. He dropped to his knees, unsure of what to do, what to say, what to think. His mind was an empty slate, erased by shock, revulsion, and fear. Deep within, however, he understood perfectly what the death of his uncle meant. In his mind, if he had bothered to dredge up the thought from the depths, there were only two suspects on the entire planet.

"David," Palasky asked. "Do you have somewhere you can stay?"

"Yeah," he responded quietly.

"Your aunt is in the bedroom."

"Same?" he asked weakly.

"Yeah," was the quiet answer.

The emotions hit him like a train hitting a stalled car. The tension in his body released, and with it released a thousand emotions crammed into a few short seconds. "I can't see Grace like this," he slowly but quietly cried out. The emotions released as he struggled to speak further. The tears flowed. His throat tightened. Pain gripped his stomach and chest. "I can't."

On his hands and knees, David's tears silently fell into his dead uncle's face. The man whom David respected yet occasionally disliked, loved yet often felt unmoved about, was dead. Phillip was his uncle, yet he was essentially his father. Dead.

Emptiness grabbed hold. Reality had come. The Kingdom, the Rebellion, his real identity, a spaceship dispatched to whisk him away- it all was now very real.

"Uh David," Palasky timidly interrupted. "I'm gonna need your help. This house has been ripped apart, yet all the expensive stuff seems to be here- jewelry, electronics, everything as far as I can tell."

"So it wasn't a burglary?"

"It looks like it is on the surface, everything ripped apart and all. But up close I'd say 'no' unless you can figure out anything missing."

David understood. The implications were far more vast than Osborne and Palasky could ever understand. "I don't understand," he lied.

The tears started again, dripping onto Phillip's face.

*   *   *   *   *   *

The deck of the Prince Tinian was quiet. Most of the ship's activities were focused on repairs in other compartments on other decks. Captain Gonchar's formidable physique loomed over Commander Bozwell, who sat in a chair in front of myriad controls at his command station.

Gonchar was new to the Prince Tinian but a legend back home. He had been a prisoner of the Rebellion for over two years before he managed to pull off an almost impossible escape. He scoffed at the thought of a quiet retirement to recover from his torturous detainment. Yesterday's scars, he often said, were today's motivation.

The addition of Gonchar to the mission was last-minute. Had he not been a celebrity on his home planet, his presence would have gone unnoticed by most observers and leaders alike. The mission was top secret, yet many people seemed to be in on the secret.

Gonchar's celebrated bravery as a prisoner of war put some in the High Command at ease about this vital mission. Admiral Praeder was known as an established leader, but two military giants on the same flight was downright comforting.

Critics said that Gonchar had a death wish. He had a need to die a hero. The mundane- though important- mission to retrieve the prince should make him feel out of place on such a mission, it was said. In fact, the military Supreme Commander had tried to convince Gonchar of just that. But he could not bring himself to turn down the request of such a hero.

Besides, while away on the trip, it gave the High Command time to figure out how to deploy the man who was considered the essence of bravery. Unlike some of the military leadership, the Supreme Commander had been uncomfortable with Gonchar since his escape from captivity. There was something different about him. For better or worse, Gonchar was a different man. Evidently, torture and confinement did that to a man.

Upon their triumphant return, the prince would be back in the fold, the Prince Tinian would be given to a newly promoted captain, Admiral Praeder would return to his position on the High Command, Gonchar would become an even bigger legend- he would no doubt find a way to paint himself as vital to the mission- and the military leadership would come up with a way to reward all involved with the extraordinarily important task.

Gonchar had been promoted from Commander to Captain upon his escape from the Rebel prison. But he was a Captain without a ship. He was a hero with nothing to do. The Prince Tinian needed a new Captain after the previous skipper had been mysteriously assassinated. Yet no one ever even considered offering the post to Gonchar: the Prince Tinian was too old of a vessel, in need of replacement in a matter of a few years. It was not ancient, but it was not state-of-the-art. Besides, such an assignment was too inconsequential for a man so deserving of tributes and parades.

During his escape, Gonchar had supposedly single-handedly killed dozens of the enemy. While unverified and a little difficult for some to believe, his exploits were revered. The fact was, he had escaped; that was undeniable. The Supreme Commander wished to deactivate him under the pretext of allowing him to recover from his trauma.

But after only a brief recovery, the publicity hound was back, wanting more. To buy time, the Supreme Commander gave Gonchar what he wanted: a trip to Earth to partake in an historic event.

Commander Bozwell had heard all of the stories and rumors that made their way through the military ranks.

Determining fact from fiction was difficult even when going directly to the source. The muscular captain understood the value of being a living legend and was inclined to protect the image- myths and all.

Bozwell found the larger bald man intimidating. Unlike Gonchar, Bozwell was of average build. He gave an impression of neither strength nor power. He had earned his rank, but he was not a sight to behold. Women did not swoon when Bozwell passed them. His voice was solid, but not powerful. His eyes were dark and brooding, not brilliant blue like Gonchar's. His steps were quick and light rather than long and forceful. Bozwell had no doubt how Gonchar viewed such men. It was obvious from the senior officer's demeanor, from his aura.

Bozwell was learning about other facets of Captain Gonchar. They had only met as their journey to Earth was about to commence, yet Bozwell believed that he understood the older man. Gonchar needed to be the center of attention, Bozwell deduced. He needed to be talked about and fawned over. He needed people to listen to him. Now, Bozwell had no choice but to listen.

"I am telling you, something is wrong with the Admiral. Something is not right." Gonchar waited for Bozwell's response, but a response was not forthcoming. Undeterred, he developed his theory further. "First, he would not bring the prince with us. Why? Now, he insists that the repairs must be perfect, even though we could return to the prince with a limp. Why?"

Bozwell was a loyal Commander who had experienced plenty of combat before joining the Prince Tinian. Unlike many battle-weary veterans, he was always gung ho about supporting the cause. Gonchar's cynicism irritated the lesser-ranked officer, particularly cynicism aimed at Admiral Praeder.

"You have to admit, we did not know whether we would make it out of Earth's atmosphere in one piece." Bozwell wisely hid his irritation. "The atmosphere is an equalizer for our advantages. In the vacuum of space, we have a destroyer that is superior to theirs."

But Gonchar was not eager to concede defeat, let alone abandon his theory. "Commander, this is a warship. By definition, we take risks."

"What else bothers you, Captain?" The sarcasm was almost visibly dripping from his mouth.

"Well, right now bothers me. Right now we should be sending a rescue team down to the planet's surface to get the prince before the Rebels kill him. With that aborted fiasco when we had him onboard, the Rebels may know who he is by now- if he is still alive."

"I believe in the Admiral and I believe he has a sound strategy."

Incensed at what he viewed as simplistic loyalty, Gonchar raised the tone of his rhetoric. "I do not call waiting for repairs a sound strategy! Since we are keeping their star between us and the Banu, they cannot see us but we cannot see them, either. And why wait until the prince or the duke signal us? What if they are unable to give the signal? Then he dies?!"

"Captain, of what are you accusing the Admiral? Incompetence?"

"Treason!" The word was delivered with the drama for which Gonchar was famous- and Bozwell understood that the man meant what he said.

*   *   *   *   *   *

Mrs. Fuller understood, or so she thought. David was a good boy who was going through a traumatic experience and needed a place to stay. He had convinced her that she was in no danger, despite the fact that murder had taken place next door. He would take up little room and need no special attention from her. All he needed from her- besides the use of her extra bedroom- was silence. Her friends, the police, and especially his former best friend did not need to know of his whereabouts lest he meet the same fate as his aunt and uncle.

While the widowed elderly woman did not understand why the police could not know his whereabouts, she knew that he was an honest, decent boy. She agreed that she would comply, even if the request went against her better judgment.

David did not explain to her where his truck was parked nor how she could escape danger while harboring him. To try to explain to an old woman about what was going on, he thought, was an impossible task. And he certainly would not bother with tales of kingdoms and spaceships.

Twelve short hours after seeing the body of his uncle, David needed solitude and sleep. There could be no doubt that this dreadful deed was done by the hand of Albert Young. He would exact revenge on the old man, but for now he just needed to mourn and recover.

After quietly eating Mrs. Fuller's delectable home cooking of pepper steak, mashed potatoes, and green beans, David slept until the sun rose again. He awakened with the same sense of depression that had accompanied him the entire previous day.

Chapter 13 - Yesterdays That Never Die

David did not know how events would unfold on this day, and if forced to do so, he could not even explain how he felt at the moment. Dead were the only family members he had ever known. His best friend was set upon the idea of doing the same to him.

Spaceships. War. A monarchy- the son of a king, no less.

He did not know what this day would bring, but he knew that today could prove to be a seminal day in his life. He had accepted his true identity now. It was all indeed real. He saw it, metaphorically, in Steele's body.

While he remained emotionally empty, he tried to convince himself that at least he was physically rested. He was still not prepared to think everything through. He always had a plan- such was his nature- but now he did not wish to think beyond the next step he would take. One foot in front of the other was all that he could presently manage as he walked across his driveway. Mrs. Fuller's spare bed had been perfectly comfortable. Now he returned to his hellish world.

A plump, gray-haired woman of sixty-four years had other ideas for David. Joan Barton was living in her own Hell on Earth. Her son Ralph and nephew Stevie had disappeared into the Bermuda Triangle of a corn field, and sixteen years later the burning embers of the desire for answers had not diminished.

Had David controlled his world, he would have successfully avoided her. But as he reached down for the newspaper that sat square in the middle of his driveway, nothing could hide him from her intense eyes. She was ready for him- ready for anything.

With mild difficulty, Joan stepped from her pickup truck and ambled toward the teenager. Besides the extra weight that she carried, both worry and arthritis wore her down and made her appear older than she was. She had no time for pleasantries- life was too short. At least it had been for her son and nephew.

"You David?"

"Yeah."

Her hard edge faded only for a moment. "I'm sorry to hear about your aunt and uncle. That was terrible."

"Yeah, thank you." David recognized the woman but did not know what she wanted.

"Those things aren't supposed t' happen 'roun' here. Sad loss." She quickly changed the subject to that which served her purpose. "Ya know my nephew Marty, don'cha?"

"Since we were little."

"I know he's a little strange, but he's a good, decent kid."

"Yep." David did not agree, but there was no need to inflame the old woman.

"I'll get to the point," Joan said, tension building in her voice. "Sixteen years ago my boy and two other boys disappeared- gone, without a trace. One of the other boys was my nephew, Stevie- Marty's brother. You probably knew that."

"Yep."

"Yep, that's why Marty's been fascinated with UFO's." She seemed to be explaining Marty to herself, attempting to convince herself that it was not Marty's fault that he was such an odd character.

"I don't get it," David responded quite reasonably.

"Look me in the eye, son," she slowly intoned as she stepped closer to him. David dutifully complied.

"My nephew believes he saw you go on that spaceship the other night and he's an honest kid. Was that you?"

Incredulity was David's only defense. "That's crazy!" he erupted. "I can't believe everybody believes that UFO nonsense! Spaceships! Little green men! You gotta be kiddin'!"

"I'll take that as a non-answer. You wanna dance, dance around somethin' some other time. Answer the question!"

"Oh come on! You're nutty like Marty!"

Mothers are not used to taking attitudes from teenagers, and Joan and her tough demeanor made her a candidate to be last in line for such disrespect. "You listen to me, young man!" she shot back angrily, her index finger jabbing the air in front of David's nose. "You'd be nutty like Marty if you believed your whole life that the brother you never knew got taken away on a spaceship! I've spent the last sixteen years tryin' to piece together what happened to my son and nephew and your face is on that puzzle! I can't see it all yet, but I see enough of it to recognize you."

Denial was failing. He fidgeted with his hands while his eyes darted up and down the street. This conversation should not be taking place in the driveway, he thought. In reality, no one could hear the two, but David was uncomfortable nonetheless. Besides, it was too late. He could not stop the conversation. So he made one last-ditch effort at obfuscation.

"And you think, what? I'm a space alien?!"

"You tell me!"

"Aw, come on!" David threw up his hands in feigned disbelief.

"Sixteen years ago my boy Ralph, Stevie, and Billy Sharp were at a party up the hill here, at the edge of the woods. They were drinkin' and smokin' dope and carousin'. The spaceship landed in the same field, in the same place as the other night. That," she growled. "There is no denyin'. Left very few marks on the ground, too, just like the one last week. I know, I checked it then and I checked it now. Wasn't one of those faked crop circle things."

The woman who looked ten years older than she really was had plenty of steam left.

"Some people got off that spaceship- or aliens. Two adults and a baby, what I hear. Ralph and Stevie and Billy went to the spaceship and were allowed to go on it. Couple of minutes later, it flew away. Not a trace was found of the boys. None."

"And they searched?" It was a stupid question and David knew it as soon as he asked it. He- like everyone else within a hundred miles- knew the story, which made the question nearly unforgivable.

"Of course they searched!" she nearly screeched. "I searched. My whole family searched. Nobody found nothin'. Not nowhere! But ever'body ignored the kids at the party who saw it all 'cause a lot of the kids were stoned. But I talked to a couple differ'nt kids who weren't straight, but they weren't bad off, neither. They saw it all, too."

"But I don't understand-"

"What this's got to do with you," she finished his sentence for him. "You got on that spaceship the other night, didn't you? Don't you deny it!" Her last sentence was delivered with a steady yet focused ferocity. It was a command that David was not going to disobey.

Joan's anger was now depleted. Softly she posed the second-most important question on her mind. "Why didn't they take you?"

Denial was no longer an option, and he knew it. He had completely failed to convince her that he was ignorant of recent events, mostly because she refused to be convinced otherwise. "The time wasn't right."

"What about my boy? Why was the time right for him and my nephew?"

He was, however, ignorant of the fate of the three boys. "I don't know anything about it."

Joan had scored a victory. David's admissions gave her hope. She softened more. "Can you find out?"

"I don't know. Did he get on the first spaceship or the second? Remember, there were spaceships two nights in a row."

"It wasn't the same one?" She was elated to be making progress, but she was too tired of a woman to show it much.

"No."

"He got on the first night." Her eyes pleaded. Her shoulders sank. Her entire frame seemed as though it could fall to the concrete at any moment.

"I'll try," he said reassuringly.

"Thank you." She had an urge to give him a hug of thanks, but she was too hard-bitten to harbor the thought for long. She could only muster a pat on his shoulder. "Thank you," she repeated as she fought back tears.

As she turned to walk back to her pickup, an important and comforting thought came to his mind. "There's one thing I do know."

She turned slowly, with neither hope nor apprehension.

"They wouldn't have taken them forcefully. If they got on that spaceship, it would've been only because they wanted to go."

"You think so?" she asked hopefully.

"Yeah. I do." Of that he was certain.

"Thank you, David." There was nothing left for her to say. She did not obtain exactly what she wanted, but she had enough to ease her mind. It was all real. It did indeed happen. The boys had climbed aboard that spaceship as the inebriated youth had claimed. She struggled into her pickup and drove away.

David watched her go, momentarily forgetting his own pain.

Chapter 14 - Face to Face

The ransacked house only added to David's tumultuous feelings. With a disconnect from reason, he wandered through the house, putting items back in place at random. He straightened a picture here, returned clothes to their drawers there. Nothing made sense to him now: why his aunt and uncle had been murdered; why the house was turned upside down; why he was picking up his aunt's and uncle's belongings off of the floor.

Upon entering the master bedroom, a flood of emotions washed over his soul. The feelings hit immediately, but were intensified as he combed through their possessions. He was uncomfortable looking in their dresser drawers and closet. A feeling nagged him- a feeling that he should box up their possessions and preserve them. But preserve them for what? For whom? His thoughts drifted until interrupted by memories.

In a dresser drawer were three photos of David and his uncle fishing at a large pond. A smile struggled to David's face as he recalled the day. Grace took the photos as seven year-old David first waited impatiently for a bite, then excitedly reeled in a small fish- he forgot what kind it was- and then posed for the obligatory holding-the-fish photo.

Typically, Phillip taught the boy what he needed to know and Grace cheered him on. He was the teacher; she was the coach. Similar, yet oh so different.

David's thoughts drifted along the same path until he spotted Phillip's pocket knife. The small knife was the inspiration for David's pocket knife- the one he had received for Christmas. Little David was enthralled with the ivory-colored handle and the three-inch blade. It was really just a common pocket knife, but he had always desired to have such an item. So on Christmas Day in his ninth year, he opened the package that brought him an elation far out of proportion to the value of the knife; but he was a boy excited by toys, gadgets, tools, weapons, and anything that could be used while on boyhood adventures.

While the purpose of this search was to find as much information about his real, extraterrestrial life as possible, and what he should do next, David found himself moving slowly, trudging through memory after memory. Having satisfactorily searched every area belonging to his uncle, he now set his sights on Grace's belongings. He sat on the bed for a moment, questioning himself about whether he really wanted to do this. He had a great love for his aunt and he had not yet accepted her death. He knew that looking through her personal property would, in a strange way, confirm her passing.

As far as he was concerned, she was his mother. She performed every aspect of the role lovingly, dutifully. Once, when he was very young, he asked her why she did not have her own children. Twelve years later he could still remember the expression on her face that day: the look in her eyes, the pain that overtook her countenance. She was unable to speak until she took a quick, deep breath. "Maybe someday I'll explain it to you," was all that she could manage. Even as a little boy he knew that he should never again ask the question.

Now in front of him was her robe, hanging from a metal coat tree. It was a soft, pink, terry cloth robe that extended almost to her ankles when she wore it. It adorned her small frame nearly every morning when she went into David's room to wake him for school. The robe was how his day started every day; the first thing he saw. The pink color penetrated through his eye lashes to his bleary, barely-opened eyes. Her soft voice and the robe were imbedded in his memory forever. Now, as the tears rolled down his cheeks, he buried his face into that robe.

As he moved past the robe, past sundry loose photos, and past memories by the seemingly hundreds- perfume, jewelry, even a pair of reading glasses- each stoked a string of fond recollections. He successfully searched every square inch of their bedroom. He was exhausted emotionally, unwilling to continue, until he shook the emotions long enough to recall his mission in the house.

*   *   *   *   *   *

David exited the attic of the house, stepping gingerly onto a six-foot A-frame ladder. Small chunks of blown-in R-30 insulation escaped the confines of the attic and fell to the hallway carpet below. He had determined that it was impossible to search every square foot due to the nature of the clumpy blown-in insulation covering the floor of the attic. He had walked on the bottom chords of the trusses to avoid falling through the ceiling below. The evenly-spread attic insulation was now clumped together in various piles as the result of his frustrating and undisciplined search. As he climbed down the ladder he was convinced that the attic excursion was a waste of time.

Back in the living area of the house, emotions shifted. The evenness of sadness and pain gave way to the roller coaster of hatred and vengeance. The degree to which chaos invaded his thoughts and emotions shaped his every move as he traveled through the house. Hunger, safety, the future-nothing mattered. Nothing, that is, except revenge on Albert Young.

Nothing else mattered until he came across shoe boxes in the den. The thin cardboard boxes held David's many baseball cards, which he had collected for twelve years. Three of the boxes had their lids removed, as if Mr. Young had quickly looked at the contents inside. Robotically, David put the fifteen shoe boxes back into the closet, one by one. He was in his own little troubled world, unaware of his surroundings.

Then he picked up a shoe box that felt different from the rest.

Rather than a box of baseball cards of long-forgotten players who would become answers to trivia questions-"commons," as they were known- the contents of this box snapped David from his near-comatose state of mind.

Numbness predominated over every move and thought until he took the lid off of the box. He knew the contents of all the boxes because he had packed them, and they all felt the same- except this one. The weight- the feel- was different.

Inside, he found a letter and six black wallet-sized objects he had never before seen. The letter immediately gripped his attention and seemingly brought a greater amount of blood to his brain.

"What communicator?" he asked aloud as he read from the letter. He lifted from the box one of the six small, black items and eyed it intently. "This is an explosive device?" he wondered out loud, examining one of the devices closely, as if he could divine the object's power. It was hard like metal but felt like plastic. It had one small, smooth area that, unbeknownst to David, was a digital readout, though now it was blank. He shoved the object into the left front pocket of his jeans. "Like a wallet," he softly said as he nodded, reading from his uncle's letter.

The single page of paper in Phillip's handwriting brought tears to his eyes. He left the five remaining small objects in the box and made his way to his upstairs bedroom. Life returned to the teenager's eyes. Through the words of a dead man, he found inspiration and comfort.

Like the other rooms, his bedroom was a mess. Clothes, shoes, baseball gear, entire drawers were strewn about. David had the feeling that whoever tore through the house- Johnny and his dad, of course- felt pressed for time, as though they knew their time in the house was limited.

It's a good thing, he thought. His dresser drawers had all been opened. Two drawers remained in the tall dresser, and the top drawer had been rummaged. Hidden on a lip formed by the frame of the dresser, above the top drawer that contained his underwear and socks, lay his palm-sized laser. It had avoided detection. David grabbed the device, then handled it for a moment as he pondered how such a small item could be so powerful. If it was anything like Johnny's laser gun, there was no question of its destructive power.

Thoughts of practice-firing the gun were ended abruptly by sounds emanating from the front of the house. He quickly stuffed the weapon into his front right pocket, where he kept his truck keys.

Within seconds, a familiar voice barked instructions.

"Check every room, every closet, every hole. If we have to tear open walls we will. Just find it."

Albert Young. Surely Johnny was with him. Albert Young, the man who killed his family, was in the living room. He could run, but to where? He could hide, but for how long? He could die, and maybe that was not such a bad option. What awaited him? He had asked himself that question many times over the past week. His home planet was wracked by war, assassinations, and rebellion. His peaceful existence was now past tense, likely to never again return, so maybe the natural fear of death had lost some of its power.

His hesitation was only slight. David walked swiftly down the stairs and to the entrance of the living room, only a matter of feet from Albert and Johnny Young.

"You killed my aunt and uncle!" he growled as he glared at Young. David was young, but he was strong- physically and mentally- and he was certainly tough.

Father and son froze. Young's only reason to exist stood before him. The attainment of sainthood in future Rebellion lore was twelve feet and one laser shot away. But, he thought, this is Johnny's moment. Johnny needs the glory more. This was suddenly too easy.

"No, I've never even been here before." Young responded casually.

"I did," Johnny said, just as casually. "I killed them both."

David's knees buckled at the thought. Phillip. Grace. At the hand of Johnny! How could that be?! His mind was overloaded with pain, hundreds of thoughts, and much more pain. This could not be possible. The disgusting creature Albert Young did not commit this heinous act. His best friend did! David quickly and loudly inhaled, attempting to keep his senses.

They had treated Johnny well. Always. They allowed Johnny to accompany them when they took various trips to amusement parks, and several times to take in Cincinnati Reds' games.

And Johnny murdered them. Viciously. Savagely. He repaid them with death.

He had never before felt such a blow. It was different than the feelings which surfaced when he saw his uncle's dead body. The loss of Phillip and Grace was great, but the emotion, the pain, the emptiness was different. It was a different kind of misery.

He lost his strength and toughness.

His best friend- not the freak, Albert Young- had murdered Phillip and Grace. David's skin tingled, as though blood ceased to flow through his body. His thoughts clouded into a dull roar, as if he were standing near a large waterfall. Sounds became muffled. He felt as though his body would shut down.

Before he completely shut down, by sheer force of will he snapped out of his plunge into physical and emotional meltdown. He had no other choice. He was facing death at any moment, and he needed to be alert if wanted to stand any chance of meeting the challenge.

But Johnny killed Phillip and Grace. That thought was the only thought that reverberated through his mind. All other thoughts were still muddled, unable to reach complete development.

David took a long, deep breath. His struggle seemed to be not only with consciousness, but with sanity. Johnny killed Phillip and Grace. It could not be. Yet, he knew it was. The thoughts repeated again and again. Johnny had become whatever it was that Albert was. A monster.

David's lapse into partial unconsciousness was brief, though it seemed like minutes to him. He struggled to regain all of his faculties as he heard the two Youngs snarl at one another.

"You've blown it twice," father snapped at son, "This is the moment I've trained you for."

"Twice?!" Glory could wait. Johnny wanted an explanation of the insult. The demanding father could dish it out, but the destined son was tired of taking it.

"Yes, twice. You had the opportunity yesterday to kill the prince and last night you should've found the communicator. Obviously you didn't search everywhere or you would've found it."

David's normal impulsive, confrontational attitude did not materialize. He had never fired his laser and Johnny- and certainly Albert Young, as well- had. He had no hope of simultaneously shooting both men. He was not even sure he had the desire to do so. Desire for anything was lacking at the moment.

Although the hollowness that he felt from Johnny's casual announcement clouded his thoughts, he understood his predicament. He could not stand around to wait to die, no matter how attractive that option seemed.

So he ran.

With the Youngs focused on each other, David fled the room in a panic. Around a corner, which prevented him from being shot, through the back of the house, out the kitchen door and through the backyard, David ran for his life. As he reached the edge of his property, a red-orange roar missed his right shoulder by mere inches, exploding into the base of a tree twenty-five yards ahead of him.

There was no need to look back. Johnny was coming. The skinny pitcher could outrun the stocky catcher, so the catcher knew he had better come up with a plan- quickly. David had both brain and brawn, but Johnny had speed and a weapon that he knew how to use.

When David reached the railroad tracks he was gassed. He lay down at the edge of the ditch, ignoring the sharp rocks that surrounded the rails. If Johnny gets any closer, he thought, I'll have to get in the weeds and water. He did not want to get into the stagnant water unless it was necessary. The mosquitoes were bad enough anywhere near the watery gullies of prior rainfalls that paralleled the train tracks, but the thought of snakes made him queasy.

He had done more sprinting in the last eighteen hours than he had since the high school wrestling season ended a few months prior. He hated running. Now he ran to live. On his feet again, David ran on the rocks, following the tracks away from his house.

The internal arguments of whether Johnny really would kill him were over. The only questions that still had to be answered were whether he could kill Johnny- if he wanted to kill Johnny; and if he wanted to even live. But for the moment, he decided that he would live for revenge.

Under the brilliant blue sky, a meadowlark sang out its happy song. A seemingly lonely frog, too, sang its praises of the gorgeous weather and sunshine. A variety of bugs called out across the countryside, announcing their presence on this muggy Indiana day. It was a day that people could agree to call "beautiful," but the beauty escaped young David's notice. It was not a beautiful day. The word had lost its meaning.

An approaching train halted the sounds of nature. David's wits began to churn.

The train traveled the same direction that David ran, so now the young man had a new fear: had Johnny jumped the train, allowing him to jump off at any moment to overtake him? He crouched down in the weeds, just at the edge of the water, until the powerful yellow engines roared by, a mere ten feet away from him, pulling its cargo at 35 miles per hour.

David sprinted alongside the train and grabbed a ladder welded onto the side of a coal car. The difference in speed ripped David's body forward, momentarily threatening his grip on the steel ladder. David had no time to worry about the pain that shot through his shoulders and arms. His legs flailed until he was able to climb two rungs with his hands and pull his legs inward, onto the bottom rung of the ladder.

The black container car brimmed with coal, with the black stuff rising to a flat, wide inverted "U" of the raw fossil fuel. As David climbed the ladder to the top of the car, he looked back in time to see Johnny, only one hundred yards back, performing the same act of successfully mounting the train.

What David could not see was that Johnny had boarded a box car. Advancing toward David would take little time.

After catching his breath, Johnny tenderly edged to the front of the car on which he now stood. The idea of jumping from one box car to the next looked easy enough, but he realized that this was a difficult task. He retraced his steps, got as good of a run that he could manage aboard a moving, swaying train, and leaped through the air.

David again lacked a plan but, as always, one came to mind. Flawed or not, he would stick with a plan for as long as possible. He trudged through the coal toward the front of the car, fighting to maintain his balance the entire way.

It was impossible for him to leap from the coal car to the box car that was directly in front of him. His footing in the coal was too tenuous to make such a leap, and the top of the box car was much higher than the top of the mound of coal.

The repetitious "clack-clack, clack-clack" of steel rails smacking wood railroad ties below and the roar of the great engines ahead of him were the only sounds that he could hear. Eventually, the locomotive's horn would blow again, but even that would not interrupt his concentration. Fearlessly he climbed down the edge of the coal car, feet dangling just above the couplers that connected the train cars to one another.

The drop was only three feet, but on a moving train he felt like a trick rider changing horses on an out-of-control stagecoach ride across the Great Plains. His feet hit squarely on the couplers but the swaying was too much of a foe. One foot slipped off, and the sudden weight shift threw him more out of balance. The stray foot shot up in the air as David frantically reached out to grab something- anything.

His right hand grabbed a steel piece of the coal car that jutted out toward him. In the half second of grasping for the steel, he could not get a firm grip. But the action, served to slow his fall and allow him to spin in an effort to avoid the ghastly death of bouncing underneath the train cars that would surely shatter and then pass over his bouncing body. He desperately wrapped both arms over the couplers as best he could. He held on tightly, but the movement of the train caused his body to slide, effectively rotating him-first to the side of the couplers, then underneath. Both feet dangled inches from the wooden ties of the tracks below. Even touching a tie would knock his body out of balance from his precarious position.

Adrenalin pumped through his body, enabling him to ignore the pain in his ribs on the left side of his torso. Mightily he struggled to push off the coal car with one foot and to slowly rotate back to the top of the couplers. He grappled with the solid steel of the couplers and a steel cable that served as a safety hold between train cars. His struggle was powered by an intense rush of strength that he had never before experienced, caused to a small degree by the pain, but largely because of the extreme terror he felt. Earlier, he had thought about giving up; now he was fighting to live with a desperation that he did not know was possible.

Once on top of the couplers again, he quickly caught his breath and methodically moved, positioning himself to regain his footing. A ladder on the box car in front of him allowed him to climb.

He should have looked back. Only the coal car and one other box car now separated the longtime friends. Johnny was not willing to waste an opportunity, so he fired at the ladder-climbing David. The reddish-orange little fireball exploded two feet from David's shoulder.

The small explosion was close enough to jar David's right hand from the ladder. With a return of the terror, David grabbed the ladder with his opposite hand. His footing slipped and he momentarily hung by his left hand.

Terror was the only feeling that David could interpret. Death might be peaceful, but bouncing underneath a moving train was not. The thought was too gruesome to retain.

Up or down, David had to decide. He quickly chose not to repeat his ordeal of dropping down onto the couplers and instead chose to risk being struck by Johnny's laser.

He had to reach the top of the box car if he wanted to avoid having Johnny catch him. He scurried up the remaining three feet of the narrow ladder as another laser round struck near his ankles. The high-pitched sound was unique and unforgettable to someone within its range. The concussion of the shot swung David's legs away from the ladder, but he maintained his grip with his hands.

Out of pure panic, David rolled once on top of the train car, spun, pulled his laser from his pocket, and from a prone position fired his weapon for the first time.

He missed his target by a country mile.

The brightness of the indigo flash surprised him, and he immediately wished that he could have found the time to practice with the device. His concentration was so great that he failed to notice the high-pitched chirp made by the blast of laser light. His concentration did nothing, however, for his aim.

He did not watch as his shot sailed far over Johnny's head and arced across the sky. If he had watched the laser light, and if time had permitted, he would have been curious whether the laser continued on for miles or dissipated in the air. He would have assumed that gravity would have taken over, but there was no time for such thoughts.

Pulling himself to one knee, he fired again. This time Johnny leaped out of the way and nearly off the box car on which he was standing. At the edge of the car, Johnny rolled until he looked toward David. From a prone position he fired two quick bursts that missed only because of the swaying motion of the train.

Johnny had obviously fired his weapon on multiple occasions. David now had a new reason for concern.

Still on one knee, David returned fire. An explosion and a short-lived fire erupted four feet from Johnny's head, on the top of the box car. David now had a new plan, and the plan's first step called for him to run to the front of the box car, farther away from Johnny. In one motion, he fired another round at Johnny, spun on his knee, and ran. Before Johnny could return fire, David was near the front of the box car.

Fearing- almost knowing- that David was not merely fleeing, Johnny climbed to his feet and ran forward, his blonde hair waving in the wind of the moving train. The leap from one car to the next barely slowed the agile young man. He hit and rolled onto the next box car, then rushed forward until he overlooked the coal car.

David climbed part way down the ladder at the front of the box car on which he rode across the countryside. The distance between the former best friends was separated only by a coal car and the length of the box car on which David temporarily inhabited, with David facing the rear of the train. Johnny was no longer in view, so David deduced that he had made the jump forward. With that conclusion in mind, David scurried down the ladder and found himself once again on the steel couplers.

This time he maintained his balance until he leaped outward, barely clearing the edge of the train car. The pain of crashing onto the rocks, feet first, then rolling hard into the weeds was a mild consequence when compared to Johnny's laser.

After lying still, the train passed and David rose to his feet. He looked nervously toward the departing locomotive. There was no time to think. Johnny would respond with a similar leap, soon.

*   *   *   *   *   *

David crawled out of the bed of the pickup truck and gave a wave of thanks to the driver. A friend's brother had passed along the country road at the right time for the weary prince. After a brief drive, only a short walk of one block separated him from his house.

Chapter 15 - Unfinished Business

Albert Young was here to complete the work that his son had started. After killing the Steeles, Johnny had searched the house, but nerves had gotten the better of him. He had heard every small noise in the silent house, so after a quick, haphazard search through the house had proven fruitless, Johnny had fled, without finding the prized communicator.

Young agreed that the police could pose a problem for them, but the habitually unhappy man remained unhappy that his son had not completed this mission. He was in the house alone. David was on his own now, so killing him should prove easy. But finding the communicator in order to lure the Prince Tinian into an ambush was proving to be more difficult.

The letter distracted him from his unfinished business. Young sat on the floor in the middle of the den, with the shoe box and its few contents at his feet.

"The communicator will signal the Prince Tinian to return for you," he read quietly. A slight pause is all that separated the words from a temper tantrum. Young exploded with rage. He pivoted to his knees and reached out to anything in sight. Almost frantically he tore into boxes, spilling out baseball cards. He shoved a wheeled chair out of his way and tore at more boxes. Nothing! He was grunting audibly. The grunts occasionally turned to deep growls.

It must be here, he reasoned. It must be! He mumbled to himself and cursed under his breath as his search lost its discipline. The whirlwind of motion and noise blocked from his ears any sound outside of the room.

David stood in the doorway of the den, laser drawn. Still on the floor, the older man turned and saw the prince standing before him.

"Where is the communicator?!" Young demanded.

David fled before Young could grab his laser.

A determined Young leaped to his feet to give chase-laser gun drawn and senses heightened. The third step carried him through the doorway of the den leading into the hallway.

The catcher could hit, and hit with power. A full swing from the aluminum bat caught Albert Young above the bridge of his nose, between his eyes. The glory of killing the prince, of returning home a triumphant warrior and agent, of helping the cause of the Rebellion by striking irreparable harm to the royal family, of receiving medals from his beloved cousin-Albert Young would not see any of it.

The body dropped to the floor, shoulders and back of the head first. David stood over the corpse, but a rush of panic overcame him. Without further hesitation, he struck another powerful blow with the bat to the dead man's skull. Panic faded.

David was back on plan. It may have been the fifth plan of the week, or even of the day, but he had a plan and this one was working. He dropped to one knee to superficially examine the body of the crusty, hard-edged man who always had seemed so paranoid and angry. He was sickened by what he had done, but he tried to push aside such thoughts and feelings. He just killed a man for the first time in his life; he was already conceding to himself that killing again might be necessary.

Lying next to the lifeless body on one side was a laser; he grabbed the weapon for himself. Inside the shirt breast-pocket was a small black item that resembled a pager. Had his home planet no imagination? He wondered to himself with a chuckle about the drab black appearance of nearly every item- everything they made was little and black, it seemed.

He ignored the details of the device, so he failed to notice that it was unlike the objects he had previously seen that his uncle had left for him. This device had small buttons on it, although the tiny buttons were not marked. It was also thinner than the explosive pack in his front pocket and the ones in the shoebox. He shoved it into his back pocket, opposite his wallet, and quickly forgot about it. There was too much going on to think about trivial matters.

His mind was heavy with death. Whatever was before him- this day, this life- pivoted on the past week. He had escaped death and now he had killed. He found out that his life was a lie, yet he was not sure whether he could accept the truth. He certainly did not understand the truth.

David's whirlwind thoughts slowed as he dropped to his knees. The feelings hit. They could no longer be pushed aside. He had killed another human being. He had hunted and field dressed deer, usually with Johnny, and he had prepared many quail and pheasant for eating. None of that was a big deal. This was. A real big deal. He had killed a human being.

The man had a soul. He had family. He had intrinsic value by just being alive. Now he was dead.

The man was also his enemy, sworn to kill him. It was either him or me, David reasoned. There was no middle ground, no negotiating.

The impact of what he had just done continued to settle in. He had killed the father of his best friend- his former best friend, anyway. He knew that if he did not get onto the Prince Tinian soon, matters would be complicated to the point that no one- on Earth or in a spaceship- could regain control. Deputy Osborne would see to that. Or Johnny.

A depressing feeling overcame him as he looked at Albert Young's carcass. Surely this will haunt me, he thought. Little did he know that Young's bloody, dead face was being etched into his brain. He would see that face for a very long time.

He reasoned that the police had no purpose in returning to the house, so he hid the body only with a pile of clothes that he brought to the den from his uncle's closet. But his understanding of police work was flawed.

*   *   *   *   *   *

Refreshed from a shower, David lay on the bed in the room Mrs. Fuller had let him use, reading and re-reading the letter from his uncle. Next to him lay the shoe box and its contents. He took out the small, black explosive pack from his front pocket, which he had previously removed from the box, and once again the six objects were together.

A knock on the door interrupted him. The door opened part way to reveal the wrinkled face of an elderly woman. Her eyeglasses rode halfway down her nose and the earpieces were attached by a thin chain long enough to allow the excess to gather on each shoulder. Her short, gray, thinning hair gave one the idea that she might soon purchase a wig the next time her daughter ferried her into Louisville.

Mrs. Fuller's generosity was the most important pillar of support since his aunt and uncle were robbed of life by Johnny and his laser. She could not understand what had happened, and she still did not understand why the Sheriff's Department was not to know where he was staying, but her motherly instincts kicked in at a propitious moment for him.

"The police are here again," she said with her soft, yet aged voice.

"I don't care, but thanks for letting me know."

"Are you okay?" The question was not curiosity as much as genuine concern.

"Yeah, sorta."

She stared at him for a long moment before quietly closing the door.

David did care that the police returned. He fretted about Young's body and whether it would be linked to him. He thought about how much he owed Mrs. Fuller. He thought about everything, but everything was too much for his mind and body as exhaustion took over. He fell asleep. Sleep did not cure his problems, but it did give him the opportunity to not feel the pain in his shoulders, from leaping onto the moving train; his ribs, from falling awkwardly onto the train's couplers; his lower back and left elbow, from jumping off a train moving 35 miles per hour. All the pain was gone for as long as he remained asleep.

* * * * * *

The nap served David well. After slapping together a ham and cheese sandwich in the kitchen and devouring it at a rate that caused sweet Mrs. Fuller to protest, he was off to his house again. Before he left, she let him know that the police had towed away someone's pickup truck and had removed what must have been a body from the house.

Young's body was gone, but David was certain that the spirit of Death lingered within those walls.

* * * * * *

With hours of daylight still remaining in the sky, David entered his house with a mixture of fear and curiosity, despite the single piece of yellow police tape that supposedly sealed off the front door. He was less concerned about the house than he was the whereabouts of Johnny. Hopefully Johnny had gone many miles before realizing that he had leaped off of the train.

The thought was interrupted by the sound of movement in a back room. With laser drawn, he entered the hallway and slowly crept toward the bedroom from where the sound came. He heard laughter as a young woman and then a young man entered the hallway, saw David, and immediately screamed in panic. David was the stalker, but he, too, was startled.

"Aw man!" the young man yelled. "Don't do that! You scared us half to death! Don't sneak like that!"

"I live here, remember Marty?!" David snarled angrily, as he tried to bring down his heart rate. He quickly tucked his laser back into the front of his pants. "Why are you here?! Who said you could be here?!" He was angry and he wanted to make sure that the couple knew it.

Marty Barton, the short, skinny weird kid had always been short and skinny and weird. His tall, bushy, light brown hair only added to the aura of a goof who was half stoned-and all geek.

His girlfriend was the perfect match for him. Kids in high school used to jokingly ask who last combed their hair, Marty or Ellen Shaw. Ellen's long, clumpy brown hair matched Marty's in color and texture, and the look begged the question of how a young woman could care so little about her appearance.

Perfect match they were. Both were 18 and headed nowhere outside of their own world. Marty was fascinated by UFO's and the paranormal while Ellen was just fascinated with Marty. Everyone figured that the two would get married and end up living in Indianapolis or Louisville behind a government building or across from a soup kitchen.

"Yeah, you live here for now," Marty responded bitingly. "But the police will own this place pretty soon, the way things are goin'."

"Whaddya mean?" David forgot all about his demand that Marty answer for trespassing.

"We know what's goin' on," Ellen confidently announced. "Well," she continued with confidence fading. "We know some of what's goin' on."

"An' we wanna ride on your spaceship," Marty completed the thought.

"Look," David sneered, the impatience boiling up rapidly. "   Marty, don't start your weird stuff with me. You too, Ellen. Just get that spaceship junk of yours out of your head."

"David," Marty happily sang out. "We saw you that night."

"What night?"

Marty did not bother with impatience- he simply laughed. "What night?!" He laughed a fake "who are you kidding?" laugh. "The night everyone's talkin' 'bout. The night the spaceships came. That was great, man!"

"It was scary," Ellen quietly added.

Marty continued the tandem explanation of their presence. "Scared Ellen so bad she 'bout peed her pants."

"I did!"

"Look, I don't know what you know," David retorted, unconvincing even to himself. "Or what you think you know, but you guys should go."

Marty's weirdness made his seriousness sound even weirder than normal. "We were there that night. In the field. And we wanna go- with you."

"Into outer space," Ellen added.

"I think you're already there," David deadpanned.

"For real though." Ellen did not miss a beat.

"In that spaceship." Neither did Marty.

David reviewed the situation. He had already confessed to Marty's aunt, and now this strange couple was adamant that they witnessed at least part of the alien extravaganza. As he mulled it over, the couple exchanged an excited glance. It was obvious to all three of them that David could not continue to plead ignorance.

"You can't go," he finally proclaimed with a voice of authority.

But Marty was ready. "Then we'll ask Johnny."

"We know he's got somethin' to do with this," Ellen again completed her boyfriend's thought. "Maybe he'll let us go."

"No!" David shouted without thinking.

After a brief silence, Marty laughed with surprise at David's outburst. "Cool off there, big boy," he scornfully reproached David. The timing was off for such a retort, given the momentary silence, but the timing and words fit

175

perfectly with Marty's weirdness. No one- except Ellen- could understand him most of the time, anyway.

"We just wanna go," Ellen said with all seriousness. "We won't touch anything or break anything. We promise."

"If you let us go, we'll make sure you won't regret it," Marty added.

Panic was starting to build within David, starting in his imagination. What Johnny might do- how he might use this odd pair of human beings- began to invade the prince's thoughts.

"You guys don't understand," he finally said after some thought. "You cannot go." To David, it was an answer. He enunciated his words and projected forcefulness to make the answer clear. To Marty and Ellen it was the creation of another obstacle that certainly had an opening somewhere.

"I think we got enough on ya that ya gotta let us go." Marty's tone was not as menacing as the words. "We know ya killed Johnny's dad and we don't wanna go to the Sheriff with that."

How could he know that? David asked himself. Certainly it was a bluff. Or had the screwy pair staked out the house and noticed that he had left not long before the police came and removed a body? But how could they know? It did not add up.

His shoulders slumped. Thoughts of his dead aunt and uncle; of having to kill that brutal Albert Young; of the spaceship and what went wrong and who he was and who he was not. His life was worse than ruined because now he knew he was not even a human. At least he did not think he was. Or was he?

His brain was overloading, and he could only do the one thing that he learned to do over the past week: run. He raced out the door, and the goofy couple who did not seem as though they were from Earth, either, watched him go.

"Wow! That really was David who got on that spaceship!" Ellen trumpeted.

"Told ya," Marty beamed.

"Ohmigod! I really really wanna go on that spaceship," Ellen half-squeaked with excitement.

"Stick with me and we will," Marty proclaimed with certitude.

For the goofy couple, this moment was a great victory.

$$* \quad * \quad * \quad * \quad * \quad *$$

David ran down the street until he arrived at his pickup. From there he quickly drove away. The thoughts that streamed through his head were the same as yesterday's, and those of the day before, and the day before that. As he drove, he turned on the radio. A Toby Keith song filled the passenger compartment, but it was still not enough to block out the repetitive thoughts. He did not know how to turn off his mind as he would a radio. As the music played, his brain repeated the same confused thoughts, over and over.

Chapter 16 - Countermeasures

The sun rose for the eighth time since the Prince Tinian landed and rewrote the story of David's life. The first rays of light found David's bed at Mrs. Fuller's house empty. Never sure of Johnny's whereabouts and in constant fear that someone would see him and casually tell Johnny where he was, the young prince stayed on a taxing, relentless edge. Sleep was no longer a routine, taking place at specific times out of habit. Sleep was now a necessity to be grabbed when possible.

He carried with him a black leather fanny pack, which he borrowed from Mrs. Fuller. Inside were his laser gun and the contents of the shoe box. The fanny pack actually belonged to Mrs. Fuller's grandson, but right now David had no concern for who owned it or about how it looked around his waist; right now, utility was his concern. He had forgotten about the black device he had taken from Albert Young, so the thin object remained in his back pocket. Young's laser rested in the pocket of his pickup's driver's side door.

He also carried, in his wallet, three hundred dollars lent to him by his elderly host. He knew that his quick grabs of fast food was not healthy, but the cash was welcome to help him keep going in food and gasoline.

As the sun's golden rays threaded through the trees behind Johnny's house, David took cover behind a large propane tank, which looked to him like a giant Tylenol pill.

He was confident that Johnny had no reason to search his own backyard.

Time passed by slowly under the Indiana sky until Johnny left the house and climbed into his red Camaro. David had ridden in the car hundreds of times. The cloth seats, the guttural rumble of the engine, and the six-speaker stereo system made for a lot of memories that were crammed into two-and-a-half short years. The car was a 1967 model, restored to cherry condition by the previous owner. The man who refurbished the car, an auto mechanic from a nearby town, had to part with it due to financial problems. David was jealous when the sweet deal fell into Johnny's lap, thanks to some unknown business dealing between the mechanic and Albert Young.

Whether they were driving home from a summer league baseball game or just out running around, David and Johnny always managed to have a blast in the Camaro. Rarely did they slow down to come close to the speed limit- the paved country roads were essentially miles and miles of drag strips. The dirt and gravel roads were fun, but the speed was reached on the paved back roads. David preferred that Johnny kept all four wheels on the ground, and Johnny complied by slowing for some of the steeper hills.

David always found it peculiar that Mr. Young insisted that no one but Johnny drive the Camaro. The boys obeyed the rule because of the old man's ability to see through his son. They were not about to cause themselves grief simply because David would have loved to drive the sporty Chevy.

When Johnny was safely out of sight, David made his way toward the house. A plank of wood a few yards from the shed, in the back of the property, caught his eye. David was certain that he never before had seen the plank, and his curiosity pulled him toward the new feature. As he neared the plank he realized that the wood served as a gravestone. He did not have to read it to understand. The wooden, makeshift headstone read: "Albert Young - cousin of Banu, the great rebel."

The name of Banu had only reached David's ears from the lips of his uncle a short week ago. The words were proof positive that Johnny knew of events in another world. David was now more convinced than ever that the young rebel knew more than the young prince did.

For the first time in his life, David broke into a house. Given the isolation of the Young house, the loud crack of glass was not a concern. David climbed through the window with the thought that he never would have believed that he could break into any house- let alone that of Johnny Young.

*   *   *   *   *   *

Tired of rummaging through the effects of a dead man and his son, David turned his attention toward the basement. In the middle of the concrete room littered with bottles of garden chemicals, spare bricks, and a washer and dryer, a ping pong table collected dust. David smiled at the memories. At fourteen years old, Johnny feared nothing more than a spike from David when the former carelessly set him up too well with a high volley. Their competitive propensities seemed to know no bounds.

When the boys were sixteen, the elder Young banned visitors from the basement. Johnny's explanations never quite made sense, and David was too afraid to ask Mr. Young directly. Mr. Young. Yes, that's how I referred to him, he thought to himself. I killed Mr. Young.

Back in the corner, next to a neat pile of bricks stacked into a square four feet high, sat the answer to the banishment from the basement. In time, David would understand that the presence of this contraption could only mean that Rebels had visited in spaceships within the past two years. But for now, he was just discovering an incredible machine that looked like a video game.

The large, black object looked nearly exactly like the big video games down at Vern's that allowed the player to sit in a seat inside a semi-enclosed cockpit. Those games were usually auto racing or jet pilot games. Only the sides were open, and then just open enough to allow a youth to pass through to enter or exit the contraption.

David climbed in and stared in awe at his surroundings. This was just like a cool video game, he thought. But the events of the past week assured him that this was not a racing game from Vern's.

Little light filtered into the basement. Besides the bulb that burned over the washer and dryer, just a small one-foot by two-foot window that was just below ground level allowed in the sun's light. An offset was dug to allow in light, and from the outside the window rested in a hole in the ground, lined with metal sheeting, just below the top of the concrete basement.

In the near darkness, David could only see one button. Naturally, the little boy in him allowed him to push it.

A low, white light instantly came on overhead- just enough for him to see a panel in front of him. The video screen whirred into action. On-screen, the schematics of a spaceship slowly spun until the image grew as David got the feeling that he was being sucked inside the craft.

A quiet but masculine voice spoke to David. "Welcome to our newest destroyer, the Banu. The Banu is the first of the "Rebel" Class and will deploy soon. Currently being tested, a fleet of these new craft will soon completely replace the "Guerilla" Class destroyers. King Chateau and his murderous Kingdom have no idea of the surprising firepower of the destroyers we are now producing. While it is just as quick and maneuverable as the old fleet, the new fleet will at long last provide the Rebellion with space-based firepower to destroy cargo ships, cruisers, and yes, even Crown destroyers. Now let us examine the capabilities of the secret weapon that will soon be unleashed on the Crown: the "Rebel" Class destroyer."

*   *   *   *   *   *

David climbed out of the alien video game slowly, still trying to absorb more than he ever could. Blessed with a solid memory, he soaked up as much as his tired mind could hold. He stood in thought for perhaps a minute, then arrived at a decision. He reached into his fanny pack and pulled out one of the six wallet-sized devices. It was time to strike back at Johnny and the Rebellion.

Somewhere, Johnny had a stash of cash, likely weapons, and maybe even communication equipment. Whatever else was in this house was about to be destroyed. Taking away the base of operations for Johnny might be a good thing.

He repeatedly poked a finger on the buttons located on the face of the device for a few seconds, then casually set it inside the virtual reality apparatus.

"That little thing can't be that big of a deal," he muttered aloud. The thought resonated to other parts of his brain, and he convinced himself that, indeed, such a little device was not sufficient. Again he returned to the contents of the fanny pack and fidgeted with two more of the devices. Satisfied, he placed the devices on top of the seat of the large, game-like contraption and walked away.

Within four steps David realized that he had committed a huge blunder, for above his head he heard footsteps. Someone- surely it was Johnny- entered the kitchen above. He broke out into a cold sweat. How could Johnny have returned so quickly?! It was miles to the nearest anything, his brain screamed. This was not possible. How long had he been inside the instructional machine? He reached into his fanny pack and pulled out a fourth of the wallet-sized devices. He quickly examined the face of the device before dejectedly returning it to its resting place. He was in serious trouble. The explosive devices lacked "off" or "reset" buttons. A particular sequence of button pushing would have solved his problem, but explosion pack functionality was another on a long list of matters relating to Craylar, their people, and their ways about which David knew nothing.

He did not know how big a one-device explosion could be. Now there were three.

The small window leading outside was large enough for even big David to pass through, but he calculated that there was no way that he could twist through the window and out of the hole in which the window was positioned outside. When they were pre-teens he and Johnny had squeezed through that very window, but David now recalled how even then he could barely turn the acrobatic feat.

The only way out was the way he came in, and Johnny was likely not prepared to listen to an explanation. If Johnny discovered the broken glass in his father's bedroom, he would certainly thoroughly search the house.

David reached the top of the stairs and slowly opened the door. With laser in hand, he slowly stepped into the hallway. No need to peer around the door, he thought just before stepping out. *He would've already blown my head off.*

David purposely let the door to the basement remain cracked open in hopes of luring his friend downstairs. Once

Johnny reached the basement, David was confident he could escape unnoticed.

When he reached the back door in the kitchen, which led to the back yard, he was still uncertain whether Johnny's suspicions had been raised. He turned the handle and was surprised to find that he could not open it. The double-key lock prevented David's passage. David foolishly panicked and rattled the door handle as if just a few shakes would unlock the door. Johnny's suspicions were definitely raised now.

Johnny's race down the hallway, from one of the bedrooms, was delayed only by the presence of the slightly ajar basement door. Laser in hand, the blonde young man's advance toward the kitchen slowed. The rattling came from within- not without- he correctly perceived.

David had killed his father. Johnny knew the taste of death and now so did his former friend. David was every bit a killer as he was now. David may have been hesitant at first, but no more, Johnny imagined. Johnny reasoned that the figurative taste of blood now put David on his level- a dangerous level.

Johnny's blood rushed through his arteries. His palms and forehead became sweaty. He understood that rounding every corner brought him a step closer to an exchange of fire. David must be here- who else would break into the house? Under the kitchen table and inside the lower cabinets he searched, never considering whether David could fit into such small confines. He trembled with excitement and dread. One shot, and glory was his. One misstep and he would meet his father's fate. Glory and revenge: two wonderful reasons to kill- no matter the target.

Finding no one, Johnny stood silently for a moment, listening. Then remembering the open door, he marched toward the basement.

David listened intently, desperately trying to discern Johnny's movements. A trick on Johnny's part and David's position as prince would last for all of one week. Remaining hidden for too long behind the living room couch and he would be trapped inside the house until finally found.

And then there were those little explosion packs, silently ticking away. Not much time was left.

David slowly, warily climbed out from behind the living room couch. Had Johnny only looked beyond the kitchen, David's hiding place would have been found. The prince's best guess told him that it was time to go. Down the hallway he raced, through the front doorway, tearing the hinges off of the old wood-framed screen door that was affixed outside the front solid-core door. He leaped off of the porch and his feet hit Earth in full stride.

In the basement below, Johnny heard the deep thuds of feet running through the living room, then down the hallway toward the front door. He could outrun big David, but the head start could be too much to overcome if David's car were hidden somewhere nearby. Johnny raced up the stairs, pushed off the door casing to make a ninety-degree right turn, and raced toward the open front door.

186

Johnny arrived at the doorway; his head swiveled to and fro to locate his adversary. Cautiously, he walked down the two stairs from the porch to the ground. As his second foot touched the ground, he was suddenly smashed from behind by a strong wave of air. The concussion of the explosion knocked Johnny down, face-first, into the hard Indiana soil.

Debris of all sorts- wood framing, wood siding, appliances, knickknacks- shot into the air and through the windows and walls of the house. What was moments ago a solid oak, antique coffee table rocketed through the front doorway, in three pieces, and over Johnny's unconscious, prone body. Debris rained down for nearly fifteen seconds.

Whenever Johnny awakened, he would discover that the back of his house was gone, and the rest of the house that was still standing was not worth standing.

*   *   *   *   *   *

In his rear view mirror, David saw dust and smoke in the air. Whether Johnny was dead or alive was now irrelevant. Prince or baseball player, war or peace, sanity or his current surroundings, he knew that he would have to accept his fate, he told himself. No matter his feelings about monarchy and friendship, he had to get off the planet as soon as possible.

Chapter 17 - Back for More

It was David's turn to frantically rip apart what was formerly the house that belonged to his aunt and uncle. Under beds, inside mattresses, in the freezer, behind the refrigerator- he madly searched everywhere for the mysterious item known as the communicator. He knew what it did; he knew the importance; he had no idea of its size or what it looked like.

All the while, he kept his mind on Johnny. For the first time in his memory, he did not care whether Johnny was injured or dead. He only cared that Johnny did not surprise him and kill him the way he killed Phillip and Grace.

For the first time, David also took stock of the big picture: If Johnny found the communicator, he could hail the Prince Tinian right into an ambush. David did not know anyone onboard the Crown spacecraft, but he did muster a twinge of concern for their safety. Yet how could the destroyer be ambushed? Why had not Johnny hailed the Banu? No Banu, no ambush. The thought of what could be gave him pause, but also brought more confusion.

He sat down on a couch that was now ripped open and missing all the cushions. If he failed, he thought, others could die. He did not realize it, but slowly, in small, indiscernible increments, he was growing more mature and thinking in a more disciplined fashion. He was growing up; how he thought was changing, if ever so slightly. He was thinking a little less about himself and a little more about the well-being of others.

David's plans were always about the moment, about escaping sticky situations- usually runners in scoring position with less than two outs- or about having fun. He liked to think of himself as a serious thinker, but he was more like a serious daydreamer. He planned and he calculated, but ultimately the plans and calculations were about unimportant diversions in life. He thought deeply and often, but not seriously, not with maturity- until now.

Unnerved by the consequences of failure, and frightened by the thought of another confrontation with Johnny, David abruptly interrupted his thoughts and continued the search for the heretofore unseen communicator.

*   *   *   *   *   *

The search dragged on. Hungry, emotionally exhausted, and suddenly overwhelmed by the fear of the consequences of failure, he decided to take a break. Before he could leave his bedroom, his mind came to attention- someone was outside. Laser in hand, David quietly hid inside the closet. If someone was looking for him, that person would find him soon enough. The element of surprise would be on David's side.

When they walked into his room, marveling at the amount of destruction to every item in sight, David wanted to scream. Screaming would not help matters, he reasoned, except that it might scare nutty Marty and his just-as-nutty girlfriend Ellen away from the house for good.

But he knew he could not get that lucky.

"What are you doing here?!" David demanded, laser still in hand.

The couple shrieked like monkeys being eaten alive. By the time they regained their composure, David was out of the closet and standing in front of Marty, face to face. Short of knocking them both unconscious, all he could think to do was to intimidate them.

"I said, what are you doing here?!" It was part demand, part question, but it was uttered with a ferocity that was not faked.

"We're goin' with you," Marty finally answered as he caught his breath.

"Don't scare us like that," Ellen demanded.

"I'm not goin' anywhere," David insisted. "Why do you keep coming into my house?! Who invited you?! Have you ever heard of trespassing?! This is my house!" His words were stated firmly and loudly, but he himself knew that they were now hollow. Trespassing was irrelevant. Only one thing mattered right now.

"With all this killin' an' craziness goin' on, somebody's gotta be goin' somewhere sometime," Marty blurted out, obviously uncomfortable with David's demeanor.

For his part, David was stuck on the logic of Marty's last statement. Marty may have sounded confusing, but he actually had a point. Somebody was going somewhere. The sooner the better.

"If I don't find the communicator soon, the only place I'll be goin' is to the grave," David mused aloud.

"Whaddya mean?" Ellen asked with a voice of concern.

"What communicator?" Marty completed the thought more precisely for Ellen.

What the heck, he figured. Why not tell them? Who was going to believe them, anyway? These two are a couple of goofballs and no one takes them seriously, he silently reasoned.

"My people are waitin' to hear from me to come get me. And don't ask me why they're waitin'! I don't understand everything." His act of intimidation was evaporating quickly. It was useless.

"We wanna go with you."

David succeeded only in piquing their interests in his predicament and in their bizarre need to see the spaceships. This had to change. Before Marty could move, David let out a low snarl, grabbed the skinny kid by the throat, and slammed him into the wall next to a dresser. The difference in size between the two made David look like a male lion about to devour a gazelle.

David withheld his bite but let out his words with a menacing snarl. "I'm not going on a romantic cruise to the Caribbean! I'm going into the middle of a civil war!" The sweat under his arms and on his face rushed out. His voice rose with anger. "Do you understand that?! If Johnny catches up with me he's gonna kill me, do you understand that?! Kill! Dead! No games, just real death!"

David let slip his steel grip. He stepped back and took a deep breath. Marty, too, took deep breaths. Slowly, the scrawny kid slid down the wall, gently landing his butt on the floor, knees in front of his face, all the while trying to breathe properly.

Ellen was unfazed. Her focus remained on David's predicament. "Why would Johnny kill you?"

With his "who would believe them?" mentality, David decided to answer the question. "Because we're on opposite sides of a war. His mission is to kill me," he patiently explained.

"But you're best friends!" she exclaimed with a naïve shock. She did not seem to grasp that the war was taking place in a different part of the galaxy.

"Were best friends." His emphasis on the first word of his response raised the eyebrows of the two unwanted guests in his house.

Ellen looked down at Marty. Her boyfriend slowly climbed to his feet, but he was too afraid of David's physical prowess to move in any direction lest he displease the bearish alien again.

For her part, she was unsure of what to say or do, particularly given the obvious pain Marty had experienced in his throat. But her fear for Marty's and her own safety was short-lived. The old subject- the main topic to them- returned.

"We just wanna go where you go. We'll take our chances."

Marty looked at her, eyes bulging. He was not prepared for David's grip again. He let out a quiet, barely audible whimper.

David could only think of the past week. He again felt tired. His emotions were spent and his eating and sleeping had suffered. He was now too drained to be angry.

"I'm goin' to Louisville if I don't find the communicator." He liked the sound of his own words. He made them up as a diversion, but it seemed like a good idea. Maybe he could just escape. Maybe they would never find him. Just run.

On the other hand, he had just given away a good idea. Marty and Ellen could never be trusted. They would say whatever was expected of them to get what they wanted. They would not hesitate to repeat their entire conversation with him to Johnny.

But who would believe them?

"What's in Louisville?" Marty finally spoke. His throat felt better and his curiosity overcame his fear of David.

"Not Johnny," David answered wistfully. His sadness reflected his view of the entire situation. Johnny, Phillip, Grace, Albert Young, the tribulations ahead. He slowly sat down onto the shredded mattress which used to be his bed.

He sat for only a few seconds before he heard the sound he now dreaded: the guttural engine noise from Johnny's Camaro. David had ridden in the car so many times and had heard it pull up in front of the house so many times, he had no doubt of the identity of the engine.

"It's Johnny! Get out of here!" he ordered as he pushed them through the bedroom door and into the hallway. "Go out the back door and run!"

The couple led the way for several steps before stopping in unison. Marty's feeble, drug-withered brain overcame his physical fears. As David bowled into them, the stumbling Marty blurted out his foolish thought.

"Maybe we can convince Johnny to let us go."

The couple, again in unison, turned to run. They ran down the stairs, but rather than heading to the back door as ordered, they ran toward the front door. David stopped in amazement as he headed toward the back door. They really are this stupid, he thought.

"Marty! Come on!"

But Marty and Ellen would not obey.

Johnny opened the unlocked front door with a laser in his hand and one thing on his mind.

"Johnny!" Marty beamed as he stepped away from Ellen to be closer to Johnny. "How's it goin', man? We wanna go-"

Johnny was not in the mood for pleasantries, and Marty was too foolish to notice. Johnny aimed the laser at Marty's chest and fired. A red-orange blast of light burst into Marty's torso, knocking the boy backward, as if he were kicked by a mule.

"Ellen, where's David?" He stepped forward, intentionally sending the message that he aimed to kill again, if necessary.

In shock, she slowly pointed toward the back of the house, toward the dining room and kitchen. She tried to speak but could only whimper a pathetic sound of horror and pain.

"Try to run and I'll kill you, too," Johnny barked at her.

She dropped slowly to her knees, looking sadly at the only person who ever understood her. Quiet sobs finally leaked out of her mouth as she cradled Marty's lifeless head in her lap. Her spirit was crushed.

"David, get out here where I can see ya or I'll kill Ellen, too!" he bellowed. He had an unmistakable edge to his voice. Merely trying to kill would no longer do. He had to destroy. He had to maintain an attitude that would propel him to his greatness.   "David!" he shouted. Again no response. His focus on the opportunity to kill was such that he did not even bother to shield himself from the inevitable blast from David's laser. When the shot came, it rocketed past Johnny's ear and slammed into the door casing behind him. The small explosion convinced Johnny to take cover behind a piece of furniture that used to function as a couch.

"You shoot at me again and I'll kill her!" he snapped.

Still no verbal response from David.

Ellen was oblivious to her dangerous surroundings. She thought nothing of her well-being, only her one true love. She rocked back and forth with Marty's head in her lap. Living and shouting and violence were just distractions at the moment. Marty was gone, and she would rather be wherever his soul was right now.

When her sobbing began, the sounds irritated the intense and murderous thug that inhabited the body of Johnny Young. "Shut up!" he growled at the girl. But she was incapable of hearing his words. Her senses shut down. Her sobs turned to wails.

Johnny tried to ignore her crying but could not. He needed to concentrate on David. He needed to anticipate David's next move. He needed to hear. Instead, the wails of a young woman in anguish over the loss of her soul mate penetrated his thoughts and interrupted his ability to make decisions.

Impatiently, Johnny glanced past the weeping Ellen, toward the dining room, but the sounds of Ellen's immense grief diverted his attention further. Out of patience, he picked up a piece of a broken ceramic lamp base and hurled it into the dining room. The only sound was that of a small crash of ceramic- no sounds of scurrying, of repositioning. Alarmed, he leaped to his feet and ran toward the back of the house.

As Johnny ran through the dining room and entered the kitchen, the sound of David's pickup starting up caused Johnny to suddenly change directions. David had fooled him. Another round lost to the mind reader.

Johnny raced to the front door, reaching the porch moments after David, behind the wheel of his truck, fired laser rounds into a tire and the grill of Johnny's Camaro. The tire popped loudly, but the sound was quickly overpowered by the explosion that thundered from beneath the hood of the muscle car. While small in display, from the sound it was obvious that the laser blast wreaked havoc in the engine compartment.

Hastily, Johnny ran into the yard for a clear shot and fired at David's truck, now nearly a block away. His first shot sailed harmlessly over the cab of the truck while the second missed one side of the tailgate by inches. He continued to run as David sped away and around a corner.

Johnny stopped in the street and dropped to one knee to fire more accurately, but by that time David's truck was already out of sight.

Dejected, Johnny looked at his car. A far deeper dejection set in. A tire was flat, but his problem was much worse than that: oil and a mixture of anti-freeze and water streamed onto the pavement, signifying the uselessness of his automobile. The hood bowed up in the front, near the bumper. He could only imagine the condition of what was left of his engine.

A sick feeling rose from Johnny's gut, up into his throat. In his own mind, he was a picture of failure. Only a matter of feet away from his enemy- the one prize which could propel him up the heights of greatness- and yet he was unable to direct a laser blast into David's body. Triumph had been so close. The taste of glory had barely eluded him.

His greatest hope was in his belief that David had not found the communicator. If he had found it, he would have already left the area and likely would have summoned his rescue. If history were to repeat, the spaceship would land only a quarter of a mile from David's house, and that encounter would likely take place this very moment.

A combination of anger directed at himself and embarrassment at what his father would think seized him. His father. This was no longer just about destiny, it was also about avenging his father's death. David had drunk from the brutal well of the civil war and he must pay for his offense. It was up to Johnny to make him pay. He killed the cousin of the Great Banu. Johnny would execute the prince's sentence.

Despite brash ruminations of his own, imagined bravery, he glumly had to admit to himself the one thing that crippled his confidence more than anything else: the catcher was once again calling the game.

Chapter 18 - Onboard

In his royal blue Ford pickup, David raced down a paved but seldom-traveled country road. The rich, cobalt sky was nearly as dark as his pickup was when clean. The green fields of soybean and now-occasional corn fields provided a comforting and attractive backdrop for any person seeking peaceful surroundings. Driving too fast to notice such a backdrop and too intent in his own thoughts to care, he hurtled toward nowhere.

A plan did not exist. He considered doubling back, but feared that an encounter with the Sheriff's Department- who were almost certainly on their way to his house at this very moment- would lead to unintended consequences; and he believed strongly in the "law of unintended consequences." No one would believe the "aliens from another planet" story, so why bother?

David without a plan was like a boat without a rudder. He felt useless, adrift. Indeed, he was mentally and emotionally adrift.

Doubling back would have allowed him to at least attempt to know Johnny's whereabouts, but fear pushed self-confidence aside, so driving madly down country roads somehow seemed like the next best thing.

Louisville was still an option in the back of his mind. He could, he decided, go for a few days, hide out in the big city, then make his way back home to search once again for the elusive communicator. But he hated cities, and he had absolutely no idea what a communicator looked like; looking now or later would not change either fact. He also realized that the longer he waited to find the device, the higher the odds would be that Johnny would find it first.

Another thought crossed his mind: if Johnny found the communicator and the Prince Tinian was led into an ambush, David would be perpetually on the run. Stranded. The Rebels could simply wait for law enforcement to find him because there was no doubt that he would now be wanted for murder; Johnny was conniving enough to pin all of the killings on an absent David.

He had to gamble that Johnny would leave without searching for the device. He hoped that the laser display and the deafening sound of Johnny's old Chevy engine being destroyed would convince his opponent that he should flee the scene.

Like it or not, David reasoned, at some point, he had to turn around and go back.

David slammed on his brakes so hard that the pedal hit the floorboard. The pickup slid toward the right edge of the dirt until he instinctively let off the brake pedal and corrected his steering.

The monstrous craft gently touched ground, blocking the entire road. The area was a tiny, shallow valley, surrounded by a sloping field of soybeans on one side of the road and a wooded area on the other. The top of the craft reached above the small hillside and would have been visible if anyone had been in the vicinity. The deep-green and charcoal craft extended fully three-hundred feet into the soybean field. The spacecraft barely missed landing on trees on the opposite side of the road.

David previously had seen the descending spacecraft-inside the virtual reality device at Johnny's house.

*   *   *   *   *   *

The bridge of the Prince Tinian was filled with tension. Every war-ready position was covered. Men stood or sat at the ready, waiting for the news from their Admiral. Artimus Praeder entered the deck; his walk showed purpose but his expression revealed a touch of confusion.

"Gentlemen," his voice bellowed, filling every free space of air on the deck. "Much time has been lost. We have uprooted a traitor, but he cowardly allowed a pill to protect him from his rightful punishment. We have had our first engagement with the new class of Rebel destroyers and were taken by surprise by its firepower. This ship has been repaired and is once again battle-ready."

The touch of confusion had been acknowledged by the stern Admiral, but only briefly. The surprising firepower of the Banu made the next course of action more troublesome than anyone had anticipated.

"Navigator, put us on a course for Earth. We are going to rescue our prince," he trailed off for dramatic effect, then continued with extra vigor. "Or die trying." His flair for the dramatic, Praeder believed, carried his men forward into battle, neutralizing fear and over-active imaginations of his crew. If pressed, even Praeder would have admitted that this moment called for a healthy dose of fear. But no one dared press him on the matter.

Captain Gonchar walked to Commander Bozwell's position. He spoke quietly, in an attempt to avoid the attention of others. "It is about time. The prince is probably dead."

The Commander flashed an irritated glance. "Still fixated on how you think things should be done, sir?" His words were barely louder than a whisper, but his hostile tone could not be missed.

"I will ignore the disrespect, Commander," Gonchar quietly but icily jabbed. "But yes, I am 'fixated.'"

Bozwell let the silence speak for him, but Gonchar was undeterred. "One word, Bozwell: treason. Just watch what happens."

*   *   *   *   *   *

A large ramp, similar to that on the Prince Tinian, lowered onto the road at the same moment that a ramp in the center of the craft lowered in the soybean field. Two creatures fully covered with militaristic protective gear advanced down the ramp and stopped in unison on the road. David's eyes darted to the ramp in the soybean field as the ramp slowly closed.

It's all for naught, he thought. Resistance would prove to be pointless. He recognized the Banu and understood that its firepower could easily vaporize something as small as a pickup truck. As he opened his door and stepped out of the truck, he reached into the pocket in the bottom of the driver's side door and grabbed Albert Young's laser gun. He consciously questioned himself about what he would do with a laser gun versus a mighty attack craft, but he nonetheless stuffed the weapon into his fanny pack as he exited the vehicle.

On a whim, he left his own laser on the seat.

The soldiers marched to David and almost ceremoniously stopped four feet away. "Come with us," ordered one of the two uniformed guards, both of whom were armed with laser rifles. Their black uniforms and helmets with dark shields that extended over their faces added a menacing quality to their presence. Black garb covered them from their oversized helmets down to the polished black boots which climbed above their ankles.

David sized up the pair to gain confirmation that resistance would be downright foolish. Had they been unarmed, he still would not have stood a chance against the two large men.

He obeyed the order.

*   *   *   *   *   *

The inside of the Banu looked exactly as it had in the computer images at Johnny's house. The replication was exact, including the whites, grays, and blacks sported by nearly every piece of equipment. Having passed through a cargo area- this was obviously not the main entrance to the spaceship- David was led through a brief maze of compartments that appeared to him to be sleeping quarters for the crew.

It was clear to David that the Banu was no longer in the testing phase.

With one guard leading and the other following, the threesome snaked their way past the galley and beyond a corridor which broadcast through its narrow opening a deep yet dull rumbling that David recalled led to the engines of the powerful vessel. He took special note of a wall that was opened that, though he could not remember with certainty, was likely the relay station that combined hydraulics, computer interfacing, and laser signals which controlled the maneuverability of the ship.

Walkways were cramped, but David was amazed at both the amount of machinery and activity which resided within the confines of the craft. Men scurried. Machines whined. Dark, open halls and walls would have made the ship seem gloomy if not for all of the activity.

This must be a momentous occasion for the Rebels, David reasoned, yet none of the few crew members he saw seemed to even blink when the threesome walked past. The sentries, with their dark visors now up, did not harass him. They just marched forward through the metallic corridors and control rooms, past objects made of substances that David was sure were not truly metals with which he was familiar.

To everyone but David, this did not seem to be a momentous occasion. On the other hand, he recognized that it was his life- not theirs- that was in jeopardy at this moment.

After progressing up a metal stairway, David and the two sentries at last arrived at the bridge. The long craft stood only three stories tall- short in height when the circumference of the spaceship was considered. The bridge was nestled in the middle of the three stories, open on all sides. Had he desired, David could have walked to the edge of the command deck and looked down at busy technicians who scurried to and fro, analyzing computer output about engine power, laser strength, shield levels, and environmental levels within the craft.

Above, forming the outer ring of the circular bridge, was a catwalk that allowed a team of men to monitor still more computers and control panels that provided support information for the bridge. Straight above, the control stations of the deck were open to the top of the ship's interior.

During the entire walk, David tried to accept his fate: he was a dead man. His stomach felt as though he had swallowed acid and his shoulders lumbered under pressure as though he were carrying Bobby and Junior. Sweat emerged from his forehead, armpits, and palms.

David looked at the two senior officers in his path, wondering if they themselves would kill him, instead of passing the duty off to some laser-wielding executioner. His thoughts strayed to his aunt and uncle. Had Phillip and Grace at least died quick deaths? Did they die to protect him, only to have him die at the hands of the enemy anyway?

Captain Arctures Cozgill and Commander Ciro Cassens viewed the expression of the young man with curiosity as he approached. The gray-haired Cozgill was tall, slender and tough. As were most officers on both sides of the long war, he was much too battle-hardened to show fear. He ruled through the intimidation produced by way of his iron grip, both figuratively and almost literally. His long fingers were famous in the Rebellion for powerfully gripping an acquaintance's hand- or an enemy's throat. His actions were consistent with his grip, and he exuded an unending aura of power.

For his part, Commander Cassens appeared much too young to be of such high rank, but the attrition of war sometimes brings young men to high rank and full maturity much too quickly. Cassens' full, brown hair flowed nearly to his shoulders, in marked contrast with Cozgill's short hair. It struck David as odd to see a military officer with long hair.

The Commander was indeed young, but predictably ambitious. While Captain Cozgill was a rabid Rebel, Commander Cassens was intellectually so. Emotion seemed to escape Cassens, making the animated Captain look like a 15-year old girl in contrast. His rise in rank was a result of pure brain power rather than an excessive hatred of the Crown.

As David and the sentries came to a stop only feet from the officers, David desperately fought to hide his fear.

Commander Cassens was the first to speak. "Welcome aboard," he said simply.

Confusion leaped into David's mind. Welcome aboard?! Was this guy twisted? The man was smiling, so he must be, David thought. Who says "welcome aboard," without any hint of sarcasm, to someone about to be executed?

David took a deep breath.

The sentries departed.

Captain Cozgill spoke as a father soothing the nerves of a new college graduate. "Relax, son. You will have plenty of time to learn to be in command. And when you are a prince, I will still assist you, even though I will only be a lowly Captain to you."

The officers laughed heartily. Bewildered, David's eyes raced back and forth between the two men. He could not see how frightened he looked, but all of the men on the bridge could see.

An uneasy silence prompted Commander Cassens to ask, "Have you nothing to say?"

David's stubborn nature kicked in. "I am prepared," he said slowly. "To fight to the death!"

The Commander smiled. The Captain nodded with approval.

"Good. Good," Cozgill said with approval. "I am pleased to hear it. We were worried that you might go soft far away from the Rebellion. Have you killed the prince yet?"

Again David took a deep breath. His bewilderment subsided as the realization sank in: he was not going to die. Not here. Not now- if he behaved properly, anyway.

"No sir, not yet," David responded tentatively. He did not have time to completely gather his wits before the conversation continued.

"Where is your father?" asked Cozgill.

"The prince killed him," David answered, confidence growing that he would live- for the moment. He was one verbal mistake from discovery, a far better state than he had previously assumed.

"I am sorry to hear it," the Captain offered. "Your father and Banu were close. They were the true leaders of the early days."

"What do you think of the craft named for your cousin?" Commander Cassens interjected.

"The new features are fantastic," David said, trying to feign enthusiasm. His anxiety decreased but the sweat did not.

"I am pleased that you approve," the Captain responded. But with impatience he put the threesome back on subject. "Now back to business. We will hunt down the prince and kill him so that our mission is complete."

"No!" David blurted. The word was out there, hanging in the air. There was no retrieving it. Quickly he thought of an additional statement to cover his tracks. "Uh, sir. I believe I need to do this myself. After all, my father should be avenged by his own flesh and blood."

Inside, David's guts turned over a little more, into a tighter knot. That last sentence should have been delivered with more oomph, he thought. More passion could have effectively concealed the fib. His breathing became more labored and his heart rate increased. He feared that he might soon lose control of his faculties.

"Your father trained you well," Captain Cozgill nearly cooed. The smiles on the faces of both men told David that he still held the advantage.

"This is my whole reason for being sent to Earth," David added, padding his fear with rhetoric, but this time with more resolve.

The officers did not miss a beat. Surely they did not suspect a thing, David concluded.

"Indeed," Captain Cozgill ventured. "And maybe the most important mission in the history of the Rebellion. The death of the prince might not have an immediate effect, but the long term consequences will be substantial. The prince is the last remaining offspring of the King. We already killed his brother's children long ago."

David tried to conceal the impact of the words. He had just learned days ago that Phillip was his father's only brother. Now, his mind tried to piece together a puzzle of what Phillip and Grace had endured before coming to Earth. They had always treated David as their own. It all made sense now. The Rebels had murdered their children, and David was the closest that they could get to having another child of their own.

As he shook off the sorrow for his aunt and uncle, David's confidence level soared, but the rise of positive emotion was fleeting, for the cerebral commander had a nagging concern.

"Tell me, though," Cassens began slowly, picking up the verbal pace as his thoughts became words. "Were you pursuing the prince? We saw no one fleeing ahead of you."

"Actually," David said slowly, trying to make it up as he went along. "I uh, I was luring him out into the countryside. I have a distinct advantage out here." He liked his own response.

"Excellent! Excellent!" Cozgill proclaimed. "A tactician! I love it! And soon you will command this very ship!" His exuberance carried across the bridge and through the abundant space above and below for all to hear.

The con was working. Never mind that David had not planned such a clever deception; it had fallen into his lap. His life was on the line and he was now as focused as ever. Three and two, bottom of the ninth, winning run at second. That's all it was, he tried to convince himself. Still, he thought, I have to carry this routine right off this ship.

His quiet fears and calculations were interrupted by a uniformed crewman's presence.

"Sir!" the diminutive crewman half-barked. "The Prince Tinian has changed its position. It is heading toward us at a low rate of speed."

"So, at this time it does not pose a threat?" Commander Cassens asked.

"That is correct, sir."

David's heart raced at the thought. They are coming back! How can I get rescued when I'm inside the Banu?! He forcibly slowed his breathing. His chest tightened, his temples felt as though they were being squeezed in a vice. His ability to think and plan seemed impaired. Only seconds before, he was convincing himself that perpetrating this fraud was easy. Now, his excitement at the news of the Prince Tinian overtook his ability to maintain his calm demeanor.

Captain Cozgill bailed him out. The elder man realized that time was of the essence, much to David's benefit. "Let us end our conversation so that you may complete our mission," he insisted. "Your father may have already explained this, but I wish to reiterate."

"Yes sir," David nodded with respect.

"You are of Banu's blood," the Captain intoned. "You will not be left behind if we can help it. However, you must be prepared for exactly that. If the Prince Tinian were to destroy us, or if we were to destroy them, either way your mission remains unchanged. You are to destroy the prince. Period."

He paused for dramatic effect.

"We cannot leave this system until he is dead. We are expendable. You are not. However, if you are in a situation where the only way you can kill him is to also sacrifice yourself, so be it. So, in a sense, even you are expendable. His death is more important than our lives. This is our number one priority."

So this is what Johnny had become, David thought. The same attitude. The same intensity. The same warped vision of life and death.

"Any questions?"

"Just one," David responded.

Had Phillip been present, he would have tightened his face and fought the urge to grit his teeth. Phillip always wondered where David got his idealism. It was worsened by the fact that David was not blessed with a wonderful sense of timing.

"Once we assume power over the Kingdom," David continued. "What form of government will we set up?"

Captain Cozgill was taken aback by a question that seemed absurd to him. "A monarchy, of course," he responded without hiding his surprise.

"I see," was David's only response.

"You better go, Johnny," Commander Cassens urged. "Please, kill the prince."

"I will," David replied. He added a short bow of the head to each officer, unsure if such a sign of respect was their custom, but he believed that he should at least do something.

To David's relief, both officers each gave a little nod of the head in response.

David spun and quickly exited the bridge. At the top of the stairs, an armed sentry stepped into his path and proceeded to lead the young man down the stairs and along the same course that David had previously taken in the opposite direction. David took quick note that another sentry did not follow him.

As they watched him go, Commander Cassens stated what was on Captain Cozgill's mind. "Quite an odd question."

Cozgill looked on, expressionless. The only reasonable conclusion that they reached was that Banu's cousin indeed had been too far from the Rebellion for too long.

Meanwhile, David followed the sentry down the corridor, toward the area in which, he believed, the relay station was located that controlled the Banu's maneuverability. He tried to recall exactly what the relay station did, but he was quite sure that, based upon his education in the basement of Johnny's now-former house, the relay station deciphered electronic commands from the bridge into actual movements of the ship.

He pressed his memory to recall how everything worked. The relay station converted commands from the navigator's station. The ship's hydraulics and thrusters were controlled by the complex computer system, which translated computer commands and laser signals, which then allowed the ship to move: via thrusts from small engines positioned in various places on the exterior of the ship for maneuvers in space, and via computer-assisted ailerons, elevators and rudders working in unison with thrusters while in the atmosphere of a planet.

The wall that had been open only minutes before was now closed. Perhaps this was good, he thought. He considered that perhaps this meant that no one was in the area to spot his next move. The deduction seemed reasonable enough.

With a quick glance behind him, David pulled out an explosion pack and Young's laser gun from his fanny pack. In one swift motion, he dropped the laser and kicked it underneath a table that sat against the wall nearest the relay station.

"Hang on just a minute," he called out to the sentry, who was now a good twenty feet in front of him. "I dropped my laser."

Underneath the table, which appeared to serve as a desk for an engineer, David deftly attached the explosion pack to a panel that covered part of the relay station. He activated the device and quickly grabbed the laser. As calmly as possible, he stood up.

Once again, David began to sweat profusely. Once again, he was flirting with death.

"Sorry 'bout that."

The sentry barely blinked, then turned to continue the brief journey. David dutifully followed- and now with an even better reason than ever to leave the ship.

*   *   *   *   *   *

When David was safely away from the craft, the engines came to life with a low but high-pitched sound, which soon transformed into a low rumble. The Banu slowly lifted off, vertically.

At treetop level, the Banu hesitated, then lurched to one side. As though in slow motion, the craft sank back to the Earth at an angle, crashing into a nearby stand of trees. The nearest portion of the craft to David was over two hundred yards away and tucked neatly amongst the trees.

"Wow. I guess it really was the relay station," he laughed with a proud sense of awe in his voice.

There he stood, admiring his work like a painter in front of a completed canvas. As a ramp opened on the Banu, David quickly snapped out of his prideful stupor. He hurried into the pickup and fired up the engine. As he hastily backed up and turned perpendicular to the country road, a small but brilliant ruby-red blast of light streaked past his front windshield. David did not notice that the deadly beam of light ricocheted off the top of a slight rise in the soybean field and launched itself into the air before dissipating in the distance.

David sped away in his pickup down the paved highway. He looked in the rear view mirror in time to see a soldier arrive on the road behind him.

The explosion of glass and light shook the pickup truck with a ferocity that momentarily deafened and blinded David. He had ducked as the ruby ball of a laser beam raced at him. Even through closed eyes the beam of light was blinding. The laser struck on the passenger side and completely shattered the back glass, then continued through the front windshield.

Glass flew everywhere in the driver's compartment. Shards of glass covered his hair and back, as well as much of the seat and the top of the dashboard. David lifted his head to resume driving. Before noticing his surroundings in the cab, he braked hard and cut the wheel to the left. A laser blast streaked by, barely missing the truck. David slowed the speeding pickup enough to make a left-handed turn onto a dirt and gravel road.

His turn was executed with too much speed, and the pickup slid into the ditch. David reacted by straightening the wheels and allowing the vehicle to drive into a corn field. Once under control, he again drove through the shallow ditch and found himself back on the road.

The back glass was gone. The windshield had a hole the size of a grapefruit in the line of sight for a passenger. The rear view mirror was contorted at an odd angle, and there were spider cracks over most of the glass. He squinted to see the road in between the cracks in the glass.

Covered with small pieces of glass, David sped down the country road. Dirt flew up behind the bed of the pickup and gravel bounced underneath the vehicle and up into the air. The dirt and gravel aerial wake that was launched from his tires and the contorted rear view mirror conspired to obstruct his rear vision, so he could not see whether the Banu gave chase. If the destroyer was chasing him, he knew that his life would end the moment the giant beam of light reached him. He would be disintegrated within a nanosecond. Not a trace of his remains, and maybe not even of his truck, would ever be found, except perhaps for burn marks on the gravel and the countryside.

He also wondered whether the Banu would launch a shuttle craft. He was too afraid to try to peer through the dust rising up from the country road behind him. He sped on, creating more of a wake, wondering with each breath whether he would have the opportunity to inhale once more.

Through no plan of his own, he had single-handedly clobbered the Rebels in his first at-bat. It was a two-run double, at the very least. He felt lucky, though he reminded himself of some baseball guy- at the moment, in the midst of the overwhelming amount of adrenalin pumping through his body, he could not remember who it was- who had proclaimed that luck was the residue of hard work. He reminded himself that he had indeed worked hard for this hit.

*   *   *   *   *   *

Admiral Praeder listened to the report with great distress. The other men on the bridge had never before seen such emotion on the stoic man's face.

"How many laser blasts?" he asked, not quite sure what the answer would mean.

"Three, sir. But we have no way of knowing what the targets were." The voice of the ensign who relayed the information cracked with tension. If the Admiral was showing anxiety, the ensign reasoned, then it really was time to worry.

"Do not lose sight of those blasts, and take us directly to that spot unless events merit otherwise. I am to be kept apprised of events so that I can determine whether a change in my orders is warranted. Further, make sure that we are not falling into a trap. Captain Gonchar will take us in. Once we near Earth, it will be slow and easy. I will give the commands at that time." Distress or not, the Admiral was always intense. His orders were always issued in such a way that no one doubted their correctness.

No one, that is, except his new right hand man, Captain Gonchar. He flashed a concerned look at young Comander Bozwell, then shook his head as if to say, "He screwed this up."

For his part, Bozwell quickly looked away from the cynical hero.

Chapter 19 - Laser to Laser

Johnny's disabled Camaro still sat in front of David's house. Good sign, David thought, as he stepped out of his beat up pickup. But he knew from the presence of two marked police cars and one unmarked Buick that he would have to do some fast talking.

There was no time for extended conversation. He had to figure out where the communicator was hidden and have the Prince Tinian get him off the planet. With the Banu surely about to return to the air, Death was catching up to him. If he could accomplish this while sparing the life of his former best friend, all the better. If not... David did not wish to think about such an outcome.

As David walked through the front door, he decided that boldness was the only tack that would prevail. He knew that Johnny could not be in the house; otherwise, the police officers in his living room would not be alive.

Deputy Osborne saw him first, but David's attention was fixed on the dead bodies- one on top of the other- that bore the markings of Johnny's laser. Marty's chest had a burn mark that Osborne recognized as a match to the wounds on Phillip and Grace. Both Marty's and Ellen's burn marks sealed off the escape of blood from the bodies, although in Ellen's case, the shot to the top of her head had also singed her thick brown hair.

"What's goin' on here, David?!" Osborne demanded. With a dramatic sweeping of his hand, he implied that his question referenced the dead bodies as well as new laser damage to the mangled furniture and walls.

"Johnny's flipped his lid," David responded without hesitation.

"Johnny Young, your buddy?"

David nodded solemnly.

"But why?" Detective Palasky asked, expressing the confusion that all of the locals would have upon hearing the news that David Steele and Johnny Young were suddenly mortal enemies.

"He thinks he's from another planet. He's goin' 'round killing folks and he's trying to kill me."

"But why have five people died in this house?! What is going on?!" Osborne demanded. Surely one did not have to be a Rhodes Scholar to understand that the sole surviving inhabitant of the house should be a person of interest. Osborne needed answers, and he was about to proceed with important questions when he was interrupted.

Deputy Todd Cole strode into the room with purpose. He did not instantly notice David's presence, his attention occupied instead by a small black item which rested in his hand. The item was made from a graphite-like substance and looked much like a thin cellular telephone, complete with a small keypad. Cole, his thick black hair curling upward, brown eyes flitting between the device and the other men, was intrigued. His small hands made the communicator look bigger than it was.

David barely knew Deputy Cole, but he was now fixated on the police officer- or at least fixated on what was in his hand. The other men, too, looked at Cole, expecting a startling or key discovery of some sort, given Cole's firmness and speed of foot.

"Palasky," he said, almost breathlessly. "Whaddya make of this?"

As Cole stretched his hand out to the detective, David's eyes lit up. Blood rushed to his head and limbs and his chest and stomach burned. For a few seconds, he felt as though he was having a heart attack. David's eyes remained on the communicator as the discussion continued. From Cole to Palasky the device was passed.

"What about it?" Palasky asked, the disinterest in his voice apparent. There were two dead bodies lying at his feet, with bizarre, mysterious burn marks on them, no less, and Cole was concerned about a little, black electronic gadget.

"It didn't seem like anything important," Cole responded defensively to Palasky's tone. "But I found it taped underneath the toilet tank in the master bathroom, which is kinda odd. It's gotta mean something."

The energy that David did not expend to reach out and gently grab the communicator from Palasky's hand was spent on concealing his excitement. This was it! The elusive communicator was now seconds from being in his hands.

"Whaddya make of it?" Palasky asked David.

"I've never seen it before," David responded honestly, as the cherished device was brought closer to him. He reached

221

out, at first slowly, as if in awe. His lungs tightened; he felt as though he were grabbing a rare vase. The communicator touched David's fingers for the first time. He could feel his heart pounding in his ears. He did not dare breathe lest he break it or drop it or did who-knows-what. After touching he grabbed- quickly.

David stepped away from the detective and instantly began pushing, in sequence, several of the twelve small buttons on the face of the device. He had memorized the short, eight-note sequence from Phillip's letter.

David's concealed elation was about to end. Behind him was a face, peering intently through a side living room window. The face disappeared, eyes absorbing all that needed to be absorbed.

"What are ya doin'?" Palasky asked, baffled by David's intense interest in the black box.

"Hang on," David insisted. He interrupted his own button-pushing out of frustration. "Dang!"

Tension in the tattered living room increased.

"Kid, what are ya doin'?!" This time Palasky's question was not one of mere curiosity. He quickly stepped forward and snatched the device from the unsuspecting youth's hands.

"That's my uncle's and I need it!" David exploded. His booming voice betrayed his instant rage. This little device had become the focus of his days, his nights, and even his dreams and nightmares. Despite all of his confusion over the weighty matters of life, over destiny and loyalty, possession, or lack thereof, of this device determined whether or not he would live beyond this day. He would not- could not- be denied. If he did not dial the correct code immediately, then his life could end at any moment.

His entire body burned with a fever of anger and dread. He knew that the deputies had the authority to detain him, and David certainly did not want to hurt the men, but gaining possession of the communicator was now the most important matter that existed in his world. The little device had value beyond the deputies' comprehension, beyond even their lives.

Authority or not, he could not allow them to keep this prized device out of his grasp. He must get it back- no matter the cost, no matter the outcome. He would have time for guilt later. This device was Life itself.

In an instant, a dozen thoughts crossed David's harried mind. Every conceivable option, from submission to murder, was silently and hurriedly evaluated. He had his principles and his values, but none would do him much good dead. Without the communicator, he would soon be just that, whether the lethal laser blast came from Johnny's hand-held gun or from the mighty blasters of the Banu. He was going to get the communicator or die. The two options necessitated actions that were harsh yet simple: kill or be killed.

As David stepped toward Palasky, he spotted movement in his peripheral vision, in the open doorway. In one motion, he dived behind a couch and shouted, "Get down!" On his way down to the floor, he grabbed Palasky by the shirt. They tumbled toward the floor, out of control. Palasky's head hit the back of the half-shredded couch, adding to the man's state of bewilderment.

The room was silent for one-half of a second before the small explosion hurled from the laser in Johnny's hand filled the air. David and Palasky disappeared from view. Osborne froze in terror, with a dumbfounded expression on his now-pale face.

But it was Cole who paid the price. The reddish-orange flash struck him just below the sternum. The most incredible burning sensation he had ever experienced engulfed his torso. In an instant, the pain spread through his limbs. He blacked out, not knowing that his body was sailing through the air, with his feet just inches from the floor. He did not have the opportunity to comprehend that his life was ending at the hands of a creature from another planet. His limp body sprawled onto the hardwood floor, eight feet from where he stood only a moment before.

David rolled across the floor and popped up above the opposite end of the couch. He let loose a wild laser shot that only served to draw attention to himself. The indigo beam of light left the house through the open door.

Deputy Osborne, still standing in the same place, was quick to draw his 9 mm Beretta, but he was not sure at whom he should fire. His hands trembled like Barney Fife about to put his lone bullet into the revolver after receiving cousin Andy's permission.

Just as Johnny was about to fire again, David launched another single shot, this time sending into the air drywall, paint, and pieces of a two-by-four that served as part of the stud wall next to the door frame. The shot missed Johnny's head by mere inches.

The debris from David's blast slapped Johnny in the head, causing the Rebel's next blast to miss badly. The shot roared past David and into the far wall, sending more drywall and paint into the air. Dust floating in the air and debris falling to the ground only added to the scene of confusion.

Now completely inside the house, Johnny had no choice but to duck behind the swivel rocker just ten feet away from his enemy.

David understood that remaining stationary cut his odds of survival. He used Johnny's dive for cover to grab the communicator from the wildly confused Palasky.

With powerful bursts of light ripping through the room, Palasky did not understand exactly what was going on. He did understand, however, that there was something important about that little black box, though he was still uncertain whether it was just a strange cell phone. He lunged at David as the younger man attempted his escape into the dining room.

David brushed away Palasky's attempt to tackle him. The big kid was undeterred by the slender detective's effort and continued forward, away from Palasky and, more important, away from Johnny. But the detective's fingers slid down until they hooked on the strap of the young man's fanny pack, slowing his flight. Reflexively, David reached down and unhooked the clasp which belted the pouch around his waist. There was no time to think about the two remaining explosion packs, Albert Young's laser, or the letter from Phillip. None of the items was worth his life. The fanny pack had to be released.

Now holding only the fanny pack, Palasky leaped to his feet and made it two steps toward David before a laser round struck the detective in the shoulder. He let out a short yelp of pain as he stumbled to the floor.

Johnny's clear shot at David had been blocked at the last instant by the now-fallen detective. His next shot at the fleeing prince was squeezed off just as he became distracted by the movement of the formerly frozen Deputy Osborne. The laser round crashed into a wall, far from David.

Osborne finally realized who the enemy was scarcely a second before that enemy blasted him in the chest. Osborne's lifeless form was knocked back into an antique oak secretary. The impact of his dead body rocked the piece of furniture, forcing it to discharge a small shower of Hummels and other dust-collecting knick-knacks that had recently belonged to Aunt Grace.

*   *   *   *   *   *

David ran. Through the house, out the back door, through the backyard, and into the countryside he fled. He looped through the large corn field, away from the railroad tracks. As he ran, he was mindful that the Rebel destroyer was near and could at any moment appear and obliterate him. His only hope was the communicator.

He fidgeted with the communicator as he sprinted, then cursed under his breath and focused on running faster. After a few hundred yards he resumed alternating between his fingers fidgeting with the communicator and cursing.

He thought he remembered the sequence that would send a signal to the Prince Tinian, but he continued his finger fidgeting, cursing and running harder. As far as he could tell, he was failing at operating the small device.

"Come on, come on, come on, come on, come on!" he demanded aloud as he ran.

David ran through the corn field, near the site where, a little more than a week before, his life first changed. But this time he was not in a zombie-like trance.

He hoped that the green stalks could help hide him. He knew that his foe was behind him, but he was not about to look back. For once, he was not afraid of Johnny, rather the laser cannons of the destroyer that could arrive at any moment. He could face Johnny- he could talk to him, shoot him, whatever necessary. But against the Banu, there was zero chance of survival.

David ran along the rows of corn in a straight line, then cut wildly through the rows in an attempt to lose his pursuer. Yet he feared that he was wasting his time. The Banu found him before and it could surely find him again. And this time, they would know that he was not kin to the Great

Banu. He was their reason for traveling halfway across the Milky Way galaxy.

The corn stalks were still below David's shoulders, not yet at their full height. The only way he could hide was to lie down in the field, but he was too scared to do so. If the Banu returned, David surely would be discovered. In fact, he wondered, is there any place where I can hide? Could they find me in a building? In my truck? If so, he reasoned that they would certainly find him in this corn field.

His thoughts returned to the communicator. He again repeated the code sequence that was supposed to summon his rescuers. He glanced at the twelve-key face on the device as he ran. Different sequences sent different messages. He only knew the sequence which beckoned for help. He had now punched in the eight-sequence signal over a dozen times, but he still was not confident whether a signal was actually being sent out into space.

For a man running as fast as he could possibly run, David put too much of his attention on the communicator. When the lack of attention to his footwork caught up to him, he stumbled, arms flailing. The communicator slipped from his hands, landing ahead of him in the soft dirt. He momentarily lost sight of the device, until his flying body fell to the ground. The communicator lay ahead of him by only a few feet, neatly resting up against the base of a corn stalk. In a panic, he crawled forward and scooped up the device, then continued his frenzied dash through the corn. If the message has been sent, he thought, I don't need this thing anymore, anyway. If.

His frantic button pushing resumed. No need to take chances. He would send his panicked message again- and again.

He had to get out of the corn and find a safe haven somewhere. But where? Where could the Banu not find him?

Before David could form one of his plans, a bolt of reddish-orange energy zipped over his head. The harmless shot dissipated somewhere in the corn field, far ahead, disintegrating a few of the stalks. Again David refused to look back as he ran.

*   *   *   *   *   *

With his injured shoulder burning horribly, Detective Palasky attempted to follow Johnny, who was now deep into the corn field. Palasky stayed on the pathway created by farm equipment, hoping that David and Johnny might at some point reverse their direction. He was, from his position, able to see Johnny's blonde head bouncing deeper into the field, in pursuit of David.

The sunlight on the pathway faded quickly. Palasky looked up and to his right to see something that he had only seen in movies: a large spaceship slowed as it neared him, only three hundred feet above his head. The giant beast of a craft rapidly eclipsed the sunlight where Palasky struggled to run.

The giant, deep-red beam that shot from the craft was bigger around than the detective's body. The roar of the blast echoed throughout the Indiana countryside. The beam instantly incinerated the man, sending dirt two hundred feet into the air. His remains would never be found. Palasky was now part of the area's spaceship lore.

The leadership on the Banu had figured out the events of the previous hour and now knew who their man was- and was not. But before the warship had the opportunity to move in for the easy kill, circumstances necessitated an immediate retreat. Johnny and the crew were expendable, but there was no reason for everyone aboard the ship to needlessly die. The Banu quickly changed course and headed north, away from Johnny and David.

The arrival of the Prince Tinian came at the last possible moment for David. Though still running, he was on fumes. He reached the end of the corn field and found himself in front of a barbed wire fence. Barely slowing, David thrust his hands onto the top of a four-foot high wood post and, using the last of his adrenalin, simultaneously carried both legs over the top wire. He did not have the energy to land on his feet.

He stayed on the ground long enough to consider just how far he had fled. He knew that this edge of the corn field was probably two miles from his house, and he had covered the two or so miles as fast as he could move in the soft farm soil.

He was now on a cattle farm, with cleared land stretching for acres ahead of him. Ahead of him, the Prince Tinian lowered itself, causing a brown Hereford calf and mother to scurry away in fright.

As the ship lowered itself onto the ground one hundred yards away, David decided to at long last look behind him. When he stood, he could see Johnny's head bobbing up and down as he ran toward David's location, but his adversary was easily five hundred yards away.

What caught David's eye, though, was just how close he had come to death. The Banu was quickly retreating into the distance. He was not sure how close the ship had been to him, although he had heard the roar of the ship's engines and the crash of the cannon firing. He had known without looking that the destroyer was flying once again, thus he knew that he was fortunate to be alive. Seeing the craft for the second time sent a cold chill through his body. When the thunderous clap of laser fire annihilated Palasky, he did not want to see what had happened. He did not know that Palasky was the target. Because the Banu was retreating now, he knew that his encounter had been too close. That was enough information for him.

He was about to learn that all of the studying mandated by his uncle, before he had met up with and confessed his true identity to Johnny, was well worth the time. The brief days of reviewing plans, learning strategies practiced by his home planet's leaders, and the terminology that he memorized for commanding a destroyer in space was about to become of paramount importance. In a few brief minutes, being the most important person on a military ship and giving orders would no longer be an abstract exercise found in his uncle's collection of papers.

*   *   *   *   *   *

Aboard the Prince Tinian, the mission was nearing completion. Grab the prince and go home- that was it. In mere moments, only the "go home" part would remain.

Captain Gonchar's apprehension led Commander Bozwell to feel that this was not going to be a routine pick up.

"Watch the Admiral," Bozwell said slowly to two armed guards. Then realizing the absurdity of his statement he added, "Watch everybody."

*   *   *   *   *   *

Although David did not know his name, the approaching man was obviously an officer. Only thirty yards from entering the Prince Tinian, David slowed to a jog as he watched the officer quickly walk down the ramp to greet the exhausted prince. David's adrenalin flow resumed as he neared safety. But thoughts of safety were shattered when the officer unhooked the laser pistol from his belt and drew a bead on David.

"He's gotta be aiming at Johnny," he said quietly to himself, huffing and puffing as he verbalized his thoughts.

"Nooo!" The deep, horrified scream from within the spaceship carried past David and into the corn field. The officer dropped to the ground as a blue-green flash shot from inside the ship into the man's back. The high-pitched sound of the blast briefly pierced the air.

Before David could process what transpired, from within the craft another quick glow of light illuminated the top of the ramp and another high-pitched squeal announced the firing of a laser.

The trembling prince stopped as the body of an officer slid down the ramp, until it came to rest against the body of the first downed officer.

Only ten yards from the Prince Tinian, and David now had his doubts whether he would live to set foot on the massive craft.

Two guards, with laser rifles in their hands and pistols on their belts, raced down the ramp.

What now? David's thoughts could be easily read on his expression. But the guards ignored David and scanned the corn field for potential threats.

Perhaps they should focus on who comes out of the ship, David thought.

Commander Bozwell rushed down the ramp as David reached the ramp's end. "Are you okay, your highness?"

"You were right, Commander!" one of the guards gushed with excitement as he returned to the ship. "Admiral Praeder killed Captain Gonchar!"

David tried to digest what he had witnessed. "What happened?!" he weakly demanded.

"I don't know. I uh," Bozwell stuttered as he glanced at the two bodies. "I'll explain later. Please get inside the ship immediately." Bozwell looked down at his feet, first at Gonchar, lifeless in the dirt at the bottom of the ramp, then at Praeder, ironically next to Gonchar in death, as one of the guards grabbed the Admiral by the ankles and dragged his body up the ramp. Two dead high ranking Crown officers. "I think I can explain," Bozwell said with great confusion in his voice.

Gonchar: the hero, the legend. Praeder: the stoic leader and consummate warrior whom men easily and confidently followed. Both dead. Bozwell did not have time to make sense of what had happened. The puzzle would have to wait for its solution at a less frenzied moment.

There was no time to grab the bodies, but they did so, anyway. Retrieving the bodies of the dead and conducting proper ceremonies were important to their culture, and this concern for the dead nearly equaled the concern for the safety of the prince. The second guard dragged the body of the once heroic- and now traitorous- Captain Gonchar.

With all now inside the Prince Tinian, the spaceship quickly closed up and flew away. The few people who saw the warship leave the Earth's atmosphere saw what looked like a shooting star going the wrong direction. The head of the vapor trail suddenly burst into a brilliant flash of white and yellow, sending a sonic boom throughout parts of three states.

*   *   *   *   *   *

In the corn field, only minutes later, the Banu also gave the locals a brief light show before disappearing beyond the bright blue summer sky.

Chapter 20 - Beyond Earth

David looked around the room, taking in his surroundings. That he was in an infirmary was obvious. The expansive sick bay could hold twenty patients at once, and when the need arose, the wall of an adjoining room could be opened to accommodate even more injured personnel. Unlike the operating room, where his singular journey from normal kid to royalty began, the infirmary was ornate and pleasing to the eye. Where there were not paintings of landscapes, framed photographs of famous Craylan sights and people, and the soft colors of various abstract paintings, a textured, gun-metal gray paint covered the walls.

The fluids being pumped into his body were of no concern to him. He felt no pain and was quickly regaining his strength. Before he could begin another visual sweep of the sick bay, a doctor entered.

A small window was too far away for him to see the slowly shrinking blue planet.

*　　　*　　　*　　　*　　　*　　　*

David was ushered to a chair on the bridge by armed guards. He did not know the proper terminology- naval terms seemed to be comparable- but the men protecting and accompanying him were guards, in his mind. Oddly enough, he did get a taste of Rebel terminology while in the Banu mock-up at Johnny's house. He assumed that the terminology and military protocol would be similar.

David had never seen the bridge of the Prince Tinian. The ship itself was much older than the Banu and not as appealing to the casual observer. Whoever decorated the sick bay, he thought, should have visited the bridge. Between the low lighting and the dark coloration of most objects, the bridge was as drab as the Craylan electronic devices he encountered on Earth, he mused.

The bridge seemed to be on a floor all to itself. What he did not immediately realize was that the crew could not literally see outside of the great warship; the bridge was buried within the center of the craft. A giant screen served as the "window," but the screen only displayed relayed information.

The number of people on the bridge varied from minute to minute. David had no understanding of what many of these people were doing. Some walked to different officers and ensigns stationed at consoles and whispered into their ears. Why not send electronic messages, he wondered? Other people would man a station for a matter of minutes, punch buttons, and then quickly leave.

Quiet voices came from every direction. For a person unable to block out extraneous noises, the bridge would have been a nightmare. It became readily apparent that, unless a whisperer approached bridge personnel, his duty was to listen to the officer in command.

Various ensigns measured environmental levels of the ship, shield levels, firepower capacities, equipment function levels, and anything else that possibly could be measured. Officers deciphered or coordinated data that they received and passed along information, where necessary.

It appeared to David that so many electronic messages were going and coming on various computer consoles that the whole system was bound to crash at any moment. Perhaps that explained the whisperers. He did not realize that flying a spaceship- a warship, more precisely- could be so complicated.

The various stations were coded in the colors of either gold or silver. Gold signified that only an officer could man the station in question, unless an ensign was given specific permission otherwise. Stations with silver surrounding the work area and decorating the control panels were open to anyone properly trained to be at such stations.

Each computer console had a typical computer screen, to which David was accustomed on Earth. Like the Banu, the crew of the Prince Tinian worked in front of computer monitors that had keyboards built into the work stations, and the monitors themselves doubled as touch-screens. Myriad colored lights, which were labeled in small lettering, decorated the keyboards. When certain lights came on, sounds were emitted from the station.

One particular sound rang from the large communications board. The shrill, repetitive whistle abruptly ended with a simple push of a button.

"Our notification of the prince's safety has been received by Central Command," Lieutenant Spencer, the Communications Officer, announced.

No one bothered to respond to Spencer's announcement. Whoever needed the information kept quiet, and everyone else continued with their duties.

The bridge was massive when compared to that of the Banu. The ceiling was not as high, but the length and width of the oval-shaped command center was substantially larger. Décor was nonexistent. The ceiling was a slick, shiny gray and was domed in order to facilitate the travel of sounds, particularly voices, which it accomplished quite well.

Between the floor and the ceiling, space was at a premium. Computer and command stations climbed the walls, although read-outs were low enough to the floor for bridge personnel to easily access necessary information. At two different stations, it was necessary to access information not available to someone standing on the floor. In those two cases, steps were built into the units.

Between lights flashing, stations chirping, voices quietly instructing or informing, and the rumbling of the ship's massive engines, the cascade of sounds was overwhelming. The ability of bridge personnel to focus on their work was amazing, David concluded.

*   *   *   *   *   *

David sat in the Captain's chair- a chair which until only minutes prior had belonged to Admiral Praeder. If the mission of delivering the prince safely home proved to be successful, Praeder would be a posthumous hero. But now the Admiral-less ship had to rely upon a Commander and his crew of junior officers to complete the mission. David naturally assumed that he was but a passenger, free to wander at his leisure. He was wrong.

"My position is behind you," Commander Bozwell informed David. "But I will be glad to stay here and assist you." The hint was quite obvious. "At your service," he continued. "Are Communications Officer Lieutenant Spencer and Navigations Officer Lieutenant Barton."

In front of the Captain's chair, close to the large screen, sat Spencer and Barton, side by side. Though their stations were twenty feet from the Captain's chair, their voices easily carried to David's ears.

Short and stocky, Lieutenant Spencer was a committed and well-disciplined member of the Crown's staff of officers. His blonde hair swept over his forehead, making him look more like a surfer than an officer.

Barton, on the other hand, was tall and stocky. Standing at six-feet, four inches tall, his muscular frame made him an imposing figure. His curly brown hair gave him a boyish look, but his bulging chest and large arms disabused any observer's notions about boyishness. Though committed to the Crown, he did not share Spencer's unassuming nature and patience.

David surveyed the two men before acceding to Bozwell's unstated wish.

"I appreciate it," David responded. "But why can't you just take control?" The words Bozwell was waiting to hear.

"On your command, I can."

Being a prince wasn't so bad, David thought. Just tell everyone else to take charge and all will be well.

"Fine with me." David's first order was not exactly delivered with Pattonesque flair.

"Commander," Barton interjected. "Permission to go to hyperspace?"

"What does engineering say about our status?" Bozwell asked.

The engineering station was off to David's right. A short, fat lieutenant who went by the name of Anders was in charge of countless consoles and the data that they produced. Dumpy in appearance- the shirt of his uniform seemed to come untucked every five minutes- the head Engineering officer was too busy to look up whenever he spoke. His direct links to the engineering department, buried in the belly of the craft, and weapons systems kept him busy. Military conditioning standards must not apply to the engineering department, David thought.

Normally, the first officer was in charge of weapons. But with the deaths of Praeder and Gonchar, Commander Bozwell was now the officer in charge of the entire ship. This mission was Bozwell's eighteenth aboard the Prince Tinian, and his surrender of the title "First Officer" due to Gonchar's presence was only ceremonial. With the Admiral and the hero having been new to the ship, Bozwell's expertise was often consulted.

Now that the prince had ceded authority to Bozwell, engineering would have to control weapons systems for the trip's duration.

Anders' voice was deep, yet crisp, as he answered Bozwell. "We are fully operational."

"Then stand by."

"Hyperspace? Wait! We're leaving?" David asked with opposition evident in his voice, his discontent momentarily drowning out his drawl.

"Well, of course," Bozwell responded. "We have to get you home in one piece."

"Not yet," David insisted.

"What?" Bozwell did not understand, and he did not have the patience to hear an explanation.

"I said, not yet." David's sudden grasp of his own importance gave him confidence that was reflected audibly.

"Sir!" Barton blurted with alarm, "the Banu left Earth's atmosphere minutes ago and is now approaching our position."

David's interest was piqued. "Is Johnny aboard?"

The crew looked at each other with uncertainty.

"Banu's cousin," David explained.

Lieutenant Spencer answered immediately. "Yes, my lord. He was picked up before they left the surface."

"My lord, we must go," Bozwell urged the young prince.

"Not yet." David was firm, confident.

242

"Sir," Anders' voice boomed as he stole a glance at Bozwell. "We are waiting for a command."

Bozwell glared anxiously at David. His eyes told David that he badly wanted to take control from the neophyte space traveler. He badly wanted to command the Prince Tinian and bring the young man home to the accolades that he knew that he, the officer in charge, would receive. But more than anything, he just wanted to end this chaos and complete the mission. The difficult part was over. All that was to be done was to outrun the Banu, which he believed should not prove to be terribly challenging.

David glared back and slowly shook his head, confirming his opposition to their desire to head hastily home.

Commander Bozwell understood his place.

"Anders, we are under the command of Prince Andrew Chateau, son of our beloved King Andrew Chateau the Second. He will give our orders."

David had never heard his true name spoken by anyone other than his aunt and uncle. He pondered it for a brief moment, then maintained his new-found confident air.

"We will not, I repeat, not be going to hyperspace just yet," he instructed. As an afterthought he added, "And call me David for now."

Barton was not so easily convinced, as was evidenced by his sharp report that sounded more like an argument. "The Banu is picking up speed and heading our way!"

"Maintain present speed and course," David instructed. "Let me know when they are close to firing range and how quickly they gain on us."

"I'm assuming," Bozwell inquired. "That you intend to destroy the Banu?"

David did not bother to answer.

"While it would not be my first inclination," Bozwell continued. "We can easily out-muscle the rebel ship."

"No, we can't," David said plainly.

"I beg your pardon, my lord." Bozwell was caught off guard. "Our destroyer has far more firepower than any Rebel ship."

"Not this one we don't. We will not go toe-to-toe with these guys."

"While I respectfully disagree," Bozwell said, almost insulted, before pausing. "May I ask what your plan is, then?"

David mulled over his answer as he alternated between biting his tongue and bottom lip. The long hesitation only heaped more anxiety onto Bozwell's nerves.

"You don't wanna know," David finally answered.

Bozwell glared at David as he made an announcement. "Clear the bridge." With the simple command, those who had been scurrying about discontinued their activities and within seconds were off the bridge. Silently yet quickly, twenty people were gone, presumably carrying out other duties elsewhere on the warship- away from what was now a war room. Only ten officers and David remained.

David turned away from Bozwell and looked toward the front of the bridge. "Someone make contact with the Banu."

The whispering between remaining comrades ceased. Only the sound of machinery was heard.

Chapter 21 - Opposing Teams

After Spencer announced that he had made contact with the Banu, the bridge again fell silent. Uncertainty filled the void, then small outbreaks of fear. If crew members- officers included- would have had the opportunity to read each other's thoughts, they would have learned that they were in agreement. Every man on the bridge possessed years of experience- experience in war, strategies, and survival. Every man on the bridge had confidence in the abilities of the others.

There had been traitors in their midst- perhaps there were still more aboard ship- but of the ten military men currently running the bridge, it was each man's conviction that the others were loyal to the Crown. They knew each other and trusted each other. They would die for each other, but they would prefer to live for each other.

The eleventh man on the bridge was but a boy in their eyes. He was young, seemingly impetuous, and, without a doubt, inexperienced. He had thus far exhibited little understanding of who he was or of his importance. To allow him to take charge of their destroyer was unwise. Yet, their loyalty to the Crown dictated that they follow proper protocol. His title outranked theirs. His life outweighed theirs. He was the reason they were so far from home, in service to their beloved king.

The senior officers- Bozwell, Anders, Spencer, and Barton- felt the most strain. The ensigns would not dare voice their opposition to the prince, at the risk that one of the officers would harshly condemn them. But the officers had achieved their rank due to their intelligence and bravery. They understood strategies; they understood danger; they understood the mission.

David, they believed, did not understand the challenges involved. He certainly could not understand the strategies. How could he? He had spent his entire life away from the protracted war. Given that he wanted to make contact with the Banu rather than destroy it immediately, it was plain to them that he could not possibly understand the dangers involved with their mission.

Maybe David understood the mission itself. After all, it was his life that was the focus. But the thought of him contacting the Banu was a bad sign. What could he possibly say- or hear- that would help matters?

The tension increased with each breath, with each thought. Every member of the crew now on the bridge felt the burden of their lives in jeopardy, and more important, the life of the prince in jeopardy.

The tension was of no concern to the teenage prince. He alone knew what he wanted to do and say. The lengthening span between conversations added to the tension, but David ignored it even though he could feel it. He was used to being in charge on the baseball diamond. Of course, the warriors would scoff at such a notion, but David was used to thinking under pressure, ignoring superfluous sounds and voices, and concentrating on implementing strategies from behind the plate. To David, this was only a difference in scale.

Spencer and Barton exchanged glances before turning in their chairs to face David and Bozwell. Neither knew who would speak first, so they ended up inadvertently speaking almost in unison.

"Uh, sir, uh…"

David sighed loudly. He did not have to be brilliant or have divine revelation to understand what was about to be said.

"Gentlemen, we are going to communicate with the Banu," David ordered with exasperation in his voice. He turned and gave a hard look to Bozwell. "It may not be the most popular move, but you will keep the men with me."

Bozwell was caught between his anger and his devotion to the Crown. He stammered as he weakly responded, "I will try… sir."

"You will do," David replied with emphasis.

Spencer gave up his opposition. "I am ready to link communications with the Banu, sir."

"Put him on-screen," David commanded. He did not even know whether such a capability existed on his ship, but he knew from his virtual education that the Banu could display transmitted images for everyone on the bridge to see.

"Yes, sir."

Johnny's larger-than-life image appeared before all to see.

"You rang?" Johnny asked, smiling.

No one else on the Prince Tinian had ever seen Banu's young cousin. They all watched intently as the arrogant Johnny and intense David verbally jousted as if no one else could hear.

"Not much to smile about, pal," David sharply responded.

"David! Look at us! One week we think we're on top of the world 'cause we're tearin' up the American Legion, the next week we're in command of unimaginably powerful spaceships! This is plenty of reason to smile!"

"I wish I could enjoy it. But you've guaranteed that one of us hasta die."

Johnny did not hesitate. "Well, that's part o' livin'."

On the surface, David appeared undaunted by Johnny's attitude. But Johnny knew better. Johnny understood the level of anguish and frustration through which David was now suffering. He also knew that David often dealt with reality by avoiding it.

"Let's put it this way," David continued his thought. "I'm sure I could enjoy this if we were still on the same team."

"Well, come on over. I'm sure my guys would love to have ya. They're a little sore 'bout the damage you caused earlier, but they'd get over it."

Crew members on the Prince Tinian exchanged quizzical glances.

"I'm sure I'm gonna become a rebel!" David hissed. It was the first time that David had vocalized his family's beliefs.

"Well, you wanted to be on the same team," Johnny taunted.

"I think," David began slowly, almost wistfully. "What I had in mind was you and me not tryin' to kill each other."

"You think I want to kill you?! Get out!" Johnny's acting skills were showing, his performance becoming less believable.

"You've fooled me pretty good so far."

"Don't speak too fast there," Johnny retorted angrily. "You killed my dad."

Spencer and Barton exchanged glances. Bozwell harbored the thought that maybe there was more to this child-prince than they had realized.

"I'm gonna have to destroy you," David said icily.

"Okay." Johnny's arrogance was on full display. The young rebel turned and spoke to an unseen person behind him. "Lower shields."

"My lord," Barton shouted. "They are lowering shields!"

"We have them!" Bozwell cried. "Prepare to lower shields to fire!"

"Okay, David," Johnny said with a mock mournfulness to his voice. "I'm at your mercy."

David, the only calm person on the bridge of the Prince Tinian, could only frown. After a moment he decided to speak. "Knock it off," was all he mustered.

"Well!" Johnny mocked. "You said you gotta destroy me!"

Bozwell was beside himself. "Now's your chance!" he screeched.

"That's right," Johnny echoed. "Now's your chance."

"Johnny..." David's words tailed off before they were uttered.

"Whaddya want me to do?" Johnny feigned exasperation. "You won't come over here. You won't kill me. You want me to come there?"

"Yeah. I do." It was David's only desire. The thought was too good to be true, yet David foolishly clung to it.

"Sir!" Bozwell bellowed. "He could destroy us all!"

"Aw come on, David," Johnny was again taunting his former friend. "I wouldn't do that."

"Yeah, I can ask Marty and Ellen about that, huh?!" David snapped. "Let alone my aunt and uncle, who you viciously murdered!"

"So whaddya want me to do?" Johnny asked, with a seriousness that signaled resignation to his friend.

Barton was the first to catch what was happening. He shouted his alarm, letting both ships know that the ploy was over.

"Sir! The Banu is maneuvering behind us!"

"Face them!" David desperately ordered.

Cries of disbelief and consternation thundered through the bridge.

"Are shields up?" David shouted.

The Prince Tinian rocked hard, accepting the blow of a laser beam from the Banu. The crew grabbed anything attached to the ship in order to maintain their footing or seats. The blow was followed by two additional blasts that knocked David and Bozwell to the floor. Johnny's smiling face disappeared from the screen as the signal was lost.

The third blast knocked Anders against his control panel. His head smacked the panel, sending him sprawling across the floor.

The deep rumble from the crash of lasers against the spaceship hung in the ears and minds of those on the bridge of the Prince Tinian. A moment passed without a sound, other than the ubiquitous rumble of the great ship's massive engines.

Ensigns and officers alike shouted information that came to them at their respective stations. The confusion was deepened by the surprise of the Banu's maneuver.

David shouted above the frantic voices of his men. "Evasive action!" His voice trembled as he gave the vague command.

"Any specifics there, Prince?" Barton shot back sarcastically.

"Full forward! And full shields!" David did not care to acknowledge Barton's breach of discipline.

Bozwell, momentarily stunned, picked himself up off of the floor.

The bridge was filled with distressed and angry voices, but before order could be restored, two successive blasts again violently shook the ship.

"What happened to the shields?!" David demanded.

"Where's Anders?!" Bozwell bellowed.

The groggy engineer could not quite shake the cobwebs from his head. He pulled his torso up from the floor of the bridge, but he looked more like a boxer receiving the ten-count from the referee, wanting to get up, but without the ability to do so.

Bozwell rushed to Anders' station and immediately began punching the over-sized keypad.

"Shields are still up," Bozwell announced. "But they have sustained damage."

"How much?" David inquired, though he really did not wish to hear the answer.

"We are at eighty percent shield strength. The aft shields took a beating, though."

A distant-sounding thud echoed through the bridge. The ship rocked slightly.

"Primary shields are holding fine," Bozwell reported, as the Prince Tinian raced away from the Banu.

Anders slowly climbed to his feet. Bozwell grabbed Anders' arm and put it around his own neck to help the woozy engineer to stand.

"I am fine," he weakly protested.

Bozwell's mind shifted back to the current crisis.

"Sir," he urged, as he helped Anders sit in the engineer's chair. "We must act now against the Banu. We are still relatively close. We can destroy it now."

"Then let's shoot back," David said, with a great degree of ignorance detectable in his voice.

"Shields are up, my lord," Bozwell explained, poorly hiding the contempt in his voice. Bozwell reasoned that he should be in command, not this naïve child.

"You should know that," Bozwell continued.

"How should I know?" David retorted. "I've never been on one of these suckers before."

"It was in-" Bozwell understood before completing his sentence.

"The chip?" David asked.

Bozwell nodded.

David took a long, slow, deep breath. "Oh boy," he muttered under his breath.

Bozwell hoped that this would convince David to turn the command of the ship over to him.

"Arc away from these guys," David barked out. "Protect our rear from direct hits, but make your way away from them and Earth."

The Commander finally mustered the courage. What nearly led to their total destruction motivated Bozwell to be forceful in his tone.

"Our rear?" Bozwell derisively repeated. "My lord, I am quite capable of commanding this ship! Shall I lead us to safety?"

"No you shall not!" David's snarl left no room for conjecture. Like it or not, he was in control. The look in his eyes left naked his rage. David had survived his first hi-tech space battle. He was trained in battle strategies of great warriors in Earth's history. He was here for a purpose. He had power, and he was going to use it- his way.

For his part, Bozwell responded with an equally wicked stare. But unlike Barton, he was not willing to risk losing his discipline. His eyes broke from the staring contest. He knew his place- for the moment, at least.

The laser blasts against the shields resumed.

"They are firing incessantly! They are going to wear down our shields!" the still-groggy Anders excitedly reported.

"They should be low on weapons generation by now," Bozwell mused aloud.

"Not with this bird," David responded ruefully.

The main lights flickered, triggering emergency lights to full illumination. A shrill alarm rang out for three seconds before fading away.

"I have never seen a Rebel ship put out such powerful blasts," Anders warned in a fear-tinged voice.

"Like this, sir?" It was Barton. Respect had returned to his voice.

David quickly walked to the seated navigations officer as the regular lights returned, allowing emergency lights to shut off. On the monitor in front of them, David watched the animation of what was actually happening. The Prince Tinian slowly banked to port, gradually putting distance between the two warships.

"Exactly!" David was excited as he walked back to the Captain's chair. "Correct me if I'm wrong, but a direct hit to our engines and we're toast."

Spencer looked over at him quizzically. Anders looked up from his console.

"Pardon?" Bozwell finally asked.

"History. Done for. Dead."

"That is correct," Bozwell responded, still confused by David's strange idiom.

"Anders, lower power to shields and increase forward power. We are leaving our left side- uh, port side- exposed, so transfer what shields you maintain to those areas."

"Done!"

The animation on Barton's console showed the ships separating at an increasing rate. The laser blasts stopped.

"They have ceased firing, sir," Barton reported.

"Great. Get the Banu on-screen."

The groans were plentiful.

Spencer dutifully tried to reach the Banu. "I cannot reach them, sir."

"Who cares about them?!" Barton's old tone returned, as he himself realized. "Sir," he added sheepishly.

"Sir! We had an opportunity to destroy them!" Bozwell was again losing patience. His frustration dripped on each word.

"Had I given the command, we would've lowered shields, but no one noticed that they were moving into position to destroy us. Had I taken your advice, we'd all be dead right now!" David snapped.

Spencer gave Barton an "oops, he's right" look.

"Sir, with all due respect, we came here to rescue you, not to get you killed," Bozwell insisted.

David had finally grown tired of the sniping. "Congratulations! You've all done a fine job and will be rewarded for your service! Now, I have a mission I aim to complete! Continue our arcing to port from the Banu and get Johnny back on screen! Those are my orders!"

A hush fell over the bridge. Everyone was amazed at David's assertiveness. The young man with no battle experience and, until recently, no understanding of his own position of honor and authority, spoke with clarity and confidence. After a long five seconds that felt like five minutes, Barton signaled that his discipline had returned.

"Yes sir."

"Attempting to contact the Banu, sir," Spencer reported.

"Sir," Barton warned. "The Banu is trying to take away our angle of retreat. They are racing to head us off."

"No problem." David's casual response was of little comfort.

Chapter 22 - Toe to Toe

While the crew worried about their survival and about the sanity of the prince, the prince's thoughts were on matters of life and death from a different perspective. He was not thinking about whether or not he would die soon. Rather, he reflected on his life in a small town on Earth; life with his best friend; life in baseball.

In David's mind, his life and Johnny's were supposed to remain intertwined for decades- if not for the rest of their lives. Johnny used to believe this, as well. Little mattered more than baseball. Though his very presence on this spaceship seemed surreal, he was alternately accepting and rejecting his new reality. No longer was Major League Baseball an option. No longer were they teammates, watching out for each other, out-thinking and out-playing opponents.

This was not how they had choreographed their lives. This was not supposed to be happening. But Johnny loved it- that was apparent- yet no one should be able to interfere with what they had mapped out.

They could never imagine anything coming between them. They even vowed that their respective wives would have to be friends- it was part of their dreams, manufactured down to the last detail. Their children would grow up together. Their dreams sometimes approached fantasy, but until a little more than a week prior, their dreams were proceeding on schedule, despite what Johnny had recently said.

Bouncing around David's brain was the expression "for the rest of our lives." But he was struggling to accept the fact that the rest of their lives could culminate this day.

At David's command, Johnny's image appeared in front of the crew. David found it remarkable that Johnny had handled the transition so well, from being a mere teenage earthling to an important extraterrestrial in a distant war. Johnny could be abrupt, even sarcastic, but what was recently the exception was now the rule.

Johnny did not wait for an exchange of forced pleasantries or hollow warnings from David. His demeanor matched what it had been since the concept of destiny had gained control of him.

"Ya know, David," he began with the manner of a Western gunslinger. "I've been thinkin' this whole thing over."

David did not wait to hear about Johnny's ruminations. His next plan was ready.

"Lower shields."

"What?!" Barton yelled.

"That's an order."

"Stand by to fire," Bozwell called out to Anders.

"No!" David was adamant.

"But sir," Bozwell pleaded. "Do you realize-"

"I thought we got over this a minute ago?!" David shouted. "I AM IN COMMAND!"

Johnny enjoyed every second. "Little problem there, David?" he asked mockingly.

"Shut up, Johnny!"

"Come on, man," Johnny pleaded, with only a touch of sincerity. "Don't get testy with me. Just listen for a minute."

"Lower shields," David repeated to Barton. "Okay, I'm listening," he replied to Johnny.

Barton could not accept the order. "I cannot put us at risk like that, sir!"

"Get him off screen!" David barked, his face red with anger.

Johnny's image disappeared, replaced by the ship's forward view of space.

"Now," David said firmly. "You just got through tellin' me   they can't fire when they have shields up! What's the problem?!"

"They could partially lower their shields quickly enough to get off a good shot," Barton explained. "Just like the Commander wanted us to do earlier."

"I know that. But what are the odds of a good hit?" David asked.

"Pretty good," Bozwell responded to the question directed at Barton.

"And how damaging would it be?"

"I do not know, sir." Barton was back to trying to be respectful again.

"Substantial, possibly," Bozwell ventured.

"Okay, I understand," David replied.

Barton and Bozwell look relieved. Perhaps, they both thought, reason will win with this kid.

"Now," David began, about to shatter their hope. "Lower shields. When shields are down, put Johnny back up."

Barton leaped to his feet. Of all the foolish commands, this was too much. He looked to Commander Bozwell for support. "Does this kid understand what he's doing?!" he shouted.

"Prince! Our lives are at stake!" Bozwell's words failed to move David.

"Mine isn't?" David shouted.

Spencer was unimpressed. "If you want to throw your life away, go ahead! But leave us out of it!"

With an urge to take matters into his own hands, Barton stormed toward the prince. Bozwell would have liked to proceed in the same manner, but he could not allow such an event to happen. Mutiny was not acceptable. Instead, Bozwell stepped forward into Barton's path.

Bozwell firmly grabbed Barton's large shoulders and spoke quietly to the incensed officer. "Remember your loyalty to the Crown."

"I left Earth years ago to find life! Not death!"

"You must be prepared to die for the   cause-   the Crown," Bozwell explained evenly.

"But not needlessly die!" Barton hissed.

"Get back to your position," Bozwell said gently.

David was focused on Johnny and his actions. He was no longer interested in keeping the men happy. That would have to wait. "Lower shields now. Bring us to a full stop."

Barton sat down in his chair and angrily jammed his finger onto the appropriate button.

"Tell me when they're all the way down," David ordered. He quickly glanced at the faces of several of the men, including Bozwell. "Put Johnny onscreen."

Johnny's image returned as Spencer complied with the order.

"I'm back," David informed his former friend.

"Shields are one-hundred percent down," Barton announced.

"Raise shields now!" David shouted.

Johnny was a step behind. "Lower shields!" His voice turned shrill with the rush of excitement. "Fire!"

The Banu's shot into the Prince Tinian had no effect. The Prince Tinian rocked only mildly.

"That was close," Barton reported.

"Nice little trick. Whaddya gain?" Johnny asked skeptically.

"I needed to see you were in charge," David explained. "And I wanted to hear you give the command." David calmly sat down in the Captain's chair.

"Well, you got what you wanted," Johnny replied with disdain. To Johnny, and to both of the crews, the move did not make sense. Only David and his mind seemed to think that something was gained. What no one realized was that, this time, it was more than idealism. "David, of course I was gonna give the command. My father taught me to err on the side of aggression. I'm not an idealist, buddy."

"I wanted to see it to believe it," David tried to explain, but now he was misdirecting from what was in his mind. Johnny knew him well. David understood that obfuscation would counteract transparency, so he continued. "I knew you'd kill, but I didn't know for sure whether you'd kill me."

"Already forgotten about all the stuff that's happened these past few days, huh?" Johnny's mocking tone was a reflection of his belief of an advantage over the always-too-nice David.

"Johnny," David explained further. "I didn't want to be haunted by 'what might have been.'" Now he was telling the truth while still disguising motive. "I didn't wanna be responsible for killing you without first exhausting every option. I had to try to reach you. I had to know for sure that you hate me enough to kill me. That's all."

"I don't hate you," Johnny responded. "You have to understand that. David, it's nothin' personal."

David was instantly on his feet. "Nothing personal?! Are you nuts?! We've been friends since we met in kindergarten! We were best friends! Then because of some stupid war we know nothing about, you're gonna kill me and waltz away! Do you even know what this war's about?! Do you?!"

"David, it's nothing personal." Johnny spoke slowly to enunciate his words, as if he could better communicate with his former friend if his words were spoken more clearly. "I looked at you as my brother- you know that. You were more important to me than my own father. But the truth about who we are changed all that. I know my destiny, David. I know. And I know that I am in control of power beyond my imagination. I also know that people come and go in life, but there is only one destiny."

"I'm sick of your destiny garbage! Answer my question," David retorted. "Do you even know what this war is about?"

"It's about freedom fighters who are opposing-"

"I don't mean some prepared propaganda! Do you really know?! Is it really important?! So important that you'd kill your best friend?!" David was not sure whether he wanted the answer to the last question. "People come and go, but not close friends."

To David, Johnny seemed as though he were emotionally disconnected from reality. It was as though his body was inhabited by Albert Young.

"David, in a few years this'll all be a distant memory to the survivor," Johnny responded. "Think about it, David. It's as if we really are children of the Sun. This is our ultimate fantasy! And I'm not gonna miss my destiny because I'm too sentimental."

David had reached his limit with Johnny's bizarre fascination with destiny. "Off screen!" he shouted. Looking depressed, he quietly gave the order as he sat down in the Captain's chair. "Lower shields. Commence firing."

Plans be damned. "One-tenth forward," came the order from David.

"Ten percent forward," Bozwell repeated to Barton.

At the exact same moment, unseen by David, Johnny gave similar commands.

Outside the walls of the great ship, the dead of space was lit up by heavy blue and red laser fire. Both ships had their shields down and were firing away. Both ships rocked and shook at the incredible impacts leveled by each shot. Only their advanced technologies kept the ships from shattering into billions of bits of debris.

The Prince Tinian moved in closer as it continued firing. The Banu rotated to face the Prince Tinian- the bows of the ships incorporated the strongest exterior surfaces. The Prince Tinian gradually climbed to a higher plane and passed over the Banu. Lasers firing, the ships continued inflicting damage upon the other. Small explosions could be seen on the surfaces of both ships.

Smoke drifted upward from the control board in front of Barton. A shriek emanated from behind the Captain's chair when a surge of energy sent an electrical shock through an ensign's body. The noise increased. Rumblings from laser impacts continued. David periodically reissued the command to continue firing. Chaos was everywhere, yet the battle progressed.

An ensign barked into a microphone the call for medics, followed seconds later by the entrance of two men who quickly but gently helped the officer wounded by electrical shock to his feet and half-dragged him off the bridge.

"Full turn! Face them! Quickly!" David stood as he gave the order.

David's shouts were barely audible over the explosions and shouts of other crew members. Each shot brought a long, deep rumbling that rattled every inch of the warship. One ensign managed to stay in his chair as he watched a schematic of the ship. The red lights in front of his eyes were too numerous to count, but he dutifully called out every possible emergency. "Sector eighteen- fire in living quarters! Sector twenty-nine- complete power failure! Weapons are receiving backup power!" His shouted cries of doom continued.

Barton picked himself off of the floor for the third time and immediately returned his gaze to the monitors in front of him. "Sir, they're going to beat us to the punch!"

"No way! Johnny never out-strategizes me! Continue firing!"

"We are past them and can only fire with aft lasers, which are weaker," Anders excitedly reported. "We should save them for the moment, sir."

"So be it. Cease firing," David commanded, sounding like an old veteran. The battle suddenly ceased.

Barton grasped his instrument panel with a death grip, his anger barely in control. "We are continuing our rotation," he growled.

Bozwell, who continued his prior regular duties of, practically speaking, being an everyman's assistant, stopped long enough to review the situation. "Sir, they are going to be able to fire before we can. But I cannot figure out how the Banu withstood such a barrage. It should have been destroyed by now!"

"They will be ready to fire in ten seconds!" Barton warned.

"Shields?"

Anders tapped his screen repeatedly before answering. "They only hit us with three good deadly shots. But one of them destroyed our generator that supplies power to the shields."

"How could the Banu have withstood this?" Bozwell mused loudly, almost as if he were in a daze.

"Barton, get us out of here! Full forward. Now!"

An explosion knocked the senior officers and David to the floor. The powerful laser from the Banu wreaked havoc in several sectors of the ship.

The play-by-play ensign continued his observations. "Sectors thirty-one through thirty-seven have lost life support and gravity! Sectors twenty-nine and thirty have been sealed off! Injuries in engineering!"

"Get us out of here, Barton!"

"Double speed!" Bozwell bellowed.

The Prince Tinian took a glancing blow as it leaped forward through the vacuum of space. Within seconds it was speeding off at over twenty thousand miles per second.

"We cannot go to double speed after that last hit!" Anders shouted.

"Calm down," Bozwell urged. "We are out of it. We will be fine now. Besides," he added as an afterthought. "We are already at double speed."

David looked at Bozwell and gave him a look of thanks. Bozwell nodded despite his frown. The Commander felt as though he had lost many years from his life within the past few minutes. He also felt that he should have never brought the prince to the bridge in the first place; he should have left him in the infirmary.

Spencer, who had been quiet during the battle, busily assisting Barton, spoke up. "My lord, I thought you said you were not going to face off with the Banu?"

Bozwell beat David to a response. "Lieutenant, if you have concerns about the Prince's handling of the matter, they will go through me." The stern but tactful rebuke was more out of duty than agreement with the prince.

David shot a quick glance at Bozwell.

"Yes, sir," Spencer humbly replied.

David slowly surveyed the bridge. Three different stations had negligible amounts of smoke billowing up from their consoles, signaling their damage. Bozwell had a minor cut on his forehead and a thin trail of blood flowed in front of his ear and to the back of his jaw.

The ensign in charge of announcing bad news- or so it seemed- revealed that all emergency and medical personnel were deployed. Barton observed that the Banu declined to follow the Prince Tinian.

"When will we have shields?" David inquired of Anders.

"If we are fortunate, by the time we get home."

David looked forward at the view of space on the giant screen before him. Slowly, he stood up from the Captain's chair and walked to and fro. "Set a course for Saturn," he announced firmly. Anders and Bozwell exchanged befuddled glances, but Barton knew exactly to what David referred.

"Sir," Barton spoke up. "You are aware that we will be heading in the wrong direction by heading toward Saturn? We will have to double back."

"Go there anyway."

David barricaded himself behind the walls of his deep thoughts as the Prince Tinian passed near the planet Mars. Soon they would pass relatively close to Earth again, but David's thoughts were elsewhere.

Currently, Saturn was on the opposite side of the sun from Earth, but traveling across the solar system was an insignificant task in a spaceship far more advanced than anything produced on Earth.

* * * * * *

The conference room was every bit as sterile as the rest of the spaceship, save the infirmary. White walls were bare. The windows that held views to the outside were tiny. Even the large, granite-like table, around part of which David, Bozwell, Spencer, and Barton sat, was plain and uninteresting. Operating rooms were more plush.

David looked haggard, and this did not escape the notice of the three other men. There had been no time for pleasantries, so they did not know what had happened in David's life. They had not even thought to inquire. Their mission was of primary concern, while small talk was of minimal importance. Nevertheless, the three officers wondered to themselves about David's physical condition and mental wherewithal.

"My lord, are you aware that the Banu has also lost all shields?" Barton asked.

"Which is why they did not give pursuit," Bozwell added as he turned from looking at Barton to David. "So you understand our firepower capabilities and limitations, correct?"

"Yeah," David answered. "And the shields, and the maneuvering. But I understand the Banu better."

The Crown officers were taken by surprise.

"What do you mean?" asked Bozwell.

"I was able to access some of Johnny's interactive equipment," David explained. "I got a look at their plans and their capabilities and a tutorial of commanding the ship. I understand basic commands and speeds and half speed, double speed, full forward and all that. But, I know more about the Banu than I do the Prince Tinian 'cause I was also on it. Destroying it isn't as easy as you think."

Barton was incredulous. "You've been on the Banu?!"

David's nod did little to appease or impress the officers.

Bozwell was indignant. "So you do not believe that we can destroy a Rebel ship with a barrage of lasers based upon

Rebel information? Perhaps they allowed you to gain access to faulty information."

Barton and Spencer nodded in agreement.

David realized that nothing he said would matter. "I know we can destroy the Banu, especially if it's low on shields, but it's much stronger than previous Rebel destroyers. This is a monster compared to the Guerilla Class ships. It has more firepower. It has a thicker skin. It's faster. Larger, stronger engines. It's more maneuverable than their old destroyers. We have to have an advantage, though. And since neither of us have shields, that's the advantage we're looking for."

It was obvious to David that the three men were not buying into David's possession of knowledge.

"Even the microchip that was supposed to be implanted did not have information about the Banu in it," Bozwell said. "It's too new and the forces of the Crown have never seen it before." Bozwell was unsure of what to think or believe.

Barton was still suspicious. "You've been on the Banu?" It was more statement of disbelief than question.

"Yes, I have."

Bozwell still had many questions. "Do you think that you have better strategies than we do?"

"Well, I haven't seen your strategies, but I would guess 'yes.'"

"And they are?" Barton asked derisively. He shot a quick glance at his superior officer, but Commander Bozwell only grimaced.

"Ya know," David began, expressing his deep unhappiness with constantly having to defend himself. The drawl melted away from the heat of his controlled anger. "I realize that you're not comfortable with me. That you're not happy with my efforts to at least communicate with Johnny. I can understand that. I can accept that. But I'm getting a little tired of the sarcasm and your lack of discipline. Is that how this ship was run, Commander?" Now it was David with the iron sarcasm.

"This ship and its crew are accustomed to exhibiting the utmost discipline, sir!" Bozwell responded sharply. But Bozwell was on the defensive. David had turned the tables, just as he intended.

"Is that so?" David continued, his words dripping with both sarcasm and authority. As his anger rose, his words were chosen more carefully and his pronunciations became more precise. "Well, I have seen very little of the discipline. I've seen more of the officers of this ship vacillating between sarcasm and anger. That's not discipline, Commander. That is a lack of discipline."

"Sir! If I may interject!" Barton began.

"No you may not, Lieutenant!" David responded bitterly, his voice growing louder. "You may sit and listen. I find it interesting that you have expressed no interest in how it was that I found myself on the bridge of the Banu. Now wouldn't that be a logical question, given the circumstances?! Huh?!"

"Well, as a matter of fact-" Bozwell began, before he, too, was interrupted by the irate prince.

"As a matter of fact, you were interested. But you're just too convinced of your own abilities to consider anything else. What I was doing on the Banu doesn't matter to you because you're more interested in having your way!"

"Okay. Fair enough," Bozwell ventured. "But perhaps you are not interested in our input enough."

"I know what your input is, Commander Bozwell. You've already made that clear."

"Then what is your plan, my lord?" Barton inquired, all sarcasm and anger erased from his voice.

"You're familiar with Saturn's Cassini Division?"

"The large gap in the rings, correct?" Barton responded.

"Yeah. Take us there. Drop us in and I'll let you know what to do next."

"Then what?" Barton inquired.

"Just follow my orders."

Barton jumped to his feet, his face reddened as he spoke. His large, intimidating frame made him look like an angry bull. "Why do I feel like we are all going to die?!" With that, he marched out of the conference room, afraid of what he might say next.

"Prince, David, please," Bozwell pleaded. "How can we advise you when you do not even trust us?"

David's anger faded. He was now speaking from the heart, more matter-of-factly. Consequently, his southern Indiana drawl returned. "If everyone kept tryin' to kill you," he tried to explain. "Wouldn't you be a little confused about who to trust? Wouldn't you play things close to the vest, worried that someone will point a laser at you? My best friend- former best friend- is tryin' to kill me. A guy from this ship tried to kill me. I've only known for a little over a week who I am. Wouldn't you be paranoid? Wouldn't you be extra cautious?"

"I understand that," Bozwell responded as he stood. "But I am a military officer, trained in combat and in leadership. It is difficult for me to turn power and strategy over to a novice." With an expression of disgust, he looked at his junior officer, Spencer.

Bozwell stood, which caused the silent Spencer to do likewise. As he prepared to leave, Bozwell turned to David for a parting shot, cloaked in a faux shroud of respect. "With all due respect, my lord. Next time, are you going to kill him or play with him?"

"He's already proven to me that he'll kill me."

"So what does that mean? Are you prepared to kill him?"

Spencer, now halfway through the doorway, leaned in to hear.

"Lieutenant," David began until he saw Bozwell's face tighten. "Commander," he corrected. "Have you ever had to decide to kill your best friend? That's what I did back there when we opened fire."

"No sir, I have not."

"The only way to outsmart Johnny is to play with him, give him confidence, jack with his mind. Right now, Johnny thinks he's got the upper hand."

Bozwell started to speak, then suddenly caught himself. He was trying with all his might to stay within the bounds of protocol, of knowing his place- a place where acting with honor, submitting to authority, and showing respect were not options.

The two officers exited. The door closed behind them.

David leaned back in his chair and stared at the ceiling. Since the day he learned of his true identity, he had felt alone. Now, amongst those who were technically his own people, he felt no different. Perhaps, he thought, it would be better to just die alone. He put his hands over his face with exasperation as dozens of thoughts raced through his beleaguered mind.

Chapter 23 - Final Analysis

David sat down in the Captain's chair with the knowledge that he instilled no confidence in the crew. The Prince Tinian had reached its destination. The Crown destroyer was at a full stop inside the inner edge of Saturn's "A" ring; in relation to the Sun, the rings were tilted at nearly a fifteen degree angle downward. The bow of the ship faced deeper inside the "A" ring, away from the planet's surface. The Sun was visible to the starboard side of the ship.

While the rings are not very thick, David knew that enough material floated around the rings to help obscure the ship. Along with the disruption of equipment by the planet's radiation, the positioning was ideal.

Anders expressed his concern. "My lord, this planet is emitting dangerous levels of radiation. We cannot stay long. And these rings appear to be planetary debris and ice. I would request that we raise shields to protect us from the bigger pieces of debris and to protect our instruments- what little shields we have, that is."

"Then do it," David said confidently, before adding. "But can they find us in here?"

"They can find us visually, sir, if they are close enough," Anders answered. "But good luck finding us visually in this mess. We have greatly cut their odds of locating us through instruments since we stopped sending out tracking signals. In fact, they probably have close to no chance through instruments."

Spencer and Barton whispered to each other before Barton turned in his chair to address David. "My lord, we believe that all communication transmission bands will penetrate the radiation. Lieutenant Anders, what do you think?"

"I agree. Communications should not be hampered. But unless we communicate with them or send out certain types of signals, we should be able to avoid detection."

"Why did you stop sending out tracking signals?" Bozwell asked. "How can we track them?"

"The prince's orders," Anders replied.

David was not concerned whether Bozwell would be unhappy about being left out of a decision. "Are we sending out any type of signals through the use of our computers or other systems? Is there anything we need to shut off?"

"No, sir," came Anders' reply.

"What is our status?" David asked, still in thought.

"We are already experiencing anomalies on some of my systems," Anders answered. "But nothing that affects the essential functions of the ship. Yet." That last word had an edge to it. "I expect both vessels to suffer equipment and instrument failures. If the instruments hold, the sensors will relay the information, but without strong shields, instruments will not hold."

"So," David ventured. "We cannot see them, but they cannot see us."

"That is correct. Your wish has been granted," Anders explained with confidence. "Our positioning seems to be perfect for not having our location discovered."

"Great. Now rotate ninety degrees and face the Sun," the prince ordered.

Barton repeated the order as he executed the maneuver. Saturn was now to their starboard.

"What is your next move, my lord?" Bozwell wondered aloud.

David looked at Bozwell and winked. Bozwell was mystified.

"How soon?" David asked, as he looked toward Anders.

"Anytime you are ready, sir," Anders answered.

"Bozwell, Barton," David barked.

The two men joined David at the Captain's chair. David's demeanor was much stronger than it had been in the conference room. The teenager was again ready to lead the men into battle. "Anders is ready to execute my plan. When the Banu is visible- and I mean as soon as the Banu is visible- we'll scream toward them at full forward. We'll transfer power to lasers, hitting them with everything we got. If we don't destroy them, we'll transfer full power back to thrusters and get out before they can draw a bead on us. Got it?"

"And you are sure that we will be able to see them?" Bozwell asked.

David was confident. "That's why we tracked their location for as long as possible. When we got close to Saturn

278

we stopped tracking them, stopped all outgoing signals, and changed course. We've laid the trap. We're within visual range of what we think is our last known position from their perspective. They'll start looking for us there. We'll be ready."

Barton looked to Bozwell. "Is it necessary to transfer power back and forth?"

"No," Bozwell answered. "Not normally. But given the ship's present condition of unreadiness and the fact that the prince wants a lightning strike, it is advisable."

"Your assessment, sir?"

Bozwell thought it over for a moment before responding. "My assessment is that he is not as dumb as we think."

The two men eyed David carefully.

"Hey," David lightheartedly responded. "My uncle trained me in military strategies. Blame him."

Bozwell flashed a rare smile. "The duke and duchess have earned themselves a place in history."

It was the first time in a while that David had thought about his aunt and uncle. However, the momentary lapse into sadness had to wait.

"You learned all of this in books?" Bozwell asked in amazement.

"Didn't you learn by books in your military academy?"

"I did not attend the Academy. I learned in battle."

David was not impressed. "I've studied my planet's- well, Earth's- greatest military minds. They may not have used lasers, but it's still military strategy, whether it's lasers or missiles or bullets or swords."

Bozwell looked at Barton. "I have to admit, I think it can work."

Spencer's panicked voice broke up David's triumphant little party. "My lord! The Banu has appeared! I have a visual!"

"Positions!" Bozwell shouted. Crew members scurried about as they prepared for their orders.

"It is approaching at a high rate of speed directly at us!" Spencer urgently warned everyone on the bridge, as Barton reclaimed his position. "They are approaching from a plane of attack that allows them to avoid the debris of the planet," he warned, referring to Saturn's rings.

"Can they see us?" David asked. The high rate of speed had him concerned.

"I cannot monitor their instruments without sending out a signal." Spencer answered.

"Anders!" David shouted. He was alarmed and could not hide it. "Change of plans. I need full thruster power now! Spencer, can they see us?! Barton, get us into the cleanest section of the Cassini Division you can find, then navigate us to the opposite side of Saturn!"

"It does seem they can, sir!" Spencer responded.

"Yes sir. Rotating ninety degrees starboard," Barton dutifully replied.

"How?!" David was angry and confused.

Barton ventured a theory. "Maybe they knew where we were all along."

Bozwell became uneasy at the rapid closing rate of the Banu, which appeared on the main screen. "Sir, we are an easy target here. We must leave this position immediately."

"How is that possible?!" David was still baffled.

"One well-placed shot could destroy us," Bozwell nervously warned.

"Ready, sir," Anders announced.

"Ready, sir," Barton echoed.

"Anders, take as little power as you can from shields. Maybe we have enough there to deflect that one well-placed shot. All other power to the engines! Barton, get us out of here now! Full forward!"

"Full forward," Barton repeated. "It will be bumpy in all this ice and debris!"

"I can only keep shields at twenty percent," Anders shouted.

The mighty ship roared away, first toward the planet, then along a semi-clear path in the Cassini Division. The crew felt no effect from the sudden catapult from immobility to high speed.

"Spencer," David barked. "Track their position! I wanna know their last known position when we reach safety!"

"I cannot get my tracking instruments back online," Spencer shouted. "The system is resetting. This radiation is creating havoc."

"Anders," David ordered. "Raise shields as much as possible. I need to be able to track them at least for a few seconds."

"I cannot without slowing us down," Anders warned. "Which do you want?"

"Forget the shields!"

"They're firing!" the bearer-of-bad-news ensign announced. As his words were completed, the Prince Tinian rocked violently.

"Please, not again!" Anders begged.

"Well, I guess it wasn't well-placed," David said sardonically. "Johnny should get a better weapons officer."

The Banu's approach was much too fast to allow it to maneuver around the rings, the planet, and the many large pieces of debris, and still follow the fleeing Prince Tinian. The Crown destroyer bolted away in time to avoid the destructive lasers of the Banu. Johnny had countered David's great plan before it could even be executed.

*   *   *   *   *   *

With the Prince Tinian out of sight of the Banu, David tried to relax. "Excuse me, ensign," David said, as he approached the doom-saying officer. "What is your name?"

"Ensign Zholtok, sir."

"It's nice to meet you, Ensign Zholtok."

"Thank you, sir."

"Ensign, do you ever get to tell me any good news?"

The young ensign's face dropped. "I'm sorry, my lord."

David laughed. It was a good feeling, he noticed. Laughter had been in short supply over the many days of his ordeal. "Don't take it wrong. I was just curious." He walked back to his chair. He had a feeling that he could not ignore: this was his ship. He could do what he thought was needed or just do what he wished. The ensign was his ensign. He was easing into the position, despite the tension and turmoil.

His thoughts flowed back to the moment. He plopped himself into the Captain's chair. Despite his laugh at the expense of the ensign, he was clearly distracted again. "Bozwell, Barton, Anders, anybody! How could he 've known?! He had to 've known where we were to come straight at us like that with that much speed!"

Bozwell poured through data on the console in front of him. "Spencer, execute a communications history. I want to know the last thirty messages to leave this ship and what they were."

"Yes sir."

"Another traitor?" Barton asked.

"Possibly."

*   *   *   *   *   *

The Prince Tinian circled Saturn inside the Cassini Division, the dark gap in the main section of rings, and had now traveled halfway around the globe from its previous resting position. The rings were tilted upward from the ecliptic at their current location. Though situated in the middle of the rings that surrounded the planet at its equator, due to the tilt of the rings, David was able to see beyond the gas giant, back toward the center of the solar system.

The Sun appeared as a small yellow disc. At a distance approaching a billion miles, the star was surprisingly bright. Earth was visible, but only to those who wished to find it. David so wished. The systems checks and histories being run on the computers bored him. The results were indeed important, but the process was not.

He stared out of the porthole of the Captain's quarters- most recently inhabited by Admiral Praeder- and marveled at the view. A little more than three-quarters of Earth's surface was visible to him- nearly "full," using the term for describing the moon in an equal appearance- but without the aid of a telescope he could not see the difference. From here, Earth looked like Venus did from Earth, only far dimmer from this distance.

David knew enough about astronomy to understand that he was an inconceivable distance from home, or at least the place he used to consider home. The so-called "blue marble" was not even that.

Barely in view from the porthole, far ahead of Saturn in its orbit, Jupiter cut its massive gaseous swath through space. Mars was visible, but too far away for David to recognize. Neptune was visible- on the same side of the sun as Saturn- but from his vantage point, Uranus was not.

David stared in wonder at Earth. He battled a brief feeling of claustrophobia as he considered his distance from his childhood home, from his high school, and from the many baseball fields where he spent his spring and summer days. If the Prince Tinian were to crash into Titan, Saturn's largest moon, or into the planet itself, David thought, then he could actually end up dying on another world. "Too weird" was all that came to mind.

Somehow, Johnny knew. Johnny was not staring through a porthole and looking at Earth in wonderment, trying to grasp his new life. He was not thinking about the past. Unlike the "old" Johnny, he probably was not even thinking about the present. He was thinking about the future. He was thinking about his destiny and his future ascension to greatness. No wonder the allure of Arizona State baseball was unimportant on that gorgeous summer day- that day when he unknowingly played his last baseball game.

David's thoughts remained with the distant planet and his former life there. Aunt Grace and Uncle Phillip. Marty's and Ellen's terrible deaths. The earnest Joan Barton. The feelings that rose up and spilled over upon learning his true identity.

But somehow, Johnny knew David's location and turned the tables. Maybe he just knows me too well, David thought.

David's vacillations between melancholy recollections and attempts at deep thought were interrupted by Commander Bozwell's voice over the intercom. "Sir, we have completed our analysis."

*   *   *   *   *   *

David entered the bridge and headed toward the captain's chair. Bozwell, Barton, Anders, and Spencer met him with the results of their hunt for electronic clues that could explain their recent debacle.

Spencer made the announcement. "Sir, the last communication to leave this ship was the final conversation between you and Banu's cousin. No form of communication went out to betray our position, and our systems have not sent out any signals whatsoever since we last tracked the Banu."

David's mind drifted off, which became apparent to the others by the way that he stared at seemingly nothing in particular.

"My lord?"

No response.

"My lord," Barton repeated. "We have a problem, but we do not know what it is."

David kept his thoughts on the planet upon which he knew he would never again lay eyes. Full of confusion, anger, and pain, his last days on Earth had become a blur in his memory. But even when the pace slowed, when he was able to drive and think, or just rest at Mrs. Fuller's house and examine his predicament, his emotions were raw, thus dulling his ability to analyze events. He had become proficient at breaking down everything that happened in a day, compartmentalizing specific aspects of events, and analyzing life from a cold, rational point of view.

Those wild last days on Earth had not been properly vetted, filtered through his unceasing, unrelenting brain. There had been no time- still there was no time. But his mere minutes at the porthole provided an opportunity for his mind to absorb and process thoughts, feelings, and events.

Even within the past few hours, since taking command of the Prince Tinian, he was a different person. The dreams of boyhood had morphed into the realities of manhood.

His necessarily accelerated emotional growth and acceptance of reality were not what bothered him the most. Neither was his tendency to fall into denial when reality was unattractive. What bothered him the most was that something was missing. A piece of the puzzle escaped him. Something unseen gnawed at him. The missing piece was within reach, within sight. But he could not find it.

While at the porthole, the recent days weighed heavily on his mind. Yet somehow, just staring at Earth and daydreaming, remembering, eased the tensions and refueled his mind, as if he had spent an hour in a hot Jacuzzi on a cold winter night. But now, standing with his four top officers, the mystery of the missing piece of the puzzle was solved inside his relaxed brain. Spencer's words rang in his head. "No form of communication went out." Those words triggered the sequence of thoughts that revealed the answer. It made perfect sense. The answer to the difficult puzzle now made it seem so easy, so obvious.

For the first time, he had hope- real hope. Not an idealistic fantasy of Johnny and David sharing the perfect friendship. Not the naiveté which had plagued some of his earlier decisions. Buried in the ordeal of the events of recent days, he discovered the answer. The answer was found where his thoughts had been: on Earth.

With the missing piece of the puzzle now in his grasp, it was a matter of mere seconds before he came up with a plan. It would be the final plan.

One by one, David slowly looked into the eyes of all four men. His soft-spoken words shocked them. "Battle stations."

The four men looked at each other with uncertainty.

"You do say that, don't you?" asked David.

"Well, yes," Bozwell replied. "But-"

"Then please take your battle stations- except Barton."

Bozwell was clearly displeased that he was to be excluded from a strategy session.

For once, David cared about the reaction to an order by one of his men. "Oh no," he saw the potential problem. "I just have a personal question for him."

Satisfied, Bozwell hurried to his station and announced David's wishes to the others.

"Are you Ralph or Stevie?"

"Ralph."

"Are you glad you left?"

"My reasons were foolish, but I never regretted it."

"The other two?"

"They both died in the war. Stevie and I went to the Academy. Billy was not allowed in and became a sentry at an outpost, instead. The Rebels raided the outpost and wiped out everyone. Stevie and I served together on the Andromeda, but we hit a mine while moving at three-quarter forward and over half the crew was killed. The rest of us were lucky the ship remained intact.

"Funny thing is, we did not go aboard that spaceship that night to go join a war. We did it because we were young and dumb and idealistic and we wanted to reach some sort of higher plane, I guess. But I believe that, after we put down the Rebellion, life will be much, much better."

"Interesting," David responded as he chewed on Ralph Barton's ancient dreams. "But why didn't you contact your mother?"

"There was no time. Things were crazy when we knew you were in trouble. But someday-" He caught himself. He did not want to get emotional in front of the prince.

"She misses you. She told me."

Barton dropped his head. "You mentioned a Marty being killed. I had a baby cousin named Marty."

"That was him," David replied gently. "Johnny killed him and his girlfriend."

The thoughts and emotions raced through Barton as he hung his head. When young Ralph impulsively and literally left his world behind, he also left behind family members who could never be comforted. They never had answers. The mystery of that night now sixteen years gone opened up tremendous holes in the hearts of the Barton families.

Ralph's life had become an amazing adventure compared to what it likely would have been had he not gone aboard. If he had it to do over, he would have chosen this life over whatever his life on Earth had in store for him.

"When we have more time," David offered with great compassion evident in his voice. "We'll talk. But I want you to know that Johnny- and the Rebellion- is about to pay."

Ralph Barton's eyes lit up as he raised his head. A faint smile crossed his lips. But rather than extend the conversation, he quickly turned to take his station.

David watched Barton take his position next to Spencer. "Spencer," he called out. "Order me a shuttle."

"For you?!" Bozwell asked incredulously.

"For me," came the reply.

"Sir! I cannot allow it!"

Bozwell was adamant, but so was David. "Spencer, do it."

"When I report to your father," Bozwell asked snidely. "Shall I classify this as a suicide?!"

David's confidence had risen throughout the entire ordeal. He was not prepared to tolerate any more of the crew's stubborn and disrespectful comments. "Bozwell!" His voice deepened on pace with his confidence. "Do you know how they found us so easily?"

Bozwell could not bring himself to reply, but the sheepish expression on his face gave the obvious answer.

David turned in place as he spoke, to make it clear that everyone was to hear the proclamation. "Prepare to destroy the Banu."

Again he looked around the bridge. "Anders. We're going to move on them quickly- full forward. Be prepared to have all available power to the weapons, but leave shields up as high as possible for as long as possible once my shuttle has left the ship. There will be no retreat for this ship.

"Barton, stay in the Cassini Division at, what? One-quarter forward? When the shuttle has launched, go to full forward. If I'm right, and I am, they will be in the Cassini Division when I want 'em to be. Johnny's running that ship. I confirmed that earlier. I don't know what he's doing right now, but I know where he'll be."

David looked at Bozwell and smiled, though Bozwell did not understand why. "Bozwell, Barton, I want us to stay in the Cassini Division. The way my plan should unfold, they'll be right in front of you before ya know it."

"Yes sir," Barton called out, though he, too, was still baffled.

Bozwell continued to stare at the prince.

"Commander Bozwell, you are an officer loyal to the Crown. When I leave this bridge, you are not to countermand my order, understood?"

Meekly and hesitantly, Bozwell replied. "Yes sir."

"The only way my plan is to be altered is to protect the ship and her crew. But that must not be allowed to happen until the time comes and my plan was to have failed." The confident prince pondered his own words. "And my plan won't fail."

Of that he was confident. The man of plans was convinced that this plan could not fail. Relief, he believed, was at hand. This terrible ordeal could at long last be put behind him. His entire life had been focused on the future. Once again, after the success of this final plan, he could return to his ways of looking forward.

Perhaps in the short term, he would no longer plot his own course in life. His was to become a life of a predetermined path, at least while he remained a prince, yet such a rigid path for the future was a relief when compared to these past few days. He was not accustomed to the mindset of a warrior, no matter how much he studied their strategies.

Until recent events, his was a mindset of an eighteen-year old boy becoming a man, focusing on fun, fame and fortune. Fighting and killing were unthinkable. Until now. Now, he was prepared to kill the one person who had always been his best friend. In the present, this was his new life. The future had been altered before it even arrived.

Every man on the bridge had a long face except David. A rush of adrenalin bathed his entire body. The thought of putting an end to this nightmare was exhilarating.

"We'll be haulin' 'round Saturn so fast they won't know what hit 'em." With that, the smiling young man hurriedly left the bridge, followed by a guard.

Chapter 24 - Children of the Sun

The first thing that David noticed about the launch bay was that it was cold. The bay necessarily was located near the exterior of the ship, and keeping the bay warm was not a priority for the craft's functions.

The bay- one of four on the ship- doubled as a hangar for three of the twelve shuttles that made up the ship's complement. Enough space was available for each shuttle to be loaded with cargo, if necessary, to maneuver from its berth, and to exit the mothership.

With modifications, the Prince Tinian could accommodate a unit of eight fighter craft. Other, much larger ships in the fleet were built for the purpose of carrying fighter craft into battle, but the Prince Tinian was not designed for prolonged combat in deep space. Because of the power of contemporary destroyers, both sides in the conflict had shunned such small fighters when on deep space missions. The armament carried on these fighters was inconsequential up against a huge destroyer, so the mothership's cargo was put to better use.

The sight of the shuttles reminded him of that first night when his people came for him. Now he could actually see the dark gray shuttles. They looked like they were built for anything other than speed or quickness, and yet these shuttles, shaped like cinder blocks with tapered ends, were quite agile. On the night when he first saw them, the bright and multi-colored lights hid their unwieldy appearances.

David's mind focused on what was ahead of him. The cold launch bay, the chunky shuttles, the memories of that night- none of it mattered as he kicked such thoughts from his mind.

As David and his armed escort approached one of the shuttles, he spotted a guard whose job was to brave the cold and guard the shuttles, though from what David was not quite sure. "Sir, please come with me and help me out with this thing," he politely ordered.

"Yes, my lord."

Once inside the vessel, David was overwhelmed by the pilot's control panel. While not as complicated as what he had seen on the bridges of the destroyers, the gauges, monitors, and other readouts were crammed into a much smaller area. Nevertheless, David would execute his plan from here.

His plan, though just one of a string of several plans that would be carried out rapidly, was nearly flawless, he thought, as he prepared to immerse himself into his next steps. He would not only fool Johnny, but he would overcome everything at once: the threat to his life that hung over his head, his propensity for denial, the doubts of his crew, and even his self-doubt. All of it would be overcome by this one, final, multi-faceted plan.

*   *   *   *   *   *

On the bridge, a sense of resignation filled the air.

"Sir," Spencer announced. "The shuttle has launched."

"I guess this means that I am in command," Bozwell ruefully muttered.

"Your orders, sir?" Barton asked hopefully.

"Full forward."

"Sir?" Barton was not happy.

"As I said, Lieutenant. Full forward. Anders, are you ready?"

"Yes sir."

Spencer spoke up again. "Commander." He paused for effect. "We are not receiving a communication signal from the shuttle."

Barton added, "The onboard tracking likely has been shut off, and we cannot track it without sending out a signal."

"The shuttle's onboard system may be damaged by the radiation," Anders theorized.

"No," Bozwell muttered, bitterness in his voice. "He has turned off everything except navigational systems. I am sure that the shuttle's shields are up to protect navigation. For whatever reason, he seems to be trying to sneak up on the Rebels."

The nine men left on the bridge felt a collective hollowness which they could not overcome. Their movements slowed. Their thoughts were left incomplete. They were overcome by a sense of failure. They had only lost one officer from the bridge, but that loss was irrelevant.

The mission had gone awry the moment that Gonchar was promoted and forced upon the crew. It was bad enough that the ship's previous captain had been assassinated- dead without a clue other than the note, praising the Rebellion, found on his chest- and the previous commander had lost his nerve. Before a permanent captain could be found, the time for the retrieval of the prince had come.

Admiral Praeder was tapped, then Gonchar was promoted and sought a seat on the historic flight. The Supreme Commander could not persuade Gonchar that the mission was too routine for his heroic appetite, thus the supposedly-great man's presence.

At this moment, no one on the crew explored the possibility that there was a reason why Gonchar had pushed hard to be "rewarded" with this journey. Everyone assumed that the man was driven by his ego; that afterward, he would trumpet himself as an irreplaceable component of the mission. The nine men who now held the bridge of the Prince Tinian did not consider that perhaps the almost impossible escape from the Rebel's gulags was indeed impossible.

The possibility remained that it was just the inability to keep secret the presence of a legend who loomed as large as Gonchar, which led to Rebel awareness and then infiltration of the operation. But that did not explain Gonchar's traitorous attempt on David's life on Earth's surface. The crew did not have time to ponder such a scenario, nor that Admiral Praeder died while in the act of saving the prince's life.

Rather than reflecting on the entire mission, the crew on the bridge instead found themselves deep in their own despair. Whether or not they themselves survived, all was lost.

"What does he think he is going to gain in a barely-armed shuttle by sneaking up on a destroyer?" Bozwell wondered aloud. He was baffled, but his state of depression was far greater than any sense of curiosity.

*   *   *   *   *   *

Onboard the Banu, the atmosphere was quite different. Between Johnny, Captain Cozgill, Commander Cassens, and the full crew, no one could contain their euphoria.

"One-quarter speed. Prepare to fire on my command." Johnny's voice was solid and nearly jubilant. He could not suppress the smile that engulfed his thin face.

"Thirty seconds until they will be in visual range," called out a crewman.

"Once in visual range, we will fire immediately," Cassens announced.

Johnny's smile completely evaporated for the first time in hours. "Something's wrong." He turned and faced his top officers. The change in demeanor was sudden, and it startled the others.

Captain Cozgill tried to reassure his young rebel. "They apparently have no idea that we can track them. They have all systems powered down so that they cannot be tracked by their signals."

"But David would know by now. He's that smart."

"Johnny," Cassens consoled. "This planet's radiation is interfering with their equipment and ours, and they have shut down all signals. That is all they know. That is what they are thinking. Their shields are likely still low and ours are much stronger than they imagine. But we will not even need shields. Johnny, surprise will swing the battle to our favor."

"Relax, Johnny," Cozgill assured him soothingly. He turned to Cassens. "Commander, on our future prince's command." Though Johnny did not carry rank, he carried prestige. He was, after all, a Banu. Cozgill would do well to honor Johnny now, for he knew that future rewards could be significant. Johnny would be honored with giving the command that would destroy the son of the hated king.

Johnny still was not convinced. "Navigator, be prepared to flee quickly."

"Johnny!" Cozgill tried to control his anger. "What has happened to your confidence?"

"I don't think you understand something. He knows how I think. We can almost read each other's minds or something. We've been close since little boys. We know each other's thoughts, each other's hearts. We've been so close it's weird."

Cozgill tried to draw from within himself an extra dose of patience. "You have him now. Put worry aside."

Johnny started to give the preparatory command, then stopped. "Stand by to fire" did not reach his lips. Instead, he slowly dropped his head, remembering. Until now, all of the memories had been forced from his mind. Destiny was his god. Friendship no longer mattered, particularly a friend who

298

stood in the way of destiny. Loyalty was irrelevant. Still, he remembered.

Johnny lifted his head as he tried not to remember, but no matter how hard he tried, the memories lingered. Nevertheless, he mustered the resolve and finally gave the command. "Stand by to fire."

Johnny knew that something was wrong. Something felt different than it should feel. He should feel glee. He should feel satisfaction, triumph. He did not. He dared not mention the subject again to his senior officers, but he was certain of his feelings.

He had pushed aside feelings for three years- since his father gradually broke him in with multiple revelations, cushioning the blow that David endured without warning.

First his father showed him the interactive machine that taught him about the Banu. Then, after the idea of spaceships and other worlds seemed more real, Banu's cousin taught his son about their identity. Then their destiny. Then their task. Over the course of three years, Johnny learned to discard feelings in favor of reasoning, and in favor of seeing what his father referred to as "the larger picture of reality."

The order in which he learned of his true identity surely would have seemed backward to others, but as Johnny often understood, the old man had his ways, and they worked. Oddly enough- and the man was undeniably odd- he could not figure out how to relate to people, but he did figure out how to read them.

That larger picture meant that relationships which did not advance the cause of the Rebellion were meaningless. Actions which did not serve as benefits to the Rebellion or detriments to the ruling tyrant and his thugs were useless. Emotions were part of a list of impediments to be avoided in the fight for the cause of the Rebellion.

Now, at this late moment, emotions were returning. Rather than gloat in the inevitable victory, something troubled Johnny deeply. Something simply did not feel right.

He remembered the good times with his friend, no matter how hard he now tried to forget. The emotions seeped through his mental defenses. He remembered the laughs, the pitches, the strikeouts, the hits. He remembered the fun and all of the good times. It seemed that there were no bad times in their friendship.

But the order was given. In seconds, David and his ship would be in visual range. All eyes of the crew were on the screen of the Banu's forward view. It was too late for such silly sappiness, Johnny told himself. The end was near.

But still he remembered.

*　　*　　*　　*　　*　　*

On the bridge of the Prince Tinian, the Banu was just becoming visible when Spencer let out a cry. "There it is! The stern of the Banu."

The stern of the Rebel ship was visible while the rest of the spaceship gradually came into view. Because of the ringed planet's radiation and the subsequent effect on much of the equipment, the two ships had to be much closer together for their sensors to alert the crews. Soon they would be within that range, but it appeared to Spencer that such detection would not come soon enough to spare the Rebels.

"Commander, they are firing lasers."

The men on the bridge visibly slumped in their seats. The silence betrayed their thoughts. Barton finally broke the silence. "He did it. He successfully killed himself because of some foolish idealism."

Again silence reigned. No one argued with Barton's assessment; no one spoke; they barely breathed.

"Stand by to fire," Bozwell softly commanded. Even if they destroyed the Banu, failure had come.

With a whirlwind of noise and energy, David burst onto the bridge. Out of breath, he completed the run from the launch bay to the deck. The launch bay ensign had, among other things, helped him to rig a device that would signal them when the device was destroyed by the Banu. Once the destruction occurred, David's sprint began.

He was tired yet energized. Before he even knew for a fact, he was positive that his plan was working. There was now no doubt in his mind. He gave a quick look at the forward view on the screen as he shouted. "Slow this rig to one-quarter forward. Stand by to fire on my command. Stand by to put the Banu deck on screen. We're firing one pulse about forty feet in front of the right rear engine, slightly below center. Got that, Anders?"

"Yes sir!" Anders exuberantly shouted, unable to hide his amazement. "We do not quite have a shot at that spot," he added with concern.

"We will," David responded confidently. "He'll turn just perfectly for me. We could shove a laser up one of the engines right now if I wanted. But if we missed they'd know we're here before they start their turn and they'd flee. I'll make sure they won't flee. Just watch this." His swagger was back. The end of the nightmare approached and he could feel it- the excitement, the adrenalin, it spurred his confidence to greater heights.

The entire crew quietly watched as the Banu began its turn. Within ten seconds, the Rebel destroyer exposed enough of its starboard side to facilitate the first phase of David's strategy.

Anders turned to Bozwell. "The hardest part was converting my calculations into 'feet.'" He tried to cover his excitement with banter, but Bozwell did not care about Anders' weak attempt at lightheartedness and did not respond.

"Just one shot, Anders. Get us ready. Spencer, put Johnny onscreen."

Anders and Spencer complied with their commands.

"Ready, sir," came Anders' response.

Johnny's face appeared on the giant screen. His face was covered with an expression of shock when he saw Johnny. His face and body tightened. Out of sight of the camera, it was evident that he was motioning someone, attempting to issue a command.

"Uh, David! What did you just pull off, bud? You sacrificed a shuttle. For what?"

Anders hoarsely whispered to David, as quietly as he could, "They are rotating to face us!"

"Fire!" David responded, quietly but sternly.

The roar and shudder of the weapons system energizing and blasting a laser beam away from the Prince Tinian could be heard and felt throughout the ship. The small, brief fireball on the surface of the Rebel spaceship did not accurately represent the amount of damage wrought by the single shot. The lack of oxygen dissipated the explosion and no sound of the impact could be heard. But its importance rang out loudly to the prince.

Johnny disappeared from the screen and the forward view returned.

"What did you do?" Bozwell asked, still astonished.

David put his hands on the back of the Captain's chair and leaned against it. He was tired, but too excited to sit at the moment.

The bright faces of his crew beamed in delight and relief.

"If the hit was good, we started a chain reaction that will disable their shields. If their shields were as weak as I think they were, no problem anyway. Between the damage we caused earlier and Saturn's radiation, shields probably weren't a problem. But I wasn't taking that chance."

"But I mean, where did you go?" Like everyone else, Bozwell was thrilled, but he did not understand where David had gone if not aboard the just-destroyed shuttle.

"I was giving instructions while the guard- whatever he was- programmed the path of the shuttle. Then I just took a couple of minutes to think about things…" His voice trailed off before continuing the thought, "and to remember what I learned about the Banu. That's all."

That's all, Bozwell thought. He just nearly scared the very lives out of all of them.

Johnny again appeared on the giant screen, his back to David and the Prince Tinian crew. He turned and glanced over his shoulder at David with a frantic look in his eyes. He knew who was the smarter of the two. He knew that David was the master at strategy.

The crew of the Prince Tinian could hear the chaos aboard the bridge of the enemy vessel. Shouting voices, full of panic. Voices trembling in fear or resignation, or both. Unless David pulled another idealistic stunt, both crews understood where the whirlwind of events was leading. Even Cozgill and Cassens now knew.

Johnny shouted at his crew, "Can't you raise shields faster?! Faster, faster! Turn this ship around faster! Disabled?! We just had them partially online! How can they be disabled?!"

David slowly walked around the Captain's chair and stood in front of it, as though he could get closer to his former friend. He did not take delight in the moment, but he felt the need to push back a little. "With two strikes, I'd call for a fastball, high and tight. Then I'd call for more heat in tight until we got 'em backed off the plate."

"Then the hard curveball away," Johnny completed the thought, as he faced the image of David on the screen in his own ship.

"And we'd get 'em swingin'."

"Set 'em up," Johnny remembered, almost fondly. "Get 'em to look the other way, and sneak one by. And if they swung at the first two, you never liked to waste one on oh-and-two. Just take 'em down on three pitches." Johnny's voice dropped as he continued. "But I think I'm the batter this time."

"Definitely," David answered unhappily. "But it's not oh-and-two. It's three-and-two, and that hard curveball just off the plate is already on its way." David hesitated as he pondered his words, before adding forlornly, "We shoulda been on the same team."

The Banu continued to rotate. Barton, caught unaware in their first encounter when he was mesmerized by the open communication between a Crown destroyer and a Rebel destroyer, carefully eyed the progress of the enemy ship. "Thirty seconds until they will have rotated enough to put us in the range of their main lasers."

"We are ready to fire any time," Anders chimed in.

"Let me know when their lasers energize," David ordered.

"You will have two or three seconds between the time they energize and fire," Anders announced.

Bozwell slowly sat back down into his seat. "No shields, and all that energy will be exposed somewhere." He faded into thought, but Anders picked up the thought and carried it.

"Somewhere in that ship, the energy will be accumulated in one spot. Apparently the prince knows where that spot is."

David slowly turned his gaze from Anders and Bozwell and looked up to the screen at Johnny. He still did not want to face facts, yet he felt a sense of determination that was welling up inside his gut. "I got ya, Johnny."

Denial was gone.

The words summoned fear- a fear that Johnny could feel burning in his stomach. Johnny knew that, even if the Banu tried to flee, David could destroy them before they made the jump in speed. And this time, David would do it. Johnny could see it in his old friend's expression and attitude.

"How'd ya know?"

"I couldn't figure out why your guys thought I was you when they picked me up," David explained. "I thought maybe they were idiots or something. Or that it was because they had never seen either one of us before- though I'm sure that helped. But after you found us so easily when we were hiding in the rings, it just made sense. It all fit."

Johnny's anxiety grew. He could see a schematic showing his ship's position. He could also see in David's eyes that the idealism was gone, yet he still made a last-ditch effort to buy just enough time to stave off what appeared to be inevitable. "David, I think you're right. I see now. It's not worth killin' each other for. None of this is. Friendship is more important."

Bozwell and Anders exchanged worried glances, as did Barton and Spencer. It had not taken anyone on the Prince Tinian long to figure out David's glaring weakness.

David smiled. "I know when you're lying, Johnny. And even if you weren't lying..." His voice trailed off at the thought, a thought that he was now able to suppress.

The crew relaxed. At long last, they were certain that their prince would remain steadfast.

"Fifteen seconds," Barton calmly warned.

David could not resist talking to his lifelong friend. Like the good friend that he was, in a bizarre way, David wanted to be with Johnny until the end. "It drove me crazy trying to figure out how you knew our location earlier. That's how it hit me. I didn't know what that thing was when I took it off your dad's body. I just stuck it in my back pocket, where it stayed ever since. When I took off my jeans to go to bed, I always left everything in my pockets."

David turned to Bozwell. "Focus just below the launch bays. There are fuel lines a little too close to the surface there. That appears to be a soft target when their lasers energize. The armor around the fuel lines won't be able to withstand so much energy around it."

Bozwell tried to whisper to David. "What if they don't energize?"

"They will," David said confidently. "They will."

"You can't do this!" Johnny was now desperate. "Think about when we were kids. Remember how we dreamed we were children of-"

"Stand by to fire on my command." David's voice rose several notes as he shouted. He did not want to hear sentimental childhood memories now. His palms were clammy and his mouth suddenly became dry. The rush of adrenalin made him feel as though his heart would not last through the encounter.

"David! I think we-"

"Five seconds!" Barton shouted, sounding like a drill sergeant, his nerves frayed.

Johnny's hardened heart crumbled inside his chest as he allowed himself to remember. The good times with his buddy, which had been blocked out until only two minutes prior, overwhelmed him.

Johnny had overcome what he thought was the temptation that his father so feared- the temptation of trying to reason with his best friend. Now, he realized, it was not the temptation to allow his friend to live, rather the temptation to remember. That's what his father had meant. With his life about to end, Johnny realized that his father recognized the weak link that could keep Johnny from destiny. The good memories should have been not merely suppressed, but expunged. Remembering would warm the young man's heart and cloud his judgment.

Now, it was too late for a life's worth of recollections to save him.

Destiny had turned Johnny's heart as cold as a stone in the bed of a mountain stream. He was left with nothing onto which he could grasp for comfort or strength. Memories would not suffice. It was too late. All of his previous decisions and beliefs brought him to this end. He understood that Death was here to destroy destiny.

Somehow, somewhere, his father was wrong about life and what was important in it. But there was no time to sort through the complications. His father's redemption, the dream, destiny, his very life- they would all be gone in seconds. Johnny knew it. And he could not stop it. David was calling the pitches.

As Johnny yelled, the despair in his voice accompanied a true sense of contrition that David recognized in his friend's eyes. "DAVID!"

David wanted to turn away from him, to avoid seeing him in that moment when the real Johnny tried to escape the brutal monster the Rebellion had created. But he had to look. He had to be there for his friend.

"Sir, they're energizing!" Barton sternly warned, his voice penetrating the bridge, where to the crew the air now seemed to be thin, as their lungs gulped for air in anticipation.

David's eyes quickly welled up with tears. "Perfect," his voice choked.

Despite the one-word response, David softly shook his head as if to say, "No." He did not wish to do this. He closed his eyes. Time stopped in his mind. Visions of meeting Johnny as a five-year old flashed by. Baseball. Their mutual friends and sharing laughs with them. More baseball. Driving fast together through the countryside as rock music blared from the stereo, not a care in the world. Parties. Double dates. Long summer days of baseball tournaments.

In a split second, their entire lives together seemed to race by on the video screen inside David's brain. But it was only for a split second.

"FIRE!" The one-word command came out as two syllables. David was certain that the single word was issued louder than he had ever yelled. Communication with the bridge of the Banu was lost and immediately Spencer replaced the image on the screen with their forward view. To David, his shouted command seemed to hang in the air as he watched the chain reaction commence from the single pulse that struck Johnny's ship. He fell back into his chair.

The Banu never had the opportunity to fire its shot. As David and the crew of the bridge saw on the screen, their own shot was perfectly placed. With the design of the Banu came a flaw that David spotted when he sat through the virtual reality tutorial of the ship. At the time, he did not dwell on the flaw. It did not seem to matter then, when destruction of the vessel was not on his mind.

His viewing of the tutorial seemed like a lifetime ago, but David retained much of the information presented. Throughout his whole life he had been blessed with a good memory. The strategies of Earth's historic military leaders were etched into that memory. But after his plan was formulated, the only thing left to remember was the location of the flaw. For all of his plans, it all came down to a matter of memory.

The energy which accumulated near the surface of the Banu made the craft vulnerable for only a couple of seconds. A direct hit rendered the ship equivalent to a massive container of nitroglycerin on a bumpy covered wagon trek across the Old West, with a lit stick of dynamite thrown in for good measure.

David's plan worked perfectly.

Within a three-second span, the Prince Tinian fired half a dozen pulses of laser rounds at various parts of the enemy craft. The shot placements were designed to disable the Banu's weapons, but within a moment, such weapons were irrelevant. Indeed, every shot after the first was irrelevant. The chain reaction of destruction ended only seconds after it had begun.

The brilliance of the fireball was nearly blinding, but just as quickly as it exploded, the flames of the fiery wreckage were snuffed out by the vacuum of space.

"Raise shields," Bozwell ordered. Then, as an after-thought, he added, "What little shields we have."

The debris of what was a Rebel destroyer littered the Prince Tinian's forward view. Chunks of wreckage harmlessly bounced off of what remained of the invisible force field that protected the Crown destroyer. The great gravitational pull of Saturn caused the preponderance of the debris to quickly arc toward the surface of the planet.

David rested his face in his hands and quietly cried. Emptiness overran his soul. He was the victor, but he felt no cause to celebrate. He tried not to think. He tried not to feel. He tried not to remember.

The cascade of debris falling toward the planet lasted for several minutes. All the while, David softly wept.

Chapter 25 - Children No More

"Are you okay, sir?" Bozwell quietly asked as he rested his hand on the prince's shoulder.

Still seated in the Captain's chair, David lifted his head to reveal his red eyes. "Yeah, I guess so."

"You did not get on the shuttle after all." Bozwell knew that he was stating the obvious, but he still did not understand what had just happened.

"I never intended to," David responded. "I had that guard help me program the auto-pilot. With all the craziness that happened when I first got on this ship, I didn't want anyone to know the plan. No offense. But I figured I could trust a guard doing nothing but guarding the launch bay."

Barton, Anders, and Spencer joined the pair.

"I am sorry, sir, but I do not understand," Bozwell confessed.

"When I killed Johnny's father, I took an object out of his pocket that I didn't know what it was, but I figured I might need it someday."

"A tracker!"

"The Banu picked me up because they thought I was Johnny. It occurred to me after they 'bout killed us when we were hiding in the rings that it all fit."

"You still had it, but you did not tell us?" Anders' excitement had still not abated.

"I forgot it was there, I was so used to it in my back pocket. Then when I figured the whole deal out I didn't know who to trust. Don't forget, that one guy tried to kill me when you rescued me. Besides, I didn't know what it was. It was just a little thing. And I just figured it out right before I headed to the shuttle."

"Yes," Barton added. "We still do not entirely know what happened when we were picking you up on Earth."

"That guy who came out first was about to kill me, but somebody else shot him."

"Commander Gonchar." Bozwell replied. "And he was trying to convince me that Admiral Praeder was a traitor."

"Well, that's why he was trying to convince you," David stated, though the fact was clear to everyone. "He was the traitor."

"So you had a tracker in your pocket?" Barton asked.

"I left it in my pants' pocket, so it was with me the whole time after I killed Johnny's dad. I pulled it from his body."

"Two Banus he has killed!" Anders exclaimed. He was both proud to serve the prince and impressed by his important accomplishments.

"Yes," Spencer added. "I caught that when they were speaking on the open line that he killed Banu's cousin. That is impressive, sir."

David was still not ready to accept that killing his best friend- or his father, for that matter- was an accomplishment. He ignored the praise and continued with his story. "I was just hoping to figure out what it was. If Albert- Johnny's dad-was carrying it, it had to be important. I just had no idea they could follow my every move with it."

Bozwell explained the basics to David. "Since it was operating separately from us, we did not pick it up when we combed through the system earlier."

Anders put his hands on top of his head in realization of what they missed. "The tracker must have operated on a frequency that would allow it to pass through the radiation intact."

"Remember when I told Johnny I just had to see him give the command?" David continued his explanation. "Well, if I knew for sure he was calling the shots, I knew I'd run into a situation later where I could think things through like Johnny. I know"- he stopped himself briefly to correct himself- "I knew Johnny and how he thought. I had to know how to think. Had his officers been in charge, things mighta been different."

"So you put the tracker in the shuttle?" Barton half-asked, half-stated.

David nodded. "Had I left the beacon on in the shuttle, it would've been too obvious. Johnny would've figured out right away that it wasn't our ship coming at him. I figured they had no clue it wasn't the Prince Tinian until they were about to fire. Why would they've thought it was anything else but this ship? Then when they saw it was a shuttle, who knows? Maybe they figured I was onboard, anyway."

Barton and Bozwell smiled broadly. Barton looked at Bozwell. "I must say, I underestimated him at every turn."

"That's obvious," David responded. He looked into Barton's eyes, then slowly, if only slightly, smiled.

"My lord," Bozwell began. "We know that you are upset about having to destroy your friend..."

"But you will come to terms with what you have done," Barton finished. "It was a necessary decision."

David could no longer avoid the truth about himself. "I guess I was in and out of denial about him. I've always believed that friendships and family and loyalty are the most important things in life."

"Sometimes," Bozwell consoled. "Doing good has to fit in there somewhere. That is why we defend your father's kingdom."

"It is why I stayed instead of going back home when I had the chance," Barton added.

David pondered their words. He had thought that behaving with decency and loyalty was doing good. Yet, somehow, his idealistic ways fell short. He knew that. He did not yet understand every aspect of what he had learned, but he now understood that doing good was not always as black-and-white as it sounded.

To do good, he had to kill. That concept will take time to digest, he thought.

He also knew that the transformation from childhood to adulthood had been an almost sudden occurrence for Johnny and himself. Dreams of baseball and life and forever were nice, but reality had a way of drastically changing the

316

importance of all that. Johnny would call that destiny, David thought.

"My lord, you are going to be a great strategist!" Bozwell gushed.

"And it may take a great strategist to end this war," Barton added.

Slow and shaking, David stood. He looked Barton squarely in the eyes, then did the same to Bozwell. "I already am a great strategist." He forced a full smile.

The officers laughed for the first time since David entered their lives.

David wiped his eyes. He was still not ready to laugh and crack jokes, but he was much better now that the deed was done, now that reality had pushed away a large portion of his idealism.

"You are going to love your new home," Bozwell promised.

"Do they play baseball there?"

"What's baseball?" Bozwell asked.

"Uh oh," David said in jest. "We may have to turn this rig around."

"Oh no! Just teach me."

Bozwell, Barton, Anders, and Spencer laughed. David smiled. This time it was a real, legitimate reaction for him.

David looked first at the man who was the only true earthling on the ship, then at the man who had become the highest ranking officer under bizarre circumstances. His appreciation for the two men existed in spite of the previous spats. "You have served me well."

He turned his eyes to Anders and Spencer. "You are brave men. I may not understand everything that I'm about to encounter, and I won't even recognize my own father, but I assure you that your friends and family will always be proud of you. Your bravery and devotion will not be forgotten."

The officers did not know how to respond. They had doubted this kid, even despised him. Now, after a whirlwind of events, the kid was a valiant man. They each silently nodded their appreciation.

David snuck a quick peek at the forward view. Even before all of the debris of the Banu had reached the outer atmosphere of Saturn, he realized that the old was indeed gone. No need to worry about returning to a place where his strongest ties were no longer present. All that remained were a few friends. His aunt and uncle, his best friend: they were dead. It was now time to meet his real parents.

"Bozwell, take the helm," Prince Andrew Chateau ordered. "Let's go home."

Brian W. Peterson grew up in a small Missouri town, where he would imagine bad and weird things happening to him, then he would write down the stories so that he could someday have material to write novels. This is novel number one. You can learn more about him at WrittenByBWP.com.

CONNECT WITH BRIAN ONLINE

@WrittenByBWP

Facebook: Written By BWP

Please leave a review at your favorite online retailer!